Deadly Prescription

Deadly Prescription

Robert E. Marx

Prominent Books

Writing: Robert E. Marx
Editing: Writer Services, LLC (WriterServices.net)
Cover Design & Book Layout: Writer Services, LLC
Cover Art: Larry Rostant

ISBN 10: 1-942389-09-4
ISBN 13: 978-1-942389-09-5

Prominent Books and the Prominent Books logo are Trademarks of Prominent Books, LLC

Table of Contents

CHAPTER 1
Dr. Merriweather and the Oral and Maxillofacial Surgery Program

The fog sits motionless in the temperate morning air, muffling the high-pitched cry of an osprey off in the distance. It's unusually warm on this particular Thursday in January. Dr. Robert Merriweather opens his front door to let Tubby, one of his three Labrador retrievers, into the front yard.

Though he loves them all, Robert has had Tubby the longest—for almost twelve years—and holds a special place in his heart for him. Tubby was, after all, around when he and his wife, Veronica, were still together. Though they have been divorced for almost five years now, he has found it impossible to separate the loving connection for V, as he called her, and this sweet, gentle animal. He was "their" pet.

So appropriately was Tubby named when they picked up the fat little ball of fur from the breeder; he never quite lost his roly-poly shape. Robert smiles as he watches him eagerly bounding out the door to fulfill his daily task of fetching the morning newspaper.

Tubby runs to the edge of the lush one-acre property, stopping briefly to mark his scent on one of the palm trees that serve as its front border along the street. Before picking up the morning edition of the Miami Herald lying partly in the road, he takes a moment to survey the quiet neighborhood, sniffing into the air. Only he is aware of something out of place.

About to whistle him back, Dr. Merriweather gasps in horror as a late-model green sedan screeches out of the driveway from across the street and barrels toward Tubby. He sprints toward his dog, but only makes it a few steps forward before the car's fender brushes against Tubby and the vehicle comes to a halt in front of his house.

Making the rest of the distance, he throws his arms around his dog. "Tubby! Are you okay?"

The dog drops the newspaper, still in his jaws, and begins to lick his master's face, seemingly unaware of the close call.

His heart pounding in his chest, Merriweather turns and glares at the car to see the blur of an object flying at him.

He ducks down and flings his arms around Tubby as the object sails overhead with a whoosh, then crashes into the wooden façade near the front door.

The car speeds away as he stands up, just in time to get a glimpse of a man with a red cap behind the wheel. *Dammit*, he thinks to himself, *I didn't even get the license plate number.*

After walking Tubby inside the house, he stops and inspects the damage. A brick had torn the American flag on his façade and cracked two boards. Wrapped around it is a white sheet of paper.

He bends down to grab it and reads the crudely scribbled note aloud. "Watch your step or next time, the drive-by will be a bye-bye."

Entering the house with the brick and note in hand, Dr. Merriweather finds Tubby waiting for him. The slightly soggy newspaper is now lying on the floor next to him.

"Well, Tubby," he says, looking down at the dog, "at least we know he's neither a poet nor a professional baseball pitcher."

Joined now by his littermates Rocky and Libby, the three dogs head to the kitchen for their morning slices of cheese. After doling out the rewards, Dr. Merriweather sits down at the glass and steel kitchen table, tries to force the disturbing incident to the back of his mind, and opens the paper to the Science & Technology section.

A smile grows on his face as he looks at the picture alongside the main article. It shows a fiftyish-looking man with graying brown hair and a goatee standing next to a young girl with hopeful eyes. The smile stretches even further as he reads the caption.

11-year-old cancer patient Lisa Golding and her surgeon, Dr. Robert Merriweather, Chief of Oral and Maxillofacial Surgery, at the University Of Miami Miller School Of Medicine. He and his team recently removed two-thirds of her lower jaw and rebuilt it with their stem cell bone protein composite.

He turns the page and looks at a much larger photo of Lisa and her parents, their arms wrapped around her as if afraid to let her go. But his gaze keeps returning to the little girl's eyes. For the doctor, it is that look, that spark of recognition that life will not only continue, but be improved, that makes it all worthwhile.

****

Just before 7 a.m., Merriweather turns onto W.152nd Street, then the west parking lot of the University of Miami's hospital called Jackson South. As usual, he parks near the back, which is what the man in the dark green sedan is counting on. He pulls into a spot one row behind the doctor and climbs out.

He watches as Merriweather walks past the areas reserved for physicians, then patients, still completely unaware of his presence.

The man zips up his Philadelphia Phillies jacket and pulls his cap lower on his head as he closes the distance between himself and the doctor. When he gets within five feet of Merriweather, he reaches into his right pants pocket and clutches at an unseen object.

"Well, hello, Robert!" says a distinguished older man who approaches Merriweather, hand outstretched. It is the Chief Executive Officer of the hospital. "I hear congratulations are in order."

Cursing to himself, the man in the red cap stops in his tracks, pulls out his cell phone and pretends to make a call. He appears to be just another faceless person heading off to his appointment.

"Yes, thank you," Merriweather says, shaking the man's hand.

"So the Chair Endowment Dedication is tomorrow," the older man continues. "I hope I'm invited."

"Of course you are," Dr. Merriweather says, smiling.

"Oh good! Say, are you going to make the Medical Executive meeting?"

"Well … I don't think so … ."

As the two continue to chat, the man in the Phillies jacket slips the phone back into his pocket and circles back to his car, already formulating another plan.

Glancing at his watch in annoyance, Dr. Merriweather rushes into the Medical Arts Building, the 5,200-square-foot clinic that serves as his home away from home. It took him several minutes to extricate himself from the CEO, and now he is running late.

He walks into his office at ten after seven to find his secretary, Isabella, already there. When she hears the door, she turns around with two steaming cups of coffee in hand.

"Well, well, I'm glad you finally arrived. It's such a lovely morning, I thought you might be hanging out in the Quad with your residents."

Robert raises an eyebrow at her. "Very funny."

It is something of a running joke between them. The Schoninger Research Quadrangle is an oasis of palm trees and umbrellas in the middle of the medical campus. At any given moment, stressed-out residents could be found there snacking, sipping coffee, or just relaxing by the large fountain. Robert never has time to go to the Quad, but on especially hectic days, Isabella teases him that he should. He knows her well enough to understand that she is suggesting he get out of her hair for a while.

She walks over and hands him the coffee, then gives him a

peck on the cheek.

"Good morning, Chief." She turns around, her long, raven black hair swinging, and heads for the inner office.

He follows her, careful to leave the door open. More than one tongue is already wagging about an office romance between them. Unbeknownst to those people, the rumors are both unfounded and, for the two of them, a continuous source of amusement.

"Is everything set for tomorrow night?" Merriweather asks, sitting down. He wonders whether or not he should tell her about the incident this morning, but shoves the thought down to focus on business.

"I think so," Isabella says, her eyes looking upward and to the right as she mentally checks items off her to-do list.

"I have arranged wheelchair access for Dr. Jacobson, Norman, and your brother. Your PowerPoint slides are on a thumb drive ... and the crepe maker, servers and bartender will be at the house by four, along with people to set up the tables and chairs." She winks. "The band will show up later."

At the mention of the band, Robert rolls his eyes at her; they had quite the battle of wills on the subject before he finally gave her free rein to choose. "I knew you'd handle the whole thing. Remind me to call Dr. Jacobson tonight to confirm that he's coming."

"Will do ... Oh, speaking of phone calls," Isabella says, "you wanted to speak to Barry about finalizing the Chair Dedication ... ."

"Right." Merriweather nods and pulls his phone from his pocket.

He chuckles to himself when Barry Withers, the Director of Gifts and Donations, answers groggily on the fourth ring. Barry is known around the hospital as a notoriously late riser; Merriweather himself once spoofed the old army commercial, joking that Barry gets less done in an entire day than most people do before 9 a.m.

"Hi Barry, it's Robert Merriweather. I'm just calling to confirm the arrangements for the Ceremonial Chair Dedication." He pauses. "Sorry to interrupt your beauty sleep; heaven knows you need it."

"Very funny, Merriweather," Barry replies, but Robert can hear the humor in his voice. Barry has known him far too long to mistake Merriweather's good-natured ribbing for anything else.

After finishing his phone call, Robert slides his phone into his pocket and looks over at Isabella. "Okay, that's handled. So what's today looking like?"

Over the next half-hour, she goes over the day's business and the upcoming court appointment. As the long list of activities is taken up, Robert stops things to catch up with how Isabella and her young son Gabe are doing. She is halfway through a funny story about Gabe at school when she stops and peers at her boss. "Okay, what's up?"

"What do you mean?" he asks, but he already knows the answer.

"You're a little distracted. Is everything okay?"

He is debating whether to tell her about the brick-throwing incident at his house when they hear a knock on the door. They look up to see Dr. James Glanville standing in the open doorway. Glanville works as the tumor and reconstructive surgery Fellow directly with Dr. Merriweather. His superb surgical abilities and research interest was why Merriweather chose him as his Fellow in Tumor and Reconstructive Surgery.

"Hello, you two. Doctor Merriweather, have you got a minute?"

"Yes, James; Issy and I are just about finished." "Yes," Isabella says, standing, "and it's well past my coffee time. I'm putting on a fresh pot if anyone's interested."

Both doctors nod, and Isabella walks out of the room.

"Do you have the reviews of the patients?" asks Dr. Merriweather.

"Yes, we extubated yesterday's cancer patient as well as the osteoradionecrosis patient from the day before," Glanville replies, grunting as he takes a seat at the table. "Both are doing well without their breathing tubes, and their flaps have good Doppler sounds from their feeding blood vessels. I discharged both of the drug-induced bone necrosis patients this morning. They're still swollen, but are otherwise healing well so far."

Merriweather nods his approval. "Good, good. Have you checked on the rats?"

"Yes," Glanville replies quickly, "that's one of the things I wanted to talk to you about. Some of the rats are acting fidgety and out of sorts—jerky movements, biting at their cages—that kind of thing."

Merriweather raises an eyebrow at him. "Really? That's unusual for rats. Hamsters and rabbits behave that way with longer-term cage confinement, but not rats."

"So?" Glanville looks at him expectantly. Merriweather pauses briefly and scratches his head. "Let's worry about that next week. I'll talk to the research veterinarian to be sure they're getting enough water and the correct diet."

Glanville jots a note down on his pad and then stands to go.

"By the way," Merriweather adds, giving him a knowing look, "did you coordinate with the residents and interns?"

Glanville gives him the thumbs-up. "Don't worry, it's all set."

"Good. I want it to make an impression on the dean and the university president."

Just then, Isabella appears at the door with two steaming cups of coffee.

"There's someone on the phone who says he needs to speak with you right now. Can I put him through?"

"Who is it?" Merriweather asks, graciously accepting the coffee.

"He wouldn't say, just that you'll be interested in what he has to tell you."

Merriweather rolls his eyes. "Right now, the only thing that would interest me is a lap dance or a fishing trip. And, at this time, I'd prefer the fishing trip."

Dr. Glanville laughs, as does Isabella—both of them used to Dr. Merriweather's offbeat sense of humor.

"Okay," Merriweather says, "put him through."

She leaves, and the ring of the transferred telephone call comes through a moment later. He puts the call on speakerphone to free his hands for note taking.

"Hello?"

"Is this Dr. Merriweather?" asks a deep male voice.

"Yes, it is. What can I do for you?"

"First, you can take me off speakerphone; we have important business to discuss."

Merriweather shoots a look at Glanville and gestures for him to sit back down. "That's okay, I do important business over the speaker all the time."

"I'm afraid I must insist that you cooperate with me, Dr. Merriweather."

"Well, if you insist," Merriweather says, motioning to Glanville to quietly pick up the adjacent trunk line.

Holding Glanville's gaze, Merriweather waits for him to gently lift the receiver to his ear, then presses the speakerphone button at the same time.

"Dr. Merriweather," the voice continues, "we are aware of your ongoing criticism of certain pharmaceutical companies and that you frequently appear in court as an expert witness against them." "That's correct," Merriweather replies with a frown. "And who exactly is we?" "That's not important. What you need to know is that your participation in these legal actions increases the cost of medicines considerably—medicines that help millions of people. It's also not very good for your career."

Merriweather feels the heat rising to his face. "You needn't concern yourself with my career," he snaps, "and I find it hard to believe that you're concerned with my patients or the cost of their medicines. Let me inform 'we' that I've reviewed the research on the cis-phosphorous drugs and found it to be manipulated, to put it lightly. Those companies also ignored the warning signs that indicated the complications now occurring in my patients that you're so concerned about. Not only that; the two drug companies that I've testified against have, to date, each made over twenty-five billion dollars on their drugs. They've also cost our patients, their insurance companies, and the Medicare system countless millions in treating the dead jawbone caused by those drugs. So, your argument about the cost of these medicines is pretty hollow, especially considering that anticipated legal fees were incorporated into the market price of these drugs long before they even hit the market." Merriweather pauses for effect. "Bet you didn't know I was aware of that, did you?"

"Well, Dr. Merriweather," the voice monotones, "I see you're as well-informed and passionate about this as you are about your research. That is why we're prepared to offer you a three-million-dollar grant for any study you would like—any one other than those particular drugs, of course. We'll even include an additional two million for you personally."

"Well, that's a very generous offer," Merriweather says. "And how are you going to sign the check? Will it be from 'We'?"

The voice laughs, devoid of any humor. "You needn't worry about that. We'll see that you get the money."

Merriweather glances at his watch. "Okay, listen, this has been an interesting conversation, but I'm afraid you've wasted your time. I'm not going to change my position or my actions." He pauses a moment, but all he hears is silence on the other end. "Now, I really must go."

"I would really advise you to reconsider—"

Merriweather replaces the receiver with a sigh.

"Wow," Glanville says, "that was bizarre!"

"Eh," Merriweather waves his hand dismissively, "it was most likely one of the attorneys representing either Apollo Pharmaceuticals or North Star Drug Company. You can bet they were recording the conversation. Anything that might imply my consideration of their offer could be used to discredit me in the courts. These lawyers know every trick in the book."

Standing up, Merriweather looks down at the phone. "But what they don't know is bone science, and they certainly don't know what to do with people they can't control."

CHAPTER 2
The Chair Dedication

With no patients or surgeries scheduled for Friday, Dr. Merriweather spends most of his morning catching up on his entries in the Electronic Medical Record. It's a task he hates due to the program's silly entry requirements and useless screens that take up time he could be using to care for patients. He begins each line with an annoyed grunt, punctuated by several hard taps to the back key to re-enter the correct number. He would call it a necessary evil, but he is not all that sure it is necessary.

Normally, it is enough to put him in a mood only a run with Tubby could cure, but today is the day of his chair dedication, and he is not going to let some inefficient computer program ruin it. He glances at the clock and smiles; nearly time for Carl and Shirley to arrive at the house. After grabbing another cup of coffee and a promise to see Isabella later, he runs back out to his car.

After thirty minutes spent battling Miami's midday traffic, which is much more congested during the winter months, a car cuts in front of him—no blinker, no warning.

"Damned snowbirds!" he yells out to himself, albeit with a bit of guilt at having been one himself some time ago.

Finally he pulls up to his home to find an older model silver Dodge Caravan minivan already in the driveway. His sister-in-law Shirley is standing at the rear passenger side, her arms wrapped around a wheelchair. She unfolds it, then opens the front door and reaches her hands out to her husband. Merriweather quickly moves to her side so he can help her move his brother into a comfortable position.

"Thank you, I could've done it myself though," she says, taking a position behind her husband and pushing him along.

"Nonsense." Robert waves her away, but his face acknowledges that she does, in fact, care for his brother every day and that he appreciates it.

He reaches down to pat his brother on the back. "Good to see you, Carl. Been too long."

"Maybe for you," Carl jokes, but he reaches up to touch Robert's hand. Humor to cover up emotions; it's a long-standing Merriweather tradition.

Too long indeed, Robert thinks as the three of them head toward his front door. He steals glances at Carl, trying to hide the shock he feels at his brother's appearance. The two were extremely close while growing up in Chicago—whether it was fishing in summer or making snowmen in winter, they were each other's favorite companion. They were later separated by divergent, yet equally ambitious, aspirations. Carl joined the navy while Robert went to dental school at Northwestern University just north of Chicago. He later returned to Chicago as one of the three candidates accepted that year for the University of Miami's oral surgical residency.

He and Carl still speak regularly on the phone, but whenever Robert stops to add up the time they'd actually spent together in the past several years, he finds it woefully lacking. He is thinking the same thing now as he looks at his brother. My God, it's also been twenty years since the diagnosis. He remembers like it was yesterday when Carl called to tell him that the weakness in his limbs and changes to his voice and vision were not "nothing," as they had all hoped, but multiple sclerosis.

He steps ahead of them to unlock the door and pull it wide.

"Congratulations on the dedication, Bob," Shirley says as she deftly maneuvers the chair through the opening.

"Thank you, Shirley. It means a lot to me that you both can be here."

"Well, of course. We wouldn't miss it."

Robert chuckles. "You might not say that in a minute."

Carl looks up at him. "What do you … ?"

He does not even get the words out before they are bombarded by the three excited Labradors that come to see the new people intruding on their domain.

Knowing his brother is a dog lover too, Robert lets them get a few good licks before reining them in.

"Alright, alright … down, Tubby," Merriweather says, patting him on the head. The three of them rush back out of the room, prancing and galloping, bumping into each other, just as Shirley stands up.

"Can I get you two some drinks?"

"Well, only if you insist," Carl says with a mischievous sparkle in his eyes.

Robert notes with relief that despite his words coming slow and slurred, his brother is still the same jokester he remembers.

"I insist," she says, smiling, then disappears into the kitchen before Merriweather can offer to help.

"So, Bob, what is a 'chair?' Do you actually get a chair to sit on?" Carl holds a little smirk on his mouth, but Robert can hear the note of admiration in his voice. Having the university name a chair after him was, after all, an acknowledgement of his accomplishments thus far. As much as Robert likes to put such public recognition aside and get on with the work, he cannot help feeling proud that he has made a tangible difference in the lives of others.

"You actually get a chair. A ceremonial wooden chair that's black with gold trim. It'll have the dedication on the back.

"Is that all?"

"Well, from the university's perspective, the donor of the chair gets two things: a relationship with the school and an opportunity to name the chair. Since I am the donor as well as the recipient, the chair will be named The Robert A. Merriweather Chair for Oral and Maxillofacial Surgery Research and Education, and I will become the Robert A. Merriweather Professor of Surgery. Most importantly, the money will go to a great cause."

Shirley walks back into the room and places down two cans of soda in front of them, along with a cup of tea for herself.

"You doctors and your fancy words," Carl teases. "What is maxillofacial, anyway?"

"Such words are used for specificity, so no one is confused with what is meant when doctors communicate to each other. It just means treating the area around the upper and lower jaw, neck, and face. The reference is that the maxilla is the upper jawbone."

"Ah, well why didn't you say so?" he says, eliciting a laugh from his wife.

"Sounds really exciting, Bob. I'm proud of you," Carl notes.

Merriweather shrugs modestly to hide how moved he is by his brother's validation.

"It's a long-standing academic tradition and a great honor to dedicate a Chair. The 2.5 million dollars goes to the university, increasing its net worth, and each year, I can draw from the interest and use it to support our research. That way, we're not beholden to drug companies or granting organizations. I can also use the money to care for indigent patients as well as our residents' educational needs. That's a really big deal; it pays for them to go take outside courses and work for charity organizations in the developing world, not to mention their required training exams and American Heart Association certifications. These are all things a county hospital wouldn't normally be able to afford."

Robert takes a sip of his drink. "But enough about work. I'm so glad you guys could make it down here."

"We're only too glad to get out of the Chicago winter for a while," Shirley says as she reaches over to affectionately pat Carl's hand. "Thanks for inviting us."

"Of course. I hope you're going to stay in Florida long enough to enjoy the condo."

Some years ago, Dr. Merriweather purchased a condo in the Middle Keys, intending it to be a place to escape his busy life. Unfortunately, he has been too busy to use it very much at all.

"You bet," Carl says, eyes sparkling. "Shirley and I will

drive down tomorrow. It'll be great to fish off the seawall at the marina again. It's about the only fishing I'm able to do anymore. I can't get into a boat, and there are only a few places you can catch any decent fish from shore."

"Well, the last time you were in town, you jacked some of the biggest snapper I've seen down here. My God, I usually have to go forty miles out into the Gulf to catch what you caught right from the seawall, but you've always been a better fisherman than me." Pausing, Robert leans in closer to his brother. "Personally, I've always figured you for a cheater."

"Is that so?" Carl responds, staring with a frown for a long moment before bursting out laughing.

"Well, what about that time in Wisconsin?" Robert says, then begins to chuckle to himself. For the next hour, the two of them share anecdotes from fishing trips everywhere from Canada to the Caribbean. Finally, the two men glance over to find Shirley nearly dozing off in her chair. This sets off another round of laughter.

"C'mon," Robert says, "we're putting your poor wife into a coma. Besides, it's time to head over to the Research Center Auditorium."

"Time for your big night, brother," Carl echoes.

Robert looks at him, thinking that even if the evening were to end at this moment, the precious hours with his brother would have made it worth it.

****

Robert knows Veronica has arrived even before he sees her. His eyes unconsciously begin flicking around the crowded auditorium and he finally spots her, all long limbs and striking red hair, standing in sharp relief from the flurry of activity. Next to her stand their three grown sons, Robbie, Randy and Ryan. They too are searching the room, then Ryan spies him and places a hand on his mother's well-dressed arm. The four of them wave in unison, wearing nearly identical smiles. The boys have always favored their mother physically; of their temperament, Robert is sure they follow his, as frequent visits usually involve their fishing and diving stories. Standing in this room, where he would receive arguably the biggest award of his career, his family stands as a symbol of all he has balanced in his career.

He begins weaving through the room toward them, but he finds himself pulled into one conversation and then another, each group offering their congratulations. He is cordial as always, all the while keeping an eye on Veronica before she takes her seat.

Robert has never considered himself a very introspective person; to him, life is more about what one does than the reasons behind it. So when Veronica came to him one unbearably humid night ten years earlier and told him she was leaving him to devote her life to animal rescue, he did not give too much thought to the why. She, on the other hand, was desperate to make him understand—she had been volunteering at the Miami Zoo, as well as at the Bird Sanctuary in the Florida Keys. It was her real passion, even more important than her marriage.

Robert still remembers the pain in his chest—similar to an

electric shock—when she told him. They had been together since high school, knew each other better than anyone, and he had known of her passion for animals, but he'd never seen this coming. There is only what one does, he'd reminded himself, the why doesn't matter. It had taken him months to realize that Veronica had grown tired of playing second fiddle to his own career, that she never would have strayed had he only let her pursue this passion together with him. And it had taken him years after the divorce to realize that not only did he not hate her, but that he loved her as much as ever. Of course, by then, it was too late.

Veronica was happily remarried and living in San Antonio, where she moved shortly after her divorce from Robert became final. Their sons remained in south Florida and close to both their parents.

After extricating himself from a group of his residents, he is heading for her when he hears a voice at his elbow.

"Been a long time coming, Bobby."

It is Dr. Jacobson, his longtime friend and mentor. Now in his eighties, he is also confined to a wheelchair, but his mind is as sharp as ever. He clutches Robert's hand and leans forward conspiratorially.

"Hope you're not getting too big for your britches."

With a smile, Robert moves his hand to his mentor's shoulder. "I wouldn't dream of it, Professor." It is a term of endearment that stuck long after Robert stopped being his resident and protégé.

"That's good to hear. Now, isn't it about time we get to the actual dedication?"

Robert glances at his watch and sees it's just ten minutes

to start time. He looks up at the entrance, any concerns immediately evaporating when he sees Isabella. Dressed in a smart gray suit and her raven hair pulled back in a neat chignon, she has assumed complete control as she greets everyone walking through the doors and instructs them where to sit.

Once everyone is in their chairs, Robert takes his place next to the stage. He looks on with satisfaction at the residents grouped together on one side of the auditorium. Their chairs are placed in a "U" formation in support of the university. Robert smiles to himself and silently thanks Glanville for arranging it.

Keeping with tradition, Dr. Gladstone, the department chairman, introduces the university president. This is followed by the dean's welcoming remarks, then ten minutes of Dr. Gladstone highlighting Dr. Merriweather's many achievements, adding how personally glad he is to have "Bobby" and his division receive this honor.

As the speech continues, Robert feels a combination of both pride and mortification. This was not his first time attending an award ceremony and Lord knows how boring they can be. While certainly enjoying the kudos, he feels pity for the rest of the audience.

Finally, it's time for Robert to take his place at the podium. He does so with a smile and the quiet confidence of one with thousands of lectures under his belt.

He uses the remote to put up the first slide on a big screen behind him that reads "Oral and Maxillofacial Surgery Chair for Research and Education." Using no notes and only an occasional glance at the small computer screen in front of him, he begins.

"President Evans, Dean Silvers, my good friend and ardent supporter, Dr. Alex Gladstone, family and friends; welcome to the first Chair in the division of Oral and Maxillofacial Surgery."

The crowd breaks into cheers, and Robert waits for it to die down before continuing.

"This chair is a blue-collar chair. That is to say, it is not the product of a single grateful donor but instead originated from two sources: the first is our continuing education programs, and the second is the numerous alumni and patients, many of them here this evening, whose generous contributions put this program over the top.

"After family, my two greatest loves have been the profession of oral and maxillofacial surgery and the University of Miami Miller School of Medicine.

"Oral and maxillofacial surgery is part medicine and part dentistry. And, because of this duality, it achieves a level of patient care and accomplishes procedures that no other specialty of dentistry or medicine can do by itself.

"It was my predecessor, Dr. Stewart E. Jacobson...."

He presses a button and the slide changes to a headshot of Jacobson, then nods to the man who is seated in the front row.

"... who, in 1981, joined forces with Dr. Gladstone's predecessor, the great Dr. Robert Giuseppe, to begin a great experiment.

"They believed that a single dental specialty dedicated to head and neck surgery could thrive, and significantly contribute to the well-being and stature of a major medical school.

"In the years since, this theory has been proven, time and time again, largely in the area of trauma care. In 1998, when Dr. Jacobson stepped down, it was this man...."

Dr. Gladstone's smiling picture appears on the screen. "... who insisted the University forgo the usual national search for a new division chief, and appointed me instead.

"'Bobby,' he told me, 'you and I can achieve great things together.' I believe we have done so, and I want to thank you, Dr. Gladstone, for the faith you placed in me and my faculty. Now, if I may, I'd like to brag a bit about the things we have accomplished."Robert quickly assesses the crowd's interest and sees they are genuinely enjoying the speech. He then proceeds to tell them about the first episode of the now well-known television program, The Doctors, during which he and his colleague, Dr. Gomez, removed a twelve-and-a-half-pound tumor from a teenage girl's tongue.

He tells them about Dr. Yoh Samanaka, a member of Robert's faculty who worked with ophthalmologists to pioneer the first tooth-in-eye surgery, a procedure that restored vision to some blind individuals.

He tells them about the books. "We are proud to say we've published nine textbooks, including a 1,250-page book on jaw and facial reconstructive surgery that won the Medical Writers Book of the Year Award. For this, I thank Heather Bellaire, the Chief Book Editor for El-Cid publishing."

Robert nods slightly to a striking long haired brunette woman seated near the back, then goes on to thank his entire faculty, especially Isabella, for all their incredible work.

"Isabella Ruiz is undoubtedly the 'first lady' of our division. She wears several hats around here, including fundraiser. She most recently raised $650,000 to build a clinic dedicated to Dr. Jacobson!"

The crowd, which has been cheering sporadically throughout the speech, now rises for a standing ovation.

"As you can see," Robert continues once they have settled down, "Dr. Gladstone was right about all we could achieve. But this Chair is about much more than TV shows and awards; it's about our patients … ."

A picture of a pretty fifteen-year-old girl's face, with red hair, green eyes, freckles and a smile that could light up a room, comes up on the screen.

"Looks normal, doesn't she? You would never know that we removed three-fourths of her lower jaw in a cancer surgery and rebuilt all of it using her own stem cells, along with recombinant human bone morphogenetic protein—a bone stimulator to most of you—and without removing any bone from her leg, hip, rib, or anywhere else. She is living proof that oral and maxillofacial surgery belongs in this medical school and in this department of surgery. And, after all, it's really all about the U."

On that cue, Robert and his residents all raise their arms to form the "U" sign, a symbol of pride for the University of Miami. The rest of the attendees playfully follow along; even President Evans and Dean Silvers. The crowd erupts into laughter, then rises for another standing ovation, this one lasting several minutes.

Once the audience finds their seats, Dr. Gladstone brings Dr. Merriweather's chair. And after reading the inscription on the back of it aloud, he asks Robert to sit down on it for pictures with his family, guests, the president and dean, and of course, Dr. Jacobson.

****

By seven o'clock, the reception at Robert's home is in full swing. Most of those who attended the chair dedication ceremony are present, along with quite a few more.

In total, there are nearly one hundred people chatting in the spacious rooms and under the several fruit trees dotting the backyard. A gentle breeze rustles the leaves and carries forth the scent of citrus blossoms mingled with the salt from the nearby ocean. *These are the nights*, Robert thinks as he steps outside, *that remind everyone why they live in South Florida.*

He is looking for his sons, who he has not had a chance to speak with all night. He did have a brief conversation with Veronica, one of those exceedingly polite interactions he found more painful than any argument. As he searches out his three sons, he sees that they are set with Dr. Merriweather's plans for a toast.

By all accounts, all are having a wonderful time, imbibing their favorite cocktails at the fully stocked bar and listening to the band he hired for the occasion. They are playing everything from Frank Sinatra and Elton John to calypso, and Robert notes with pleasure that everyone seems to be enjoying the eclectic blend. He makes a mental note to thank Isabella and to remind her that she once again knew what was best for him.

Toward the end of the evening, Dr. Merriweather gains everyone's attention by clanging on a glass with his knife. It takes a minute, but the crowd gradually quiets from a dull roar to an occasional whisper, and the current song comes to a close. When the guests turn to Robert, they find him standing behind three men, each sitting in a wheelchair.

"Today, there's been a lot of attention on me and the division of oral and maxillofacial surgery. However, we have three very special guests here tonight who deserve some recognition—a group we affectionately refer to as the 'Wheelchair Brigade.'"

A tentative laugh goes up from the crowd, a few still debating if they found the joke appropriate.

Robert gestures to his three sons, making their way through the crowd with small trays. "My sons are coming around with glasses of the eighteen-year-old Johnny Walker Blue I reserve for special toasts. If you're like me and don't usually drink, either make an exception, or ask them for a glass of orange juice instead."

Once the drinks start to pass around, Robert stands behind the first wheelchair and puts his hands on the frame.

"For those of you who do not know him, this is my dear brother, Carl. He was my protector growing up, and I loved him for it. However, despite my reputation as a good fisherman, this guy always out-fished me."

Robert laughs, squeezing his brother's shoulder.

"I propose a toast to a great fisherman, Carl Merriweather."

A sea of glasses rises up at once, along with an enthusiastic cheer.

Robert steps towards Dr. Jacobson's chair, and his voice takes on a calmer tone.

"This is the man who started it all—my mentor and a teacher of so many professional and life lessons. He also out-fished me … but he cheated."

Chuckles go through the crowd.

"When I first arrived in Florida, I had only fished fresh water. So, as he and I began fishing the ocean, I would catch these large, oval-shaped, white, shiny fish with big eyes. Dr. Jacobson told me, 'Bobby, that's a horse-eye jack. Throw it back. It's no good.' I later came to find out that those fish were African pompano, one of the most delicious fish you can catch." The crowd laughs, and Dr. Jacobson twists his head to look up at Robert, his eyes as alive and devilish as ever.

"Today, I propose a toast to Dr. Jacobson—one of the best doctors, the best fishermen, and the best liars I've ever met." Again the crowd cheers.

Finally, Robert comes to Norman Edelson's wheelchair. "I am standing behind Norman, a true American hero. While our politicians continually tell us that they're fighting for us, Norman actually did. He was a World War II, 101st Airborne Division paratrooper. He parachuted behind enemy lines in the Battle of the Bulge and earned a Purple Heart for his heroism. Now, at 93, he is one of the few remaining true World War II veterans. He also happens to be married to another of my heroes—the lovely Diana, who has helped countless patients during her twenty years as my own hospital volunteer. He has earned our gratitude and certainly this toast. Let's hear it for Norman Edelson."

"Here, here!" the crowd yells, before tipping back their drinks.

With the reception breaking up around midnight, Dr. Merriweather catches up with Miriam Reyes, Dr. Jacobson's caregiver, before she leaves.

"So, are we still on for tomorrow?" he asks.

Miriam nods. "Yes, would nine tomorrow morning be an okay time for Dr. Jacobson to come in?"

"Yes, I'll make sure the stem cell research he wanted to see will be ready for him."

Miriam smiles warmly at him. "Gracias … and gracias for the party."

"It was my pleasure," Robert says, but his eyes are already on Heather Bellaire, who is heading to her rental car. "I'm glad everyone enjoyed themselves."

He says goodbye to Miriam, then hurries to catch up with Heather.

The two remain quiet until he opens the car door. "Will we be able to get together while I'm here?" Heather asks, looking over his shoulder to make sure no one's listening. "I miss you."

"I would love that," Robert whispers, "but with my brother leaving tomorrow for the Keys and Dr. Jacobson wanting to spend time with me, I can't. I'll see you soon up in New York though."

Heather climbs into her car and looks up at Dr. Merriweather.

"I miss you too." He gently but firmly closes the door, then watches as her car disappears into the balmy night. He neglected her tonight, as he had at past events when his ex-wife and sons were around, and he feels just as guilty about it.

Deep in thought, he turns back towards the house and the other guests waiting to bid him goodnight. He doesn't notice the green sedan parked behind a hedge in his neighbor's yard or the person inside, watching him and waiting.

CHAPTER 3
Tragedy

Dr. Merriweather loves Saturday mornings at the hospital—the relative calm of the Medical Arts Building, the way his footsteps echo on the spotless marble floors of the empty lobby, the opportunity to get things done without being pulled in fifty different directions.

This Saturday is even better than most, as he is still on a high from last night's festivities. The chair dedication went off without a glitch. His only regret is that he did not get to speak with his sons very much. He makes a mental note to call and organize a fishing trip. They will go down to the Keys, away from the busyness of their everyday lives, and catch up with no interruptions.

When he walks into his office, Isabella is waiting for him with a cup of coffee and a satisfied smile.

"That was a great event last night."

"Yeah, thanks largely to you. What would I do without you, Issy?"

"Well, probably not this HIPAA stuff." She gestures toward the small mountain of papers on her desk.

Merriweather chuckles. "Thank you for coming in on a Saturday. I hope it didn't mess with any of your plans."

"It's not a problem." Isabella gives a modest shrug before going back over to the desk where a stack of HIPAA compliance forms and subpoenas relating to upcoming trials lie in wait.

He gives her one more look of appreciation before powering up his computer. Just then, Diana Edelson peeks her head around the corner.

"Hey, Robert. Do you have a minute?"

"For you, Diana, I have at least two," he says, gesturing for her to take a seat. "Coffee?"

Diana shakes her head. "No … thanks. I was wondering if I could get some unofficial medical advice from you."

"Of course … is there a problem with Norman's dialysis?"

Diana gave a warm, slightly sheepish smile. "No, it's about me this time. For the past six years, I've been taking Bone Max for osteopenia, and I have to say … after seeing some of your patients, I'm becoming really concerned."

Merriweather nearly jumps out of his chair. "What? Why didn't you tell me this before? Of course you should be worried! Bone Max causes ninety-six percent of all the oral cis-phosphorous necrosis cases I've seen! What's the dosage?"

She tells him, and Robert starts shaking his head. "Diana, that's way too high a dose and for far too long. Have you had any jaw or leg problems?"

"Knock on wood, no," Diana replies, rapping her fist against his desk. "I've spoken to my doctor about my concerns, but she wants me to keep taking it. She said it's a must for post-menopausal women."

Merriweather sighs. "That's not your doctor talking. That's the marketing department at Apollo Pharmaceuticals. Just this year, the FDA ordered them to add a statement to their product label that doctors should consider taking their patients off of it after three years.

A flash of alarm jumps across Diana's face. Before she can react further, her concerned colleague switches to a softer tone.

"Look, it's okay. You're not experiencing any symptoms, so there's no need to panic. I'll examine you Monday. We'll take a few x-rays. I'll also talk with your doctor. She may just not be up on the latest FDA reports."

"Okay …" Diana trails off as they hear a shuffling sound coming down the hallway.

"Good morning, Dr. Jacobson," Isabella calls out from her desk in the room adjacent to Dr. Merriweather's office. Both of the room's occupants turn to look as he walks into the doorway, leaning most of his weight on his walker.

"I hope I'm not interrupting anything."

"No, of course not," Merriweather says. He pauses for a moment. "Where's Miriam?"

Jacobson raises an eyebrow. "She's visiting some relatives here in town. I'm not totally dependent on her, you know. She's going to come and get me when we finish."

Diana rises out of her chair. "Well, I'll leave you gentlemen to your visit." She mouths thank you to Merriweather, then says, "It was a pleasure seeing you again, Dr. Jacobson. Have a safe trip home."

"Thank you, Diana."

She gives him a cordial nod before disappearing into the hallway.

Capitalizing on the moment of silence, Isabella peaks her

head in and says, "I should get going too. My son has a birthday party to go to. I'll drop him off and should be back in about a half-hour to finish these forms up."

"Is that Hispanic time or Gringo time?"

"Hispanic time, if you must know," she quickly replies, with a smile. Isabella had learned to hold her own early in her employ with Merriweather. It's one of the many qualities he admires in her.

"Well, in that case it will be over an hour—maybe two," Merriweather says, enjoying the look of shock on Dr. Jacobson's face. "Before you go, please set up the presentations I prepared for the professor."

"Of course, with pleasure." Isabella guides Dr. Jacobson to the chair in front of Dr. Merriweather's computer. She readies things with a few clicks.

"Okay, I'll be back soon."

Isabella nearly makes it to the door when the phone rings. She spins on her heels back into the room.

"No, no. Go … I got it." Merriweather says, waving her away and putting the call on speaker. "Yes, what is it?"

The voice on the other end talks fast and panicked. "Hello, sir … it's me, James … I'm in the emergency room. We have a woman here with a stone in her submandibular gland. She's really swollen, and her tongue's pushed back into her airway. I think you need to come here right now."

"Will do," Robert says, ending the call and turning to Dr. Jacobson.

"I'm sorry, Professor, but it looks like I have to get to the emergency room."

Dr. Jacobson looks up from a Power Point slide and waves him away. "Go, Bobby, go help that woman. I'm fine."

Dr. Merriweather nods before rushing out.

With the room now quiet, Dr. Jacobson starts looking through the slides with growing fascination. Each includes before and after pictures of Merriweather's patients—and proves the effectiveness of his methods.

After just ten minutes, he is so engrossed in the slideshow, he doesn't notice that someone has entered the room.

"Dr. Merriweather?" a gruff voice asks.

Dr. Jacobson blinks and starts to turn his head. "No, it's this old—"

The first blow knocks his head forward into the monitor, cracking the glass. Dr. Jacobson manages to give out a small moaning cry as his assailant winds up to deliver another. The second strike scatters Jacobson's skull. Lying unmoving on the desk, he doesn't feel the following blows as blood splatters on the walls and floor and oozes along the desk, soaking sticky notes and sheets of paper. Still, the killer continues, grunting with the effort of each swing. It is the only sound in the room, but for the grotesque squishing of the weapon against pulverized flesh.

****

Dr. Merriweather closes the hanging curtains around Ms. Krajek's gurney in an attempt to shield her from the chaos of the emergency room. As he approaches the bedside he holds her gaze, trying to calm the panic in her eyes.

"Ms. Krajek, the x-ray shows you have a stone in your spit gland below your left jaw. There's also a serious infection there. It's making your tongue and the bottom of your mouth swell. That's the reason you're having trouble swallowing, okay?"

The woman nods, her eyes wide and her breathing fast. Dr. Merriweather takes her hand.

"My greatest concern, though, is that the swelling is starting to hinder your breathing. To fix it, we're going to need to do what's called a tracheostomy."

Ms. Krajek's eyes start to jump back and forth, her breath now labored.

"It's okay," Merriweather says, squeezing her hand. "It's a routine procedure. We're just going to make a small opening in your windpipe, which will allow you to breathe easier until the swelling goes down. We will remove it as soon as this occurs. Now before we go, I need you to sign this consent form. It'll let us remove the gland and the stone so we can get you feeling better."

Dr. Glanville steps forward from behind Dr. Merriweather and starts reading aloud the form displayed on a laptop. Ms. Krajek reaches over to sign it electronically, while Dr. Merriweather talks to the anesthesiologist and emergency room nurses.

"Dr. Morales, we need to get this woman to the OR immediately. She is losing her airway fast and I would prefer not to have to do a tracheostomy in the hallway."

"Okay, we're ready," Dr. Morales replies. "I'll try to get as much oxygen through as possible on the way."

Ms. Krajek is gasping for air as they rush her into the main hospital towards the operating rooms. Running behind them is a nurse waving a group of papers.

"You can't take her to the OR yet," she says, "the C-250 form and the C-274 forms aren't signed."

Ignoring her, Doctors Merriweather and Glanville exchange a knowing look as they continue wheeling the gurney toward operating room number two. Nothing irritates Merriweather more than bureaucracy, especially when a patient's life is on the line. When they reach the OR, they find the scrub nurse and circulating nurse already waiting.

The irate woman follows them in, where Dr. Glanville intercepts her and signs the two forms—the C-250 to handle Ms. Krajek's personal items, and the C-274 for patient rights. He hands them back to the nurse and is barely able to hide his own disdain as she turns on her heel and stalks away.

He has been gone under a minute, but when Dr. Glanville returns, he finds Ms. Krajek semi-comatose, with a bluish tinge to her skin. With one gesture from Merriweather, Glanville moves around to the other side of the gurney.

"We haven't got time to move her to the OR bed—we'll do it right here."

Glanville nods, and Merriweather picks a scalpel blade off the instrument stand.

"Better work fast, I've completely lost the airway," Dr. Morales says, beginning to put the EKG pads and the blood pressure cuff on the patient.

"Stop while I do the timeout!" the circulating nurse screeches.

Without even a pause, Dr. Merriweather makes an incision and separates the strap muscles in the neck.

"I need to do the timeout!"

"Dr. Glanville, retract the thyroid gland upward," Dr. Merriweather says. Dr. Glanville nods and complies.

"Dr. Merriweather!" shouts the nurse again.

Still ignoring her, Robert makes a vertical incision through tracheal rings, exposing the windpipe. He then inserts the tracheostomy tube into the trachea and hooks it up to deliver pure oxygen.

Almost immediately, Ms. Krajek's skin turns back to a near normal pink. Only then does he turn to face the circulating nurse.

"Paula," he says coldly, "a life is more important than the damn timeout. Forget the administrative bullshit for now and help us suture this woman's tracheostomy in place."

It is a tone he does not use often, which makes it all the more intimidating when he does.

Paula's mouth pulls into a tight frown and she refuses to look at him. "Yes, Doctor."

"Thank you. Now give me a tracheostomy collar. The emergency is over."

She gives one to him without a word, and Dr. Merriweather returns to his patient. Her skin's already a completely normal color and her oxygen is up to 100%. The entire procedure had taken all of ninety seconds.

"Thanks to our quick work, the odds of brain damage are very low," Dr. Merriweather announces to the others, "but I'd still like to be sure. Dr. Glanville, after the surgery,

Robert E. Marx

please request a neurology consultation and electroencephalogram for Ms. Krajek.

"Got it."

"Okay, now let's get her onto the operating room table and remove the stone and gland that is causing all this infection."

Before they can prepare any of the instruments, Isabella's voice comes through the OR speaker phone.

"Dr. Merriweather … come, come quick. Dr. Jacobson is … hurt—it's really bad. I-I called the fast response team but …" Her voice catches. "Please come back here right away."

His heart in his throat, Merriweather steps back from the patient and rips off his gloves. "I know you know how to do this procedure," he says to an equally shocked Glanville, "but bring Dr. Sanders in here to help you and call Dr. Brewster to take my place as the faculty. I know he's in the hospital somewhere."

Glanville nods. "Yes, of course."

"Thanks." Before the nurses can say anything, Merriweather races out of the room, leaving the doors swinging back and forth behind him.

The hallway seems to stretch endlessly before him and Robert is in a full sprint by the time he rounds the corner and opens the door to his office. He arrives just in time to see the hospital's Emergency Response Team rushing inside. He enters right behind them and sees Isabella standing by her desk, arms wrapped around herself. She catches his eye, slowly shakes her head, then looks back at the emergency team, now gathered around the area where he'd left Dr. Jacobson less than an hour before.

39

His mentor's body is slouched limply in the chair, his hands still placed on either side of the keyboard, suggesting at first glance that he may be asleep. Then Merriweather sees the back of the skull, now a mess of pulpy flesh and exposed bone and brain. A thick, dark red fluid is spread over the floor.

"Oh my God," Robert gasps as he rushes to Jacobson's side, "No, no, no!" He gasps again when he sees Jacobson's eyes wide open and bulging.

"I don't understand," he says to no one in particular. When Isabella had called to say Jacobson was hurt, he had assumed he'd fallen, perhaps hit his head. He never imagined something like this.

Processing more of what he is seeing, he notices the blood splatter around the room. He feels a firm but gentle hand on his shoulder, then a member of the response team says calmly, "I'm sorry, Doctor … we need you to step away from him."

He stares blankly at the man for a moment through water-filled eyes.

"Who would—? He never—"

Struggling for control, he glances at his friend again, then slowly backs away. Behind him, he hears Isabella's ragged breath and turns to her.

"He's right, this is a crime scene. We shouldn't touch anything."

She nods, just as they hear blaring sirens approaching nearing the hospital. Within minutes, several uniformed cops race into the office, guns drawn. The entire hospital has been put on lockdown.

CHAPTER 4
The Murder Scene

Detective Andy Molinaro looks young for his age. At least, that's what most people say when they find out he's forty-five years old; aside from a few speckles of gray at the temples—his hair is dark and thick and cut in a way that accentuates his dimples and chiseled jaw. Molinaro's been turning heads since high school, not that he's ever noticed.

He'd been a quiet boy growing up and kept mostly to himself. His outlets were the arts and solo sports, like running and weightlifting, which had added just the right amount of lean muscle mass to his six-foot-one frame.

His partner Enrique Gonzalez, is the complete opposite. A poster child for the processed food industry, he'd had a fit of anxiety when Hostess announced they were discontinuing their Twinkies product. The buzz around the department was that he'd gone to at least twenty convenience stores and cleared their shelves of the golden treats. His favorite pastime was watching TV and smoking hand-rolled cigarettes.

Molinaro often tells him that he needs to lay off the junk food; not that Gonzalez ever listens. Most nights he suffers through the healthy (and tasteless) dinner prepared by his wife, so if he wants a little treat during his shift, what's the harm?

He is munching on an apple fritter—his second of the

day—when he and Molinaro arrive at the University of Miami Jackson South Hospital. They walk through the lobby of the medical arts building, noticing the blood droppings on the floor now already marked with bright yellow cones. As they enter the crime scene, their nearly identical black suits scream law enforcement to anyone who sees them. At the door of Merriweather's office, Gonzalez shoves the last oversized bite of fritter into his mouth.

"Those things'll kill you." Molinaro raises a single brow to his partner.

Gonzalez reaches down to button his suit jacket only to find the two sides don't quite meet over his paunch. He hears a snort and looks up to see Molinaro smirking at him with brows raised.

"What? This is an old suit, and it's a known fact that this material shrinks over time."

"Whatever you say, Rick." Molinaro rolls his eyes.

"I'm serious. I read it somewhere."

Molinaro ignores him with an intentional exhale and side-steps past some C.S.I. team members who are going in and out of the door. Other techs remain in the hallway, setting down numbered cones to mark what look to be more drops of blood. The detectives eye each other; someone, presumably the killer, had fled toward the back entrance and was possibly bleeding, carrying the bloody murder weapon, or both.

Molinaro ducks underneath the police tape and takes a step into the room. "Holy shit," he says just loud enough for his partner to hear him.

Gonzalez comes up behind, raising an eyebrow at his

partner. "What's the matter, Andy? You've seen grisly crime scenes before."

"Not that—take a look at the walls. There isn't a single space without some kind of plaque or award. This Merriweather guy's the real deal."

"Speaking of which, where is the good doctor?" Gonzalez asks as he lets out a deep, resonating belch.

Molinaro steps back, fanning the air in front of him. "Man! What the hell did you eat today, a week-old rat?"

"What? I don't smell nothin'—oh, now I do. Whew! Must be the midnight snack I had last night. Couldn't tell what it was in the fridge or if it had sauce or cheese. Must've been mold."

"Good God, man! Don't do that again. Step outside or something. Christ!"

"I didn't know it was coming! Caught me off guard, I guess."

Molinaro shoots him an annoyed look, then catches the attention of a passing CSI.

"Dr. Merriweather—where is he?"

The CSI points to a door on their left. "Next office. Merriweather's assistant is in there too. She called it in."

Gonzalez turns to his partner. "Andy, you go talk to them while I see what the lab boys figured out."

"Sounds like a plan." Andy disappears into the other room.

Gonzales turns to the three people crowded around a computer desk. One tech is crouched down, examining the floor, while the other two are bent over the body—an elderly man with the back of his head half-gone. He is sitting in the chair with his upper body sprawled on the desk.

"Well, boys and girls, what have you come up with so far?"

"Right now, not much beyond the obvious," a young woman replies as she straightens to face the detective. "Meet the late Doctor Stewart E. Jacobson."

"Okay, now we've met. What happened?"

"Blunt force trauma. No sign of struggle though. He probably didn't even see it coming."

Gonzales leans down and takes a look at the injury. The blood, now dry, leaves Jacobson's white hair red-stained and stuck to his scalp.

"What was it?" Gonzales asks.

The woman looks at one of the other investigators before shrugging. "We're not sure yet. Whoever did this took the murder weapon with them. We've found some foreign metal fragments embedded in the skull, but we don't know what it's from.

"How long ago?"

"About an hour, according to the body temperature and minimal level of decay."

"Huh," Gonzales replies, then falls silent as he looks around the crime scene. It catches the woman by surprise when he speaks up again.

"What about the perp?"

The woman grabs a paper off the table and looks at it.

"Physically, all we know is he's right-handed. But from the blood drop pattern, we can tell he walked out of here—slowly-didn't run—and did so pretty much immediately afterwards."

"Is that everything?"

"Yeah, that's all we've got for now. I'll let you know more when we complete our investigation."

Gonzalez nods, more to himself than to the tech, then moves to the wall to look at Merriweather's awards. Who is this guy … and what the hell happened to make somebody so incredibly angry?

****

In the adjoining room, Andy Molinaro is thinking much the same thing as he sits across the conference table from Dr. Robert Merriweather and his assistant, Isabella Ruiz.

"You knew the victim rather well?" he asks, looking at Merriweather. Next to him, Isabella is quickly burning her way through a box of tissues.

"He was my mentor," Merriweather says, controlled but clearly upset. "Like a father to me."

"Can you think of anyone who would want to hurt him?"

"No," Merriweather says simply, looking at the table. Tears bristle, but he manages to blink them away.

A sympathetic frown tugs at the detective's mouth as he jots a few things down on his notepad.

He then turns to the woman. "What about you, Ms. Ruiz? You found the body, correct?"

She pushes her long black hair from her face, revealing

lovely blue eyes that are swollen with tears.

"Yes … I returned from an errand and he was …" She looks like she's about to start sobbing again but holds it together. "I didn't know Dr. Jacobson very well, he retired many years ago, before I started working here. But I certainly can't think of anyone who would want to hurt him. He was just a sweet old man." She sniffs.

Molinaro turns back to Merriweather. "Do a lot of people have access to your office?"

"Not on a weekend, no, but we keep the door unlocked while we're here. Dr. Jacobson's caregiver … umm, Miriam … was going to come and pick him up after he was done using the computer. She's usually with him twenty-four-seven."

"Where was she?"

"With some nearby relatives …" His voice trails off and his eyes go wide. "Oh God, I hope she's okay!"

Isabella's head swivels to look at Merriweather, panic spreading across her face as well.

Molinaro's hand comes up in a placating gesture. "We're going to check that out now. Do you have any way to get in touch with her?"

"Well, I know her number is in Dr. Jacobson's cell phone."

Molinaro stands up. "Okay, stay right here. I have a few more questions, but I'll get someone to make sure she's safe."

The two nod numbly at him as he walks from the room and pulls aside a young, uniformed officer standing in the outer office. A moment later he is back in his seat, still clutching his pad and pen.

"Alright, someone is going to call her, break the news and make sure she's okay." Molinaro doesn't bother telling them that they will also need to clear Miriam as a suspect. "Now, I know it's been a long morning, but I need to ask you about a few more things."

They both nod again, then Dr. Merriweather holds another tissue to Isabella. Molinaro notices the way her hand reached up to take it almost before he made the move.

"Dr. Merriweather, was there anyone else in your office this morning before you left for surgery?"

"Only Diana Edelson. She's my patient advocate and a volunteer. Been here for eighteen years. She left right after Dr. Jacobson arrived."

"Is it unusual for her to come to your office on a Saturday?"

"No, she's here every Saturday," Merriweather says, shaking his head. "She rounds with me and the residents, helps the patients with the logistics of leaving the hospital or contacting family members."

"Anything else?" the detective asks, his pen running across the paper.

"Yeah, she usually comes by the office afterward to go over schedules for upcoming clinic and surgical cases." He sighs. "Today was no different."

"Okay, can you give me her phone number? I'll need to speak with her—just part of our routine."

Merriweather recites the phone number from memory.

"Thanks, Doctor. Now, I have to ask—did you leave the operating room at any time during the surgery?"

"No, I was there the entire time, until Issy called me."

"And you, Ms. Ruiz?" Molinaro asks, "You were with your son … ?"

Isabella nods.

"Was your husband with you too?"

She shakes her head. "No, I'm divorced … I came back a-and there was blood on the floor … and I looked in … and …" Isabella bursts into fresh sobs.

Resisting the urge to squeeze her hand, Molinaro instead passes her a business card. "That's enough questions for now. If you think of anything that might help, call me, okay?" He then closes his notepad, drops it into his pocket, and stands.

Stifling another sob, she tucks the card into her jacket pocket, then rises along with Merriweather to thank the detective.

Molinaro has his hand on the door when he turns back to them.

"Oh … ah, I do have a request for both of you. We'll need to examine your clothes. It's standard procedure. Is this what you've been wearing for the past three hours?"

"Yes," they respond in unison.

"Good, then I'll need you to take them off in the company of one of our CSI team members." He notes their blank but conciliatory nods—then adds, "We want to eliminate as many suspects as quickly as we can. If you don't have a change of clothes to wear home, we can provide jumpsuits for you. Dr. Merriweather, I see you're in surgical scrubs. Does that mean you have street clothes somewhere nearby?"

"Yes. I can change into my own clothes. They're in a locker next to the operating room. While I'm there I can get some scrubs for Issy." He turns to her. "That okay with you?"

Isabella is not paying attention. Merriweather and Molinaro follow her line of sight out the door, towards the slumped over form in the chair.

"Y-yes," she stutters after a moment, "that's fine. I can get Gabe from the birthday party later."

"Thank you," Molinaro responds. Then, with a final sympathetic look at Isabella, he leaves them alone with their grief.

****

After dropping off their clothes with the CSIs, Merriweather and Isabella leave, both looking drawn and exhausted. Over the next couple of hours the CSI team finishes photographing, collecting prints and cataloging its contents, then the body is carefully removed from the office for transport to the morgue.

Gonzales and Molinaro stick around until the room is sealed up, then they head out to the car to regroup and compare notes.

"What do you think of the doctor and his secretary?" Gonzales asks as he slips into the driver's seat.

Molinaro shrugs. "In my opinion, there's nothing there. They seem genuinely broken up about the old man. Don't appear to have a motive either."

"Appearances can be deceiving, Andy."

"True, and I've seen incredible acting before too. We'll know more after the clothes are examined. There's no way the perp could have avoided getting some of the victim's blood on them, not with that degree of splatter."

"Any other leads?"

Molinaro takes out his notepad and flips through a few pages. "Yeah, I'm really interested in the victim's caregiver, a Miriam Reyes. We got her on the phone and she wasn't that far from the murder scene. Sounded devastated. That's not hard to fake over a call, though."

He pauses to flip to the next page. "Her alibi's not perfect, said she was with her family, but apparently they don't speak English—they're from Nicaragua. When I visit I won't let on that despite my Italian good looks, I'm fluent in Spanish."

"Good plan, Andy," Detective Gonzalez says, chuckling. "But seriously, you might be on to something. Caregivers get fed up with their patients sometimes. Wouldn't give her a raise, wouldn't support her citizenship application ... who the hell knows, could be anything."

He starts the car, but leaves it in park.

"While you do that," he continues, "I'll check out the victim's family. See what he's been paying her, and if he left anything in the will. Also, if you're going to check Ms. Ruiz's alibi, try to get her to talk about Dr. Merriweather. Secretaries have all sorts of juicy details about their bosses."

"Will do."

"Good, is there anything else?"

"Just one, that woman—Diana Edelson. She was in the office before Jacobson got in. I got her address and phone number from Merriweather."

"We'll check her out too," Gonzalez says, sighing. "Looks like we got our work cut out for us."

He turns to Andy. "C'mon, I know a great new burger place."

CHAPTER 5
Behind Closed Doors

Of the twenty-one chairs around the oval mahogany table in Halstead, Butterworth and Payne's conference room, only one is empty. It's also the only one that counts, for it belongs to Barrymore Halstead, the firm's founding partner. Listed by Newsweek Magazine as the third largest law firm in the United States, Halstead has three floors of New York's Tony Seagram Building and employs hundreds of people, including attorneys, support personnel, and law school interns hoping to land a plumb job.

The lively chatter around the table ceases abruptly as Halstead walks into the room. As always, the six foot two inch slender man with neatly combed, fully gray hair is dressed for the part in an impeccable three-piece Brooks Brothers suit, his trademark blood-red handkerchief tucked in the left breast pocket.

An imposing figure, Halstead walks to the head of the table, places a thick folder upon it and, without preamble, begins to speak.

"I don't need to remind you how important Apollo Pharmaceuticals Inc. and North Star Drug Company are to this firm."

The lawyers around the table nod; the retainers alone from the two companies are enough to ensure everyone at the table a sizable year-end bonus.

"Therefore, I do not have to remind you how much is riding on the upcoming lawsuits against them. No one in this room wants another 'Dolor-Not' fiasco."

The mention of Dolor-Not sends a chill up the spines of the attorneys—the younger ones because they had studied it as a cautionary tale in law school, the more seasoned attorneys because they had worked it or witnessed the fallout.

Seven years earlier, Apollo Pharmaceuticals had made headlines around the world after it was discovered they had knowingly relied on faulty research to obtain approval for their "Dolor-Not" painkiller.

With the hubris common to most corporations of their size and stature, they thought a clever marketing campaign (including the name itself, "dolor" meaning "pain" in Latin) would deflect consumer concerns about a new drug. And they succeeded until an email was discovered that revealed they had buried their own statistics of a fourfold increase in heart attacks over other painkillers. Even worse, Apollo had published tainted data in the New England Journal of Medicine as part of the cover-up. Thanks to clever lawyering, they won ten of the first fifteen lawsuits that were filed. However, there were thousands of other claims waiting in the wings, resulting in a very public class action suit, a settlement of epic proportions, and years of negative press. Entire law firms, including some of Halstead's biggest competitors, had folded under the backlash.

Now Apollo's drug "Bone Max" and North Star Drug Company's "Bone Protect" have come under fire.

"Given the history here," Halstead growls, "there is absolutely no room for error. Did you hear me? None. Or every head in the room is going to roll." His piercing gaze scans the room, managing to make contact with everyone around the table. "And another thing—I don't want to hear anything about settlements or mediation. Our clients are ready to go to the wall on this." Halstead turns to his right, where George Payne, senior partner and the lead attorney on the cases, is sitting. "Where are we with this, George?"

"Well, to date, there are 792 cases filed against Apollo and 913 cases against North Star. Thirteen have come to trial. We've won four and lost nine. After a thorough risk assessment, we settled six others. The settlements were less than what we could lose in a jury trial."

Payne cowers lightly in his chair even before Barry Halstead speaks. He knows his boss all too well.

"Now that's not very good, is it?" Halstead says, his jaw flexing. "That's not what Halstead, Butterworth and Payne is all about. What is the problem here, George? Give it to me straight."

George Payne motions to Ferris Neuman, a senior associate who would sell his own mother to make partner. Neuman has been assisting Payne with the pharmaceutical cases.

"Well, sir, both of our clients have some serious vulnerabilities."

Halstead waves impatiently. "Go on."

"Well, both of them have damaging internal emails and memos identifying flaws in their research, including a lack of due diligence with regard to 'serious adverse events' associated with the drugs. Some emails have even identified payoffs and granting research dollars to support certain influential physicians. Others refer to their efforts to bury studies that prove their drugs work at lower doses." Neuman pauses to skim his notes. "There are emails from their marketing directors seeking to promote the drugs for purposes not approved by the FDA. The worst, though, is a list of physicians—mostly oral and maxillofacial surgeons—who lecture on the osteonecrosis—or 'dead bone jaw' associated with the drugs. There are notes with the list that indicated a willingness to threaten these doctors. Some—"

"That's enough," Halstead snaps. "Don't those idiots know by now that these things can be subpoenaed? It's like putting all your emails on the Jumbotron at Giants Stadium for the world to see. Morons!"

The entire group flinches when Halstead pounds on the table.

"That's not all," Neuman continues timidly. "Opposing counsel has several strong expert witnesses."

"Do tell," snorts Halstead.

"An FDA Medical Affairs Officer, for one. She's notoriously anti-pharma and continuously testifies that our clients refused for years to place FDA warnings on their drug labels and that when they did, they corrupted the exact wording of the warning. The other side also has at least two very credible case-specific witnesses who relate well to juries. They've testified in similar cases. They'll review each case file and conclude that the cis-phosphorous drug from either Apollo or North Star was the direct cause of the osteonecrosis of the jaw—or 'ONJ'—in that specific patient, often quoting the publications and books of a Dr. Robert Merriweather out of Miami."

"Finally, there is Merriweather himself. He's the lynchpin, the one who first discovered ONJ and how the cis-phosphorous drugs cause it. He is the go-to guy on this topic, so it's hard to find doctors who'll go against him on the stand. He is also very good with juries, and—"

Halstead cuts him off again. "I get the picture, Neuman. Any way we can convince this Merriweather not to testify for them? What if we offer him more to come to our side?"

George Payne shakes his head. "It's been tried. This guy doesn't care about the money. For him, it's some kind of good versus evil thing."

Halstead is quiet for a minute. "Okay, first step is to hit them with Daubert hearings…."

There are snickers around the room. Multiple Daubert hearings would deplete the plaintiffs' financial resources while racking up our firm's billable hours. The group grows quiet when they see Halstead's angry stare aimed at a few of the interns standing at the back of the room.

"Excuse me, back there," Halstead snaps, "are we interfering with your conversation?"

One red-faced young woman steps forward. "Excuse me, sir, um, we had a question. We were, uh, just wondering—"

"Ask the damn question," roars Halstead.

Now visibly perspiring, she asks, "What exactly is a Daubert hearing? I don't believe we covered that in our classes."

"What's your name, young lady?"

"Brenda—Brenda Peabody."

"Well, Ms. Peabody, normally I would tell you that this is not the forum for such questions and that you and your colleagues should have waited to do a Westlaw search rather than wasting our valuable time...."

"Sorry, uh—"

"But this one time, I will answer your question. A Daubert hearing, if granted by the judge, limits and challenges their expert witnesses as to what they can testify to at trial. These hearings are a great strain on the other side's resources, as it requires them to pay for the witness' travel, their hotel, and their fees. It's also a great strain on the witnesses, for it requires them to rearrange their schedules, get on a plane and fly to wherever the hearing is. After a dozen or so times, many get tired of it and will drop out of a case or two—maybe even their entire commitment. It further allows us to see how they will answer at trial, and, if we are good, we just might expose a weakness or inconsistency in their testimony. It's literally no risk for us and a burden for them. I hope that answers your question, young lady."

"Wow, it certainly did, Mr. Halstead. Thank you," gushes Ms. Peabody with an appropriate amount of awe.

"So, George, schedule a Daubert hearing for every case. If the judge balks because they've already been certified as experts in the other cis-phosphorous cases, let me know. I know him personally and will take it up with him myself." He eyeballs Neuman and Payne. "You two just focus on running their asses all over the country. We'll see how long they hold up."

"Yes, sir," they say in unison.

"Also, I want someone to go over every lecture and publication Merriweather has ever done with a fine-tooth comb. I mean every screen image, every damn thing. Look for any inconsistency between his lectures, his books, his publications, and his previous testimonies. Put as many people on it as you need to, George, understand? And while you're at it, get someone to look into his professional and personal life. I want to know if he ever had a DUI, beat his kids, had a medical malpractice suit, or even ran a damned stoplight."

"And, finally, at every trial, emphasize the expert witness fee he gets. Paint him out to be a hypocrite—going after big, rich pharma when all he wants is a 6 hefty payoff."

"That's, um, the problem, sir," says another, equally timid junior co-counsel on the other side of the table. "Dr. Merriweather doesn't get any of the deposition or expert witness fees. All checks are written out to the University of Miami. He always testifies that all payments are to repay the University for his absence and that his salary is fixed and doesn't change with the expert witness fees or deposition payments. The jury really likes him for that, and the other side always makes sure they compare him to other, paid witnesses who keep their fees as personal income."

Halstead waves away the young man's concerns. "Keep looking for personal stuff. In the meantime, we'll bring up any bonuses he gets and any lecture fees he gets, and be sure to point out any perks he receives by lecturing in these courses. A lot of these doctors lecture for an hour and then frolic at Disney or take in Broadway plays at the expense of the institution. Now, we all have work to do, so let's get to it. If we do our jobs right, I expect us to win more of these cases in the future."

With that, Halstead leaves the room and as always, seems to drain it of energy. George Payne stays behind and parcels out assignments to everyone, then watches them file out before turning to Ferris Newman and the two other attorneys who have stayed behind.

"Our previous efforts to get Merriweather out of the way have been unsuccessful. I'm open to suggestions now. If we can get him out, the dominos will fall."

CHAPTER 6
The Other Board Rooms

The boardroom at Apollo Pharmaceuticals is half the size of the one at Halstead, Butterworth and Payne, but the meeting taking place inside is no less intense.

Founded in 1957 by internist Dr. Angelo Apollonia, Apollo was still in its infancy when the thousands of thalidomide cases began to emerge. Unbeknownst to the pharmaceutical company that had developed thalidomide, the drug that had been created to prevent morning sickness in pregnant women, it was inhibiting the development of new blood vessels. It was not until a number of babies were born without hands or feet, and sometimes with only half an arm or leg, that the devastating side effect was discovered.

Horrified by the cases and the international fallout that ensued, Angelo Apollonia vowed that his fledgling drug company would engage in rigorous testing before bringing a drug to market, followed by a strong post-marketing surveillance program.

Over the years, Apollo Pharmaceuticals gained a well-deserved reputation for integrity and the marketing of good medicines. However, that all began to change in 1992 when Angelo Apollonia retired. The new CEO, David Steiner, was not a physician but an Ivy League-educated MBA, and he changed the culture of Apollo Pharmaceuticals from a doctor-driven model to one focused solely on the bottom line.

By the time Angelo Apollonia passed away in 1995, Apollo was unrecognizable from the small, reputable startup he had founded nearly four decades earlier.

It was Steiner's profit-above-safety attitude that brought about the Dolor-not scandal and the subsequent two-billion-dollar settlement. It had taken nearly fifteen years for Apollo to fully recover from the loss of credibility in the medical community and the trust of the public. For reasons that stymied everyone, Steiner had somehow managed to survive the scandal and remain at the helm, even as the company moved forward with its latest blockbuster drug known as Bone-Max.

Now, in a meeting with his medical director, marketing director, the lead research team of five PhDs, and Apollo's general counsel, David Steiner moves to the next topic on his agenda: the status of Bone-Max and the new spate of lawsuits associated with it.

"Okay, fill me in on the status of Bone-Max," Steiner says to no one in particular.

The others shoot glances around the table, each hoping someone else will be the first to speak up. Finally, Gordon Hardgrave, Apollo's Global Director of Marketing, clears his throat.

"Bone-Max made 3.6 billion in revenue last year, as it has, plus or minus a couple hundred million dollars, each year. We've now grossed thirty-two billion dollars for Bone-Max, which should continue until the patent runs out three years from now. We believe this is largely due to marketing Bone-Max as a preventative measure and targeting physicians rather than the public. Due to our efforts in this regard, most physicians believe that every postmenopausal woman over fifty needs a cis-phosphorous drug and that Bone-Max was the first and best drug to prevent and treat the inevitable osteoporosis and fractures. The numbers indicate that they have been prescribing Bone-Max without reservation and plan to continue for the rest of their patients' lives."

Steiner's eyes flit around the room, gauging the expressions of the others before returning to Hardgrave. "Good. What is your sales projection when it goes off patent?"

"Traditionally, sales are cut in half when a drug goes off patent, but we are still looking at 1.8 billion a year."

There is the hint of a smile, then Steiner issues his version of gushing endorsement. "Not bad." There is a palpable release of tension in the room, but it is short-lived. "Now, tell me, how are those pesky lawsuits coming?"

This time Lou Magi, Apollo's general counsel, speaks up. "Not well, David. As you know, we lost most of the initial suits, settled others, but there are many more—eight hundred by last count—and there are new suits being filed every day. Good news is Halstead's the best firm in New York. We've only paid out forty million."

The CEO snorts. "Let's not forget that retainer we paid to Halstead ... highway robbery." He pauses, and everyone holds their breath to see which way he is headed. "But, I must admit, forty million is a very acceptable number." Again, the tension in the room subsides; no one ever knows when Steiner is going to applaud or explode. "So, Lou, suppose we make this all go away, settle the rest of the cases like we did with Dolor-not? It worked for the tobacco companies, right?"

Magi thinks for a moment. "I'd say less than three billion. Still not bad, especially when we take into account the twenty-percent markup on Bone-Max for legal expenses." Magi allows himself a smug smile; the markup was his idea. "I see no reason to admit to the side effects. Besides, exposed dead bone in the mouth and a couple of leg fractures are not as dramatic as the heart attacks that Dolor-not allegedly caused."

Steiner nods. "That's all good news, Lou. But, as you know, I pay you to tell me the bad news as well as the good." The others chuckle nervously. "Any flies in this ointment?"

"Yes, there is one," answers Lou Magi. "Dr. Robert Merriweather—one of the plaintiff's expert witness and a real loose cannon. Merriweather's the main reason we lost the cases we did and why we were advised by our attorneys to settle the others."

"Tell me more about this Merriweather."

Magi quickly hides his look of surprise. Everyone in the pharma community knows of Merriweather. "Well, he's a professor of surgery at the University of Miami Medical School and is highly regarded. In the context of the lawsuits, this isn't so much of a problem. However, he could be a public relations nightmare with his lectures and publications. This guy's on a mission, David, and well connected. I'm worried he might reach out to someone in Congress and convince them to initiate a Department of Justice investigation. I don't have to tell you what'd happen if the DOJ gets involved. They'd rip through our files and subpoena everyone and everything. We'd be fully exposed, and our chances of getting FDA approval on any new drugs would be in the toilet, not to mention the fines we'd have to pay on what's already out there."

Steiner is quiet for a moment, the first look of real concern crossing his face. "That would be bad." He glances around the room, again gauging the nervous faces. "Have we tried offering him a consultantship ... research grants?"

Medical Director Frank Imhoff now speaks up, "Indeed, we offered him both. He turned us down each time. We even invited him to lead a discussion on our experts' panel designed to show we were interested in this ONJ problem. He accepted, then outlined how we should've anticipated the ONJ caused by Bone-Max, and he criticized our research protocol for not requiring oral examinations. As I see it, he knows too much about our research protocols and what we presented to the FDA. We can't let that come out in the courts. It would be Dolor-not all over again."

Fifty blocks away, those in the boardroom at the North Star Drug Company subsidiary are facing a similar situation. Unlike Apollo Pharmaceuticals' humble beginnings, North Star Drug Company came into being as the result of a merger of ten smaller European drug companies. Over the past fifteen years, it has emerged from Stockholm, Sweden as an international pharmaceutical giant. Much of North Star's success had come from its first blockbuster drug, Bonafide, which was introduced to physicians in 1998 as the first cis-phosphorous drug useful in treating cancer patients.

Although Bonafide did not treat the cancer per se, like all cis-phosphorous drugs, it prevented bone renewal by killing off the normal cells in the body that dissolve old bone and replace it with new bone. It just so happens that cancers use these cells to do their dirty work for them. Cancers influence these cells to excavate cavities in bone into which the cancers grow. This bone metastasis weakens the bone and releases an excess of calcium into the blood stream, often leading to mental confusion and, sometimes, even death.

Bonafide was roundly accepted by physicians and was very beneficial for the patients, for the physicians themselves, and, of course, for North Star Drug Company. Patients benefited by avoiding the pain that resulted from the bone metastasis. Physicians benefited because Bonafide, which had to be taken intravenously, could be administered in their offices. The doctor didn't even have to see the patient. Instead, the nurse or physician's assistant would set up the IV to the tune of $1,500 per visit.

The two-hour treatment was painless and, since per North Star's instructions Bonafide had to be administered on a monthly basis, quite lucrative. Thousands of physicians jumped on the Bonafide bandwagon, often administering treatments to several patients each day. As for North Star, it pulled in $2,000 per dose via insurance approval. Bonafide was a win-win-win for all involved.

Beginning in 1999, numerous publications touted the drug for its positive results in breast cancer patients, multiple myeloma patients and prostate cancer patients. Most of the sources for these articles were physician consultants paid by North Star, but no one seemed to notice. Applications expanded, and North Star's revenues grew to over two billion dollars a year. It was the best of all worlds for North Star, that is, until the reports of exposed jawbone began to emerge.

The first hint of trouble came in 2002 when Drs. Merriweather and Romano published their initial findings. But, as they published separately, they made few ripples in the pharmaceutical pond. The ripples turned into a tsunami when Dr. Merriweather's prediction of an epidemic of jaw necrosis came true, and numerous publications, each reporting dozens of cases, flooded the scientific literature. The FDA was soon inundated with Medical Watch reports identifying the "dead jawbone" problem linked to Bonafide. The matter worsened still when Dr. Merriweather coined the term "Drug Induced Jaw Osteonecrosis" (DIJON), creating a publicly recognizable name and implying causation to North Star's drug.

Additionally, Dr. Merriweather's criticism of poor research design and oversight caught on. He argued that the dose was too much for too long, especially since the drug appeared to accumulate in the bone, reducing by half only after eleven years. Furthermore, the jawbone is more susceptible to cis-phosphorous drugs. Five doses, Merriweather contended, would yield the same beneficial effects as the recommended often twenty or more. Indeed, the drug reached toxic levels in the jaw with repeated monthly doses, causing DIJON that, according to Merriweather, North Star Drug Company should have been able to anticipate.

To add insult to injury, while on the lecture circuit Dr. Merriweather often pointed out that neither the North Star Drug Company nor Apollo Pharmaceuticals ever included an examination of the mouth or jaw. He also criticized them for not having anyone trained in dentistry on their research team.

Now, twelve years after the first reports of DIJON came to light, North Star Drug Company's CEO, Anders Christiansen, has flown in from Stockholm to discuss strategy with its US subsidiary.

Like his Apollo Pharmaceuticals counterpart David Steiner, Anders Christiansen is an MBA business executive and no stranger to the challenges of juggling business competition with Certification Europe (the European equivalent of the FDA) approvals and, unfortunately, lawsuits. Now, as he is about to address the sixteen department heads sitting around the glass-top table, he looks out the boardroom window, with its expansive view of New York harbor and the Statue of Liberty, and wonders what happened to the free market.

"Ladies and gentlemen, I have what you Americans like to call the good news and the bad news." He waits for the polite laugher to subside. "First, the good news—our transition from Bonafide to Bone-Protect had been seamless and enormously profitable. Before going off patent in 2005, Bonafide grossed over eighteen billion US dollars, mostly from the sales within the US itself. This is thanks largely to the peer-reviewed papers published by our physician consultants, which outlined the advantages of Bone-Protect over Bonafide, particularly the timesaving and economic advantages of a twenty-minute IV infusion over the two hours formerly required. Of course, having eleven of our physician consultants on the National Association of Bone Research Task Force has not hurt our cause." Again, Christiansen waits for the deferential chuckles to subside. "Now, not only do we have the Task Force's endorsement, but none of the generic drug labs dare to produce the generic form of Bonafide. We are alone and atop the marketplace with over three billion in US dollars per year revenue from Bone-Protect."

The room erupts into applause, and, one by one, each of the sixteen people rises to his or her feet to pay homage to their leader. When word that the CEO was crossing the pond to address them came down, they'd feared heads were going to roll. Now, it seemed that bonus dollars would be flowing instead.

The celebration faded apace with Christiansen's smile. "Now, the bad news. The law firm you hired has lost most of our cases, and there have been settlements in too many others. The other side is trying to rack up wins and individual case settlements before the magistrate forces an across-the-board settlement. Of course, we want to keep that per-case settlement figure down while at the same time delaying each case for as long as possible. To that end, I've instructed Mr. Halstead to use anything in his legal bag of tricks."

"You see, many of the plaintiffs still have cancer that has spread to their bones, and, despite the new chemotherapeutic drugs they are receiving—unfortunately produced by our competitors—" Christiansen pauses here for effect, then quickly coughs and moves on when the room sinks into an uncomfortable silence. "Yes, as I was saying, many of these patients will die before their trial dates. We'll get a number of cases dismissed on that alone. In the meantime, we'll bury that unfortunate study your office initiated. The principle investigator on the study has been made aware that this data would be extremely damaging to North Star. I do not have to explain to you what cutting the dosage in half would do to our profit margin. I've also reminded him that if this data should be released, no further research grants would be forthcoming, so I think he won't be a problem for us. However, we are facing a reduction in Bone-Protect prescribing, thanks to the reports of Dr. Robert Merriweather and other oral and maxillofacial surgeons."

"Now, many physicians in medical oncology are afraid of these jaw necrosis problems and are only infusing it once every three to six months instead of our recommended once a month. This brings me to the other part of our strategy, which is to begin a media campaign of our own. We'll get our physicians to write and speak on the positive effects of Bone-Protect and to minimize and trivialize the jaw necrosis problem. I've consulted with a few of them, and they feel we can convince a lot of people—including those we may find on our juries—that it is the cancer, not Bone-Protect, causing the dead jawbone problem. They also believe they can be quite persuasive in convincing the courts that these issues are actually jaw infections misdiagnosed." Christiansen shrugs. "Perhaps they were even caused by the unsterile techniques these doctors use in their offices. I'm no doctor, but it seems quite feasible, does it not?"

Christiansen smiles as the sounds of applause echo through the room once more.

CHAPTER 7
The Funeral

Diana Edelson's condominium sits on a lovely cul-de-sac in a gated community that would be considered exclusive by most. Palm trees cast cooling shadows along the winding streets and upon the Spanish-style stucco buildings, with their pink tile roofs and stone walkways.

It is with a heavy heart that Robert pulls his car to a stop in front of her condo and walks to the front door. He has barely rung the bell when Diana pulls the door open, which he finds odd until he realizes the guards at the gate had already announced his arrival. He shakes his head, trying to clear away the mental fog; he cannot recall a time, apart from the months following his divorce, when he felt so out of sorts.

He takes one look at the rings under Diana's eyes and knows he's not the only one losing sleep over the events of the past few days. Whether they knew Jacobson or not, everyone at the hospital was traumatized by this most heinous violation of a place they considered safe.

"Hello, Robert. Please … come in," she says, giving him a slight but warm smile.

"Good to see you, Diana. I just wish it were under better circumstances."

He steps into the foyer, taking in the spaciousness of the

place, the high ceilings and rustic Tuscan tiles. "You have a beautiful home."

"Well thank you, dear. Norman is in the other room watching TV." She waves an elegant hand toward an archway at the other end of the foyer. "Go say hello to him. I'm going to grab my sweater." She pats his arm affectionately, then starts up the winding cast iron staircase to the second floor.

When she disappears from sight, Robert walks through the doorway and into a narrow hallway lined with photos. A television is blasting a few doors down and he heads toward it, dismayed to find that the stench of cigar smoke is growing stronger with every step. Frowning, he mentally chastises himself for not leaving his jacket in the car. He has never seen Norman without a cigar.

Sighing, he mentally adds the dry cleaner to this week's to-do list and tries to prepare himself for the pungent, gray cloud that surely awaits him. When he walks into the room, he finds Norman sitting in a leather recliner, trademark stogie clamped between his teeth.

"Norman," Robert calls out, trying to breathe through his mouth as he walks over with his hand outstretched. "Always good to see you."

Norman picks up the remote and mutes the television before taking his hand in a surprisingly strong grip. His other hand pulls out his cigar from his mouth.

"It is, Robert, lousy circumstances, though. Sorry to hear about your friend." He shoots Robert a sympathetic look, then holds up the stogie. "Hey, you want a cigar, Robert? It's a special blend ... Dominican."

Robert smiles and shakes his head. "As someone who treats

mouth cancer, I'm good, thanks."

Norman shrugs and takes another puff. "Been smoking these things since the War. Guess I've been lucky."

Actually, Robert knows that cigars and smokeless tobacco don't actually cause mouth cancer, only cigarettes do. He just doesn't want to offend Norman by stating his true feelings—that he finds the smell of cigars disgusting no matter what country they come from.

"You know what you're most lucky about?"

Norman gives him a quizzical look.

"Diana," Robert says with a grin, and he means it. At eighty-five, Diana Edelson is as spry and attractive as a woman twenty years her junior.

Norman nods, chuckling. "And don't I know it, Bobby. I've known her for more than seventy years now, and I still thank the Big Man upstairs every day for it."

They hear the clicking of Diana's pumps across the tile, then she appears in the doorway with a knowing smile.

"Oh my, were you two talking about me? Must have been, you stopped talking when I came in. Something good, I hope?"

"Of course ..." both men say in unison, grinning like two youngsters with a shared secret. Then, as if everyone suddenly remembers the somber occasion they are faced with, a thick silence settles over the room.

"Well, I guess it's time we head out," Robert says, finally pulling his gaze from the floor.

Diana nods with a forced smile, then she leans down to place a kiss on Norman's forehead. "We'll be back in a few hours, dear."

Robert sees the warm look that passes between them and cannot help feeling a pang of sadness that has nothing to do with the loss of Dr. Jacobson. It was the sort of look he thought he'd share with Veronica when they were in their golden years. He recalls being surprised with how easy it was to just be with her, how she was equally accepting of his flaws as she was his virtues. She most admired him for his dedication to his work, which ironically had been their undoing.

Diana's polite cough brings him back to the present. Embarrassed, he looks up to find the couple staring at him patiently.

"We know this is hard for you, dear," she says, assuming he was thinking about his lost friend.

Robert nods, then holds his hand out to Norman again. "Hope to see you again soon."

"You too, Robert. In the meantime, look after my wife." Norman sticks the stogie back in his mouth. As they walk out the front door, Robert and Diana hear the television sound come back on.

On the way to the funeral service, Dr. Merriweather rather sheepishly admits that he is unfamiliar with the protocol of a Jewish funeral.

"So that's why you asked me to go with you!"

Robert is about to object when he realizes Diana is joking.

"In all seriousness, Diana, thanks for coming with me today. It may sound crazy; I speak publicly all the time, but this one actually makes me a little nervous."

Diana places a sympathetic hand on his shoulder. "Are you

nervous because it's a Jewish funeral, or because Dr. Jacobson was so important to you?"

"A little of both, I guess. I wasn't just close to Stewart, but with his family too, and it'll be difficult to see them under these awful circumstances." He sighs. "I even tried to help his daughter once with her high school algebra. Boy, was that a disaster! A few minutes in, and I realized I'd forgotten more algebra than I ever knew."

"Stewart knew my sons too—when they were young we all used to go fishing together." He laughs sadly. "'Dr. J', they called him. They wanted to be here today. So did Veronica...."

On the night of the chair dedication, Veronica had gone directly from Robert's house to the airport. Veronica had flown back to Texas, Randy and Ryan back to their homes near Miami while Robbie headed to New York, where he had business to attend to. The following morning they had all been devastated to learn of Jacobson's murder, but their various obligations had made it impossible to return to Miami in time for the funeral.

"You'll do fine, Robert," Diana says, "just as you always do. Now ..." her voice becomes more businesslike, "... here's what to expect. The rabbi will begin by reciting the 23rd Psalm, then he'll go into the eulogy. When he finishes, he'll ask family members and friends to give their eulogies. That's where you'll come in. I think you should keep it short and mostly about his professional position— how it affected you and the others in your program." She laughs softly. "I don't think you should lapse into any of your fishing stories." Robert nods, chuckling. "After all the eulogies, the rabbi will sing 'EL Mole Rachanmin', which means, 'God, full of compassion' in Hebrew. He'll end by leading everyone in reciting the Kaddish. It goes, 'Yiska dol v iskadash shema rabe.' I'll have to help you with that one."

"Thanks, you're wonderful." Robert gives a sigh of relief as they pull into the parking lot.

The funeral service proceeds just as Diana outlined, with a twenty-minute eulogy by the rabbi followed by more than an hour of eulogies from Dr. Jacobson's family members. Finally, Dr. Merriweather's turn comes. As he moves in front of the crowd, he considers the length of the service to that point, the restlessness of those in attendance and Diana's admonition to keep it short.

"I stand before you humbled by the life of the man we honor here today. And I speak not only for myself, but also for all those who trained under him. From Dr. Jacobson—Stewart—we learned not just about surgery, but about life, about family, and about commitment. Most of you know that we affectionately called him 'The Professor.' Many of you may also know that he was an all-American center for his college football team and was inducted into their Hall of Fame. But what does a football center do to earn this? He blocks out the defense so other members of his team can score and gain national attention. That's what The Professor did for all of us divas of surgery. I can say without question that he is the singular reason for our own achievements. Sacrificing the limelight so we could excel is what Stewart was all about."

Robert pauses to wipe away a tear and notices several mourners dabbing their eyes as well. "I'll leave you with this one final personal note: in my fifty-five years, I have seen many friends come and go, but Dr. Stewart Jacobson is the one I find impossible to say goodbye to."

As Robert takes his seat, he sees several of Dr. Jacobson's family members crying openly. He can only hope, as the rabbi returns to begin the Kaddish, that he has done The Professor justice.

After the service is over, he and Diana stop to talk with Dr. Jacobson's two sons and daughter. He encourages them to be strong and take solace in the fact that their father was now happily beside their loving mother, his wife of forty-seven years, in Heaven.

Robert offers Diana his arm again, and the two slowly proceed outside to the parking lot.

He is just about to open the passenger door of his car for her when he hears a man say, "Dr. Merriweather, can we have a few minutes of your time?"

Startled by the unfamiliar voice, Robert instinctively places an arm in front of Diana. They both turn to see Detective Enrique Gonzalez standing there, looking a bit sheepish at having scared them.

"Man! Detective Gonzalez … don't do that," Robert snaps.

"Um, I'm sorry I startled you two. My partner says with this belly people can see me coming a mile away." The detective rubs his stomach, attempting to lighten the mood.

Robert takes a breath and allows his body to relax. "No … I'm sorry. Guess I'm a bit jumpy lately."

A few feet away, he sees Detective Molinaro getting out of an unmarked car.

"Mrs. Edelson, if you'll excuse us for a few minutes, I need to speak with Dr. Merriweather alone." He nods at Detective Molinaro. "In fact, Mrs. Edelson, since you were at the clinic the morning of the murder, my partner would like to ask you a few routine questions as well."

Still looking a bit shocked, Diana takes a second to respond. "Of course, Detective." She then accepts Molinaro's arm and allows herself to be escorted to the detectives' car.

Gonzalez gestures toward Robert's car, indicating he would conduct the interview there. Robert swallows his annoyance at being stopped after the funeral and reminds himself that they are trying to find his friend's killer. With a curt nod, he opens the driver's side door and slides behind the wheel, then waits for the detective to get in the passenger side.

"Dr. Merriweather, let me begin by saying that we have cleared Dr. Jacobson's caregiver and Ms. Ruiz."

"Well, I could've told you that," Robert says.

Gonzalez ignores the sarcasm. "We also now strongly suspect that this wasn't a random killing and that Dr. Jacobson was not the intended victim." He pauses to contemplate how to best convey his suspicions, then gives up and decides to give it to Merriweather straight. "Dr. Merriweather, we believe the killer was after you."

The detective stares at Merriweather, clearly expecting him to object, or at least register shock. Instead, Robert just looks over at Gonzalez with a resigned frown. "You know, I actually thought about that."

"My partner spoke extensively with Ms. Ruiz. We've also done some checking into your professional dealings. I'm sure it comes as no surprise that there are a number of people who might have a grudge or two against you. There are the confrontations with the human resources people and the computer guys at the University, not to mention all the plastic surgeons who want to lynch you for taking over their 'territory.'" Gonzales gives him a pointed look. "That's a pretty impressive list, Dr. Merriweather. Now, not that I'm looking to make more work for myself and Detective Molinaro, but are there any more I should know about?"

Robert is silent for a few moments. "Well, you can add to the list the chairman of the National Association of Bone Research, with whom I had a knock-down, drag-out fight over his bias in their position paper. I found out he was receiving over a million dollars in grants from North Star Drug Company and then, of all things, selected eleven other people paid by North Star to be on the Society's task force. But seriously, Detective, we're talking about a group of professional disagreements—nothing more. Even the turf battles we have with plastic surgeons are part of the ego and economic battles people in my field have historically engaged in. They've never resulted in murder, and I don't believe they have now."

"Let me be the judge of that, Doctor," Gonzalez says as he makes notes on a small pad. "I'm going to need you to come down to the station. I know you're busy, but I want all the details about these run-ins, whether you think they're relevant or not."

Robert shifts uncomfortably in his seat. The word run-in had reminded him of the man who threw the brick at his house the morning of the chair dedication. When he looks up again, Gonzalez is peering at him.

"Something else I should know about, Doctor?"

Robert toys with the idea of telling him but quickly dismisses it. Surely, it would just muddy the investigation further.

"No, Detective, I was just thinking about something I have to do later."

"Okay." He meets Robert's eye. "In the meantime, you need to be very careful. If you were the target, whoever did this to Dr. Jacobson may very well try again."

"Thanks for the warning, Detective. I'll certainly be on the alert, but I must tell you I'm not about to give up on my work or living my life. I have patients to care for, residents to work with, and trials to prepare for—these things are not negotiable."

Gonzales shakes his head, thinking that sometimes the smartest people were also the most foolish. "Sure, Doctor."

In the unmarked police car, Detective Molinaro also informs Diana Edelson that Dr. Merriweather was the intended target. After allowing her a few moments to express her horror and disbelief, he moves on to her whereabouts the morning of the murder.

"Well, I left Dr. Merriweather's office about eight-thirty that morning; I'd consulted with him about Bone Max—a medication I'd been taking for seven years. I was concerned about what he told me, so I drove to my doctor's office to see if she had Saturday hours so we could talk about it. I got a little lost on the way—a senior moment, I guess. Anyway, I got there around nine-thirty but her office was closed, so I went home and picked up my husband, Norman, so we could go to the medical supply store—we needed to fix a loose wheel on his wheelchair. We were there for, dear

Lord, nearly two hours while they worked on it. Then we went home."

"That'll be all for now," Molinaro says, jotting it all down. He'd check the timeline with the medical supply company and security gate at her complex later. A mere formality, for sure, but Molinaro is known for leaving no stone unturned. He offers Diana a friendly smile. "Thank you, Mrs. Edelson, for your time."

A few minutes later, Robert and Diana pull out of the parking lot and head back toward her condo. "That detective was actually asking my whereabouts as if I might've been after you." Diana laughs. "As if this old body could do anything if I was."

Despite the gravity of the situation, Robert finds himself laughing as well. "I don't know, Diana; maybe after twenty years of volunteering, you've grown tired of me. You may have an eye for one of my younger faculty members or, more likely, want to adopt my dogs."

Diana looks at him with mock disgust. "Now that's not at all funny, young man."

They spend the rest of the ride updating each other on some of Robert's charity cases. Many of these patients were from the developing world and had been brought to the States for treatment by Merriweather and his team. Several stayed with Diana and Norman for weeks—sometimes even months—during their treatments.

The conversation was a welcome diversion from Dr. Jacobson's death, but Detective Gonzalez's warning was never far from Robert's thoughts.

CHAPTER 8
The Meetings

Two weeks later, the hospital is back to normal. The police tape around the entry to Dr. Merriweather's office has been ripped away, the walls have been repainted and the plaques adorning them cleaned of blood. Every corner is once again pristine, all vestiges of the brutality wiped away. The staff rushes through the halls with their usual efficiency; after all, there are other patients to care for, other tragedies to avert. They do not have time to dwell on the past. At least that is how it appears on this Friday morning. Anyone looking past the bustle of activity would see the furtive glances, long stares and lulls in conversation and realize that the entire building is abuzz with an undercurrent of tension.

For Dr. Merriweather, that tension is much more palpable. That morning, he had looked around the office he'd always considered a second home and realized it would never be the same, clean walls or not. Two days after the funeral, Dr. Jacobson's ashes were spread over the Atlantic waters off Islamorada in the Upper Keys, as per his wishes. Robert attended that ceremony, along with several others honoring his friend over the past few weeks, all the while feeling like he was moving through a heavy, numbing fog. Now that the dust has settled, he feels the horror and shock even more acutely. Not that anyone would notice; as always, Merriweather moves through his day with stoic efficiency, with no hint of the heaviness of his heart. Only Isabella senses his mood—a combination of sorrow at losing his friend and guilt at knowing that he had been the intended target.

That night, Isabella and Detective Molinaro are also thinking about Dr. Jacobson's murder—at least, that's what they are supposed to be thinking about. Molinaro had been casual when he asked her to dinner, saying they needed to discuss the case further and might as well do it over a meal. Isabella looks out over the lovely restaurant with its cozy, candlelit booths and isn't fooled for a minute. No cop would suggest interviewing a witness at Vialetto's, especially on a Friday night. She observes Molinaro over the top of her wine glass and decides to play along.

Divorced for five years now, Isabella has not dated since her husband moved away. She doesn't have time for men, she often tells herself; she is too busy with Dr. Merriweather's many projects and the responsibilities of raising her nine-year-old son, Gabriel. Not that she doesn't have offers. Many of her boss' colleagues—captivated by her slender, fit figure that curves in all the right places, the sultry mouth that when she smiles causes men to lose their train of thought, and her take-charge attitude—had expressed an interest in getting to know her outside the hospital. She's always refused, so Isabella had been surprised to find herself looking forward to this dinner, although she is not quite sure whether it is the handsome detective sitting across the table from her or the recent tragedy at the hospital that changed her mind.

"Would you like another glass of wine, Isabella?" he asks her, holding up the bottle of an Argentine Malbec. At

Isabella's nod, Molinaro reaches over and pours, surprised to find his hand is shaking slightly.

At first glance, Detective Andy Molinaro, with his tall, muscular physique and killer, if rarely seen, smile is the very image of a ladies' man—except that he's just not. As a result of his years spent in military law enforcement, followed by service in the FBI security division, he'd never developed the charming smooth talk to go along with his looks. Instead, he is often tongue-tied and jittery around women, especially those he finds attractive. The irony is, most women find his shyness adorable, but he is too busy being self-conscious to notice.

As the musician at the piano bar plays soothing music, Andy cautiously sips his wine, hoping it will relax him.

"So," Isabella says, startling him.

He coughs, bringing his cloth napkin to his mouth just in time to keep from spraying red wine spraying all over the table. "I'm—I'm sorry, what you were saying?"

Not wanting to embarrass him, Isabella suppresses a smile. In truth, she finds his boyish nerves very appealing. "Are we really going to talk about murder all night, or is this going to be a real date?"

Molinaro feels the blood rushing to his face. "Well, um … there is one more thing I want to ask you, then yes … um … I would like this to be a real date."

Isabella finds herself smiling ear-to-ear. It feels somewhat foreign, as do the sensations tingling about her body. At this point, she is glad she'd chosen the more daring glossy red lipstick when getting ready for the evening.

"Okay, then." She raises the glass to her lips, then pauses.

"Bet you're glad I am no longer a 'person of interest.' If I were, a date might be a little uncomfortable for both of us."

Molinaro laughs, relieved that she has broken some of the tension. "That's true, and you are completely in the clear. Actually, the question is about Dr. Merriweather. Do you know if any of the faculty resents him for any reason? You know, maybe someone wants to replace him or feels that he hasn't supported them? Someone jealous of his position?"

Isabella shakes her head, not missing a beat. "Not in the least. Dr. Merriweather has the complete support of his faculty. I should know; I type all their correspondence. Dr. Merriweather has supported their academic promotions, helped them write their papers for publication and always gives them credit for their work. You should've heard his chair dedication speech. He referred to the faculty as integral to the success of our division." She shakes her head again. "No, I can't imagine any of the faculty wanting to get rid of him. They go nuts whenever they hear he's been offered a research position somewhere else, and—"

Molinaro smiles and holds up a hand. "Okay, okay, I believe you. I just had to ask." He leans slightly forward, trying to shift into date mode. "Now, tell me about yourself. Were you born in Cuba?"

"No, my parents were, though. I was born in Youngstown, Ohio, but we moved to Miami when I was six."

"I'm sorry," Molinaro says quickly, "I didn't mean to assume...."

"Not at all," she says. And just when Molinaro is convinced he messed the whole thing up, she reaches across the table to pat his hand. He feels his face turning red again. Fortunately, the waiter approaches the table to go over the specials.

Sensing his nervousness, and since she's been to enough business dinners at Vialetto's to know the menu by heart, Isabella takes charge, ordering the lobster ravioli as an appetizer, followed by the salmon Champaign risotto for each of them.

She catches Molinaro's raised eyebrow and laughs. "Oh, do you mind that I ordered for you? I promise you'll love the risotto. Dr. Merriweather and I always order it when we come here."

"It's fine," Molinaro replies, trying to hide his annoyance at hearing she's eaten there with her boss. "I make enough decisions on the job." He leans forward again. "Now, back to you, Ms. Ruiz...."

"Right. Well, as I said, my parents were Cuban, but I'm an all-American girl. My father, God rest his soul, was a boat builder, here and in Cuba, and when I was a kid he taught me all about boating and fishing. I still have the first boat he ever built. It's called The Release, and it's the most popular backcountry boat around." Isabella pauses as their appetizer arrives. "Go ahead—taste."

Molinaro uses his fork to cut a ravioli in half, figuring it would be wiser to eat slower than normal, then pops the small piece into his mouth. "Wow—this is amazing."

"Told you." Isabella puts a ravioli on her plate. "Anyway, my son Gabe and I take it out fishing, and Dr. Merriweather has even come with us a few times. It's good for Gabe to have a man around ... Lord knows Edgar, that's my ex, never was much of a father."

Now it's Isabella's turn to look uncomfortable. "I'm sorry. I didn't mean to go on so much about myself, and I certainly didn't mean to talk about my ex-husband."

Molinaro waves away her apology. "Not at all, but what I really want to know is how come you got divorced?" He forces himself to meet her eyes. "I can't imagine any man wanting to leave you."

Feeling the heat rising to her cheeks, Isabella sidesteps the compliment. "Actually, I'm still not quite sure why the marriage fell apart, but I can tell you that I initiated the divorce. Things were great for the first eight years. He was a detective too." She smiles. "Sometimes he told me about his cases, which I loved. I'd even like to think I helped him solve one or two." Isabella's voice grows serious. "But after Gabe was born, he completely changed. He lost interest in me and our son. He didn't even want to be a detective anymore! You can imagine my reaction when he came home one night and told me he'd retired from the force and was starting an exotic plant import business with growers from Central America."

This is certainly not the story Molinaro expected. He is about to ask a question when the waiter returns with their salmon risotto. He leans back in his chair as the young man places the steaming dishes in front of them, and after inquiring if they need anything else, rushes off to another table. Molinaro takes a bite, nods his approval, then urges her to continue.

"Turns out Edgar's plant business was a success, but it took him out of the country for long stretches of time. When he did come home, he ignored me and Gabe. All he wanted to do was play tennis and golf. At first, I thought he was involved in something illegal, like drug shipments, but that wasn't it. Then I thought he might have a mistress in

Central America. I even flew down there once, showed up unannounced, but there was no sign of another woman. The man had just changed." Isabella shakes her head sadly. "Anyway, after dealing with it for years, I decided I couldn't take it anymore."

She eats a forkful of risotto, indicating she'd reached the end of the story. "Wow, this is even better than usual." She raises her eyes to meet Molinaro's and finds him staring at her. Suddenly, she feels all jittery, like a high school kid on her first date. "There, I just poured out my history to you. Your turn, Detective."

"Well, for starters, my first name isn't detective, it's Andy. By the way, can I call you Issy? I heard Dr. Merriweather call you that and it seems to fit you."

"Of course you can."

"Okay. Well, Issy, I've never been married—never even been close, actually. Guess I've always been too much of a workaholic. First it was the military, then the FBI, which I thought would be exciting but actually turned out to be more of a security post. Too much bureaucracy." He shrugs. "Four years ago I came here, joined the Miami PD and partnered with Gonzalez. We hit it off right away, and not to brag, but we have a hell of an arrest rate. We'll solve this murder too, but it's a tough one."

Molinaro sits back in his chair, surprised at the ease with which he's able to talk to her. He's not sure if she feels the same, but he takes it as a positive sign when Isabella orders tres leches, her favorite dessert, and even a second cup of coffee. Still, the dinner is over far too quickly, and the next time the waiter comes around he reluctantly asks for the check.

"Well," he says as they walk toward their cars, "I hope we can do this again sometime."

Isabella looks at him with a mischievous spark in her eye. "Are you kidding? It's only 10 p.m. on a Friday night in Miami. This night is far from over."

Molinaro raises a quizzical eyebrow at her.

Isabella pulls out her key chain and clicks it in the direction of a silver Acura. "I'll drive."

****

At the same time Isabella and Molinaro are leaving Vialetto's, Robert's flight is landing at La Guardia Airport. After getting off the plane, he heads right for the baggage claim area, where he sees Heather Bellaire's trim figure standing next to carousel one. She is scanning the crowd of weary travelers, her face breaking into a wide smile when she sees him. He's grinning too as he saunters over to her, bag in one hand, suit jacket slung over the other shoulder.

"You look as lovely as ever," he says as he pulls her into a tight embrace.

A statuesque brunette in her mid-forties, Heather is wearing a smart white blouse and a black skirt two inches above the knee. She pulls back from Robert just enough to kiss him briefly on the lips, then the two of them walk hand in hand out to her car.

"Go ahead, Bob," she says, handing him the keys to her white BMW. "I know how you love to drive in New York."

"Thanks." He pops the trunk and places his bag inside

before slipping into the driver's seat. Heather gets in on the other side, then leans in for a deeper kiss.

"Hmmm," Robert says, his left hand running over her breasts then down to her thighs before finally slipping under her skirt.

They hear giggling and realize they are being stared at by a group of twenty-somethings walking by the car.

"Maybe we should adjourn this until we get to my place."

Laughing, the two of them fasten their seatbelts, then Merriweather eases the sedan out of the airport and onto the Grand Central Parkway, heading east.

The trip from LaGuardia to Heather's Upper West Side apartment should have taken only twenty minutes, but with New York City traffic it took nearly an hour.

As they chat about their day, Robert keeps his eyes on the brake lights in front of them and tries not to be distracted by the weight of Heather's hand on his thigh. Finally, they pull up in front of Heather's brownstone, where, thankfully, she has a parking spot reserved.

As soon as the engine is off, they jump out of the car and hurry quickly toward the front door like two newlyweds on their honeymoon. As soon as they are inside with the door shut behind them, he pins Heather against the door, looks into her eyes and lowers his lips to hers while his hands move to the hem of her dress. Returning his kiss, Heather places her arms over his shoulders, offering no objection to the slow raising of her skirt. He slowly pulls her panties down to her ankles, then waits for Heather to step out of them before unbuttoning her blouse. She leans back against the entrance door, and Robert kisses each side of her neck before moving downward, over her breasts to arrive at the midline of her abdomen. With Heather's hands combing through his hair, he buries his head between her legs. Within minutes, Heather's knees begin to buckle as her first orgasm rips through her body.

Panting, she grabs him by the shoulders and pulls him up to full height. "I need you inside me. Let's go to the bedroom."

They head down the hall to her room, peeling off the rest of their clothes as they go. Heather lays back on the bed and places her legs over his shoulders. Although passion would dictate a quick entry, he knows to start slowly, teasingly. Heather gasps and pulls him toward her. It has been five years since their first discreet tryst while away at a professional conference, yet somehow it always feels like the first time.

An hour later, they lie cuddling in her bed, with Heather's head on his shoulder, her nails gently running back and forth across his well-developed chest. She'd often joked about how grateful she is that he was active in his younger days; between playing sports, his military service, and scuba diving, he had remained in excellent shape.

"I am so sorry about your friend," she says quietly. "I know he meant a lot to you. How are you holding up?"

"Okay, for the most part. Between the residents, surgeries and the research rat problems, I've been too busy to think about it much. Even preparing for these upcoming trials has been a welcome distraction. The thing I can't get over is that I was the target—I was the one they were after. Poor Dr. Jacobson was just in the wrong place at the wrong time."

Heather draws herself up to look at him, her eyes wide with alarm. "What? What do you mean they were after you? And, Bob, why am I just hearing about this now?"

He sighs. "Because it's not something you say over the phone. Besides, I knew I was coming up here for the Daubert hearing nonsense and would finally see you." He places a gentle kiss on her forehead. "Now, let me make it up to you with one of my famous shoulder rubs that you like so much."

Smiling now, Heather rolls off him and onto her stomach. Robert straddles her and begins rubbing her shoulders with just the right amount of pressure. Eyes closed, Heather moans with pleasure. "That feels so good."

"Am I forgiven?"

She giggles. "Keep going and I'll think about it."

He smiles and moves over to her neck, eliciting another groan. A few minutes pass in silence, and Robert is sure Heather has fallen asleep. Suddenly, though, her eyes flutter open.

"We never had a chance to talk about the chair dedication...."

"I know, but with everything going on ..." He trails off sadly. That wonderful night just a few weeks earlier now seems like a million years ago.

"I noticed your sons were there. How are they?"

"Oh, Heather, what can I say? They're the greatest. Ryan just took over the fuel management division at Ryder Trucking, Robbie's dental practice is booming and Randy's orthopedic foot and ankle practice is booming too."

She pauses, just long enough to be significant. "And Veronica is looking well. How is she doing?"

"Veronica is fine, loves those poor animals," he says evenly. "Although I was pulled in so many directions, I really didn't get a chance to talk to her much." Or you, he finishes silently. He had barely looked in Heather's direction that night, and although he kept telling himself that he had been too busy, he wonders whether he just hadn't wanted Veronica to see them together.

In the aftermath of Jacobson's murder, he hadn't given it much thought, but now, under the weight of Heather's questioning stare, he feels the guilt rise up within him. Even though they live in different cities, he knows Heather would take their relationship to the next level; she had hinted as much several times over the years. But while he cares for her deeply, he can't bring himself to commit. It would mean that he and Veronica are really through. He looks at the beautiful, desirable woman lying in bed next to him and feels like an utter fool. Veronica has her own life, Robert, time to get over it. Unfortunately, getting over his ex-wife seems to be the one goal he cannot achieve, no matter how he's tried.

"Speaking of exes," he says, smoothly changing the subject, "Is yours still threatening you?"

After years of fighting, Heather had finally decided to end her marriage to William, an intelligent but often out-of-work English professor. Enraged that anyone would dare leave him, William vowed to make her life miserable. Now, seven years after their divorce, his anger has not abated;

in fact, it has only grown stronger. Recently, he has been sending her angry letters and emails. He also stopped paying child support for their two sons while at the same time threatening to fight for custody.

Heather pulls herself up to a sitting position and crosses her legs. "It's worse than ever. He hasn't sent money for the boys in months, and he's constantly accusing me of being an unfit mother because of my schedule. I know I travel quite a bit, Bob, but it doesn't affect them. They're fifteen now, they have a short walk to school, and they have a nice bunch of friends. They are never alone. Besides, when I'm not home, my niece comes over to stay with them. I love my work, but even if I didn't, it's not like I could quit." She snorts. "God knows William doesn't make enough at the junior college to support them, especially since he spends most of it on pot and alcohol."

Dr. Merriweather strokes Heather's cheek. "I know you're a great mom, and I know how hard you work to keep it all together. Is he any kind of real dad to them?"

Heather wrinkles her face in disgust. "Hell no, he never was. He doesn't do anything with them, doesn't even talk much unless it's to badmouth me. They told me he drinks and smokes in front of them."

Robert looks down at his hands, genuinely worried for Heather and at the same time relieved that the conversation had shifted away from him. "What did you ever see in him?"

He'd only met the man once, at a trade show nearly ten years earlier. William and Heather were still married then, and although there was no hint of trouble between them,

Robert could tell he was an overbearing jerk.

Heather shrugs. "My parents had passed away and I felt a bit lost. William was teaching at Yale and seemed to have a future there. You know he was my English professor, right?" Robert nods. "It was flattering when he pursued me, and eventually I gave in. I know that's not a great explanation, but it's the only one I have. Now, he is obsessed with ruining my life and would try to ruin yours if he knew about us. His jealously seems to get worse the longer we're divorced." She grows quiet for a moment, and Robert can tell she is holding something back.

"Heather, what is it?"

"The day after the chair dedication, I ran into him at the Miami Beach Hotel. He was at some convention. He pumped me about what I was doing in Miami when there was no publishing meeting or medical trade show going on. He asked me who I was with and what I was doing, as if we were still married and I was cheating on him. Then he threatened to take me to court for being an unfit mother. He also said that anyone I was involved with would also pay."

"Heather, this is not good," Roberts says gravely. "Have you thought about getting a restraining order?"

Heather shakes her head. "It would just enrage him more. Besides, I don't think he'd really do anything. He's just blowing hot air." She smiles. "Besides, I'm taller than him."

"That you are, lady, but it won't do you any good if he comes at you with a gun or knife. We need to talk more about this, but, right now, I think we should get some sleep. We have a lot of work to do on the pathology book, and we only have half the day before you have to get the boys and I have to meet the lawyers to prepare for the hearing."

As if on cue, Heather yawns, then lowers her head back to Robert's chest.

****

"Can't you at least give me a hint of where we're going?" Molinaro asks as he grips the door handle, adding silently, And can't you drive a little slower? The Land Rover has been flying ever since she pulled away from the curb on Le Jeune Road.

Isabella laughs as if reading his thoughts, and lets up on the gas a little. "And spoil the surprise? For now, let's just say it's a place you've probably never been before."

Molinaro smiles nervously. He's thrilled that their date is continuing, so long as it doesn't involve dancing. Back in college, he had been notorious for his lack of rhythm and the butt of many jokes because of it.

Fifteen minutes and several sharp curves later, his worst fears are confirmed when Isabella turns onto Calle Ocho, a street in Little Havana known for its excellent Cuban restaurants, cigar factories ... and nightclubs. Andy can hear the music blasting from several of them as Isabella slows the car to a crawl.

"Let's see ... it should be right up here ... . Yes!" Isabella points to a small building to the right, with a sign over the door that reads Hoy Como Ayer. She pulls into a parking spot and turns to him. "You're gonna love this."

Andy doubts it, but he nods enthusiastically as he climbs out of the car and follows her to the club.

The place is tiny and, except for the stage in the front, packed with tables. The lights are dim and tinged with red. Isabella grabs Andy's hand and guides him through the thick cloud of cigar and cigarette smoke toward two empty seats near the back.

"They should be coming on soon," she yells to make herself heard over the blasting salsa music. No sooner has she spoken when the lights dim even more until the room is nearly dark. Andy jumps in his seat as all around him people begin cheering and clapping at the several figures, each carrying what looks to be an instrument, walks onto the stage. When the stage lights turn on, he sees the shiny brass of trombones, trumpets and a saxophone. Behind them, a man sits down at a drum set Andy hadn't noticed before.

A second later he jumps again at the high-pitch scream of the trumpet. Another cheer goes up from the crowd, many of whom clearly know the song, then they are out of their seats before the conga player hits his first beat. Andy watches them enviously as they glide and twist to music, wishing he could do the same. Suddenly, he realizes Isabella is standing next to him, her hand outstretched.

"Oh … I … uh…."

Isabella's eyes challenge him. "Are you going to tell me you don't salsa? I'm shocked."

"No, um, I mean … I don't dance at all."

"Well that's going to change … now."

Knowing she won't take no for an answer, Andy allows himself to be pulled into a standing position.

"Don't be afraid, Andy," Isabella says, placing his hand on her hip and smiling. "I'll be gentle."

****

Barrymore Halstead hadn't chosen the penthouse on E. 81st Street because it was his favorite; he had chosen it because even in this city of excess, it was the most opulent. Granite countertops, hardwood floors polished to a high shine and a marble tub were easy enough to come by in Manhattan if you have the money. The expensive ornaments that line his shelves all have a story to them, stories of winning over on others. But they pale in comparison to the Faberge egg that sits within a crystal case, lighted above and below by Halogen lights. Rumored to be worth thirty-three million and believed to have been obtained by "questionable" means, to Halstead it was a symbol of superiority. And to display these things within a 5000-square-foot space with a panoramic view of the city—that makes a real statement. It is exactly the statement he plans to make for his guests tonight. Officially, he had invited CEOs David Steiner of Apollo Pharmaceuticals and Anders Christiansen of North Star Drug Company for dinner, but everyone knows tonight is about business. When he hears the doorman buzz to announce his guests' arrival, Barrymore slides into the jacket of his impeccable gray Armani suit and adjusts the signature red handkerchief in the left breast pocket, then crosses the room toward the door.

"David, Anders ... how good of you to come. Please ..." Offering them a magnanimous smile, Barrymore waves the two inside, noting with satisfaction the looks of surprise on their faces as they take in the enormity of the space. The server comes to take their overcoats and drink orders, then Barrymore leads them to his drawing room. A few moments later, the server returns with three dirty martinis and announcement that dinner will be served shortly.

"Gentlemen, you are in for a real treat tonight," Barrymore says. "My chef and I have planned an exceptional menu."

After twenty minutes of excruciatingly boring small talk, Barrymore leads them to an oval mahogany table with an inset glass top ringed by mother-of-pearl. As if on cue, a fortyish man dressed in white appears at the side of the table, an obsequious smile pasted to his face. "Gentlemen, we will begin with caviar flown in from Kazakhstan, along with sautéed wild arctic char from the Dubawnt River System in Nunavut, Canada. We will then proceed with a pacific puffer fish fillet cleaned and dressed by the most highly trained fugu chef in Japan—"

"… So you needn't worry about those pesky poison sacks," Barrymore interjects.

David and Anders laugh politely.

"For the main course," the chef continues, "Yak veal, just flown in from China a few hours ago."

"Sounds wonderful, indeed," says Anders, while David nods his agreement. The significance of the over-the-top dinner menu is not wasted on them; both know Barrymore would never have invited them over if he did not have a specific agenda in mind. Nevertheless, they make it through dinner and desert without a single mention of business.

Afterward, the three men return to the drawing room,

each with his choice of brandy or Port and a newly acquired Cuban Cohiba cigar. After inquiring about what they thought of the meal, Barrymore rises from his seat and faces them.

"Gentlemen, I'm sure you have heard about the recent murder at the University of Miami … where Dr. Robert Merriweather is on staff?"

"Yes," Anders says solemnly, "terrible business."

"Well, what you may not have heard is that the police believe Merriweather was the intended target."

"That comes as no surprise to me," David says coldly. "Surely, the man has many enemies."

Barrymore nods and takes another sip of his brandy. "Right. Well, if that is true, then it was a superbly botched job." His face stretches into a smile. "What I would like to know, gentleman, is which one of you two ordered the hit?"

CHAPTER 9
The Daubert Hearing

Robert looks around the small, dilapidated eatery with disdain. When Roger England, the attorney representing one of the plaintiffs in one of the North Star lawsuits, suggested a breakfast meeting to discuss the upcoming Daubert hearing, this was not the place Robert had in mind.

"I know, I know, it doesn't look like much, but we can't talk business at Bubby's on a Sunday morning; it's a madhouse in there. Besides, this place makes a breakfast burrito that will knock your socks off."

Robert looks around again, noting the four plastic tables in the corner, all of them empty but for a guy with a ratty jacket and dirty hair. Robert just hopes he's not the chef. "Don't suppose the lox are any good here?"

Roger raises an eyebrow. "Only for the adventurous." He steps to the counter, where a disinterested-looking woman is waiting for their order. "Two breakfast burritos and two large coffees, please."

"Just coffee for me," Robert says.

"One burrito, two coffees," the woman repeats.

"No, we'll take two burritos. Trust me, Robert."

"Okay, fine." Robert makes a mental note to buy Tums after they leave and to suggest that he and Heather go to Bubby's on his next trip to the city.

The woman places two black coffees on the counter and gestures vaguely toward the station of cream, sugar, and assorted plastic cutlery. "Burritos'll be right out."

Can't wait, Robert thinks as they go to doctor up the coffees. He blows on the steaming brew, then takes a sip to gauge how much milk he'll have to put in to mask the taste. He finds it strong but surprisingly good and decides to leave it black, as is his preference. He grabs knives and forks for them, then stands there watching as Roger pours nearly half his coffee into the trashcan and fills up the cup again with cream until it is a light tan color. He then picks up five sugar packets, tears them open, and dumps them in.

"Robert, you know this is just an attempt by the Halstead firm to harass us," he says, stirring the coffee. He raises it to his mouth and sighs. "There is no doubt you will be certified as an expert witness."

They no sooner sit down at a table when the woman carries their burritos over. Each is large enough to feed a surgical team at the hospital.

"I know," Robert says as he skeptically eyes the burrito. "I have met George Payne before and would like to think I'm wise to at least some of his antics."

Roger England picks up the gargantuan burrito and takes a large bite. "Hmmm ... Robert," he says, eyes closed as he savors it, "you gotta try this."

Robert uses the plastic knife and fork to cut off a small piece, which he pops into his mouth. It is a surprisingly fresh combination of buttery eggs, cheese and peppers.

He nods appreciatively at England. "It's delicious, thanks

for twisting my arm."

"No sweat." Roger smiles, then takes another healthy bite.

As they eat, the talk turns to Merriweather's upcoming testimony, which is to focus on "general causation." As with the previous trials in which he has testified, his job is to educate the jury about what osteonecrosis is and how the drug Bone Protect causes it.

First, though, Dr. Merriweather needs to know about the specifics of this patient's case. In between bites of burrito and sips of coffee, Roger explains that she's in long-term remission from breast cancer, thanks to surgery and chemotherapy. However, for the past four years she has been suffering from exposed bone in the right side of her lower jaw—the result of a lengthy course of Bone Protect. During that time, intermittent infections have occurred due to the portal of entry for bacteria. This progressed to a jaw fracture, a foul odor and taste, and an inability to eat due to the jaw deviation and loss of teeth in her dead jawbone. The ongoing pain has led to an addiction to prescription narcotic painkillers, and she now requires a gastrostomy, or feeding tube, in an attempt to regain the twenty-five pounds she lost due to the jaw pain and other symptoms.

George Payne, North Star's attorney, will attempt to convince the jury that these maladies can be attributed to her cancer. Robert knows this tactic well, as he has seen it in many of the four hundred of his own patients and the two dozen legal cases he has been involved with. And, as in many of the other cases, the patient's cancer has been effectively dormant for some time, rendering Payne's argument a disingenuous one.

"The former FDA Medical Affairs Officer and the case-specific expert witness will go on first," Roger says, "and I hope to get you on the stand after the lunch break. My direct questioning will be short and straight to the point—namely, your qualifications. That's what a Daubert hearing is all about. It is not to try the case at this time. In fact, I really don't want any of my witnesses to tip our hand on how we will approach the actual trial."

Robert nods. "Got it."

"That said, Payne is really going to go after you because you demonstrate that the Bone Protect issues are pervasive, not just specific to this patient."

****

The next morning, Robert takes a cab from Heather's apartment to 500 Pearl Street, where the courthouse in which the hearing will take place is located. As the driver navigates the narrow, cobblestoned street of Lower Manhattan, Robert stares out the window at the throngs of suits rushing toward their offices or perhaps the New York Stock Exchange a few blocks away. But he's not really seeing them; he's remembering the look on Heather's face as she said goodbye to him an hour earlier. She had seemed to be silently pleading with him, although for what he did not know.

His thoughts are interrupted by the loud blaring of a horn; apparently his driver cut someone off as he pulled up to the courthouse. All thoughts of Heather forgotten, Robert hurriedly pays the man and heads into the building.

After clearing security, he heads for the courtroom, where Judge Thomas Lockhart, a thirty-five-year veteran of the bench, will preside over the hearing and hopefully rule in the plaintiff's favor.

Robert has been in plenty of courtrooms before, but this may be the largest and fanciest. It is set up as all of them are, with the judge's bench in the center of the far wall under the large, ornate seal of the United States District Court for the Southern District of New York. To the right is the witness box, to the left is the jury box, and they, along with lawyers' tables and eight rows of visitors' benches, are all done in dark, highly polished cherry wood.

When he enters the room, he sees Roger England and his co-counsel are already seated at the plaintiff's table on the left side. Seated immediately behind the table are the two other witnesses plaintiff's counsel hopes will be certified as experts. Since that determination will be made by the judge, the jury box will remain empty. George Payne and the rest of the Halstead team have not arrived yet, and, but for the sound of shuffling papers and the bailiff clearing his throat, the room is eerily quiet.

Robert heads over to the other two witnesses, his echoing footsteps drawing a nod from Roger.

Just then, George Payne, followed by two pale, overworked associates, files into the courtroom and the three take their seats at the table to the right of the room.

"Ready, everyone?" Roger whispers.

Robert and the other witnesses nod just as the bailiff clears his throat.

"All rise," he announces as the door near the bench opens

and Judge Lockhart, a rather short and paunchy man with disheveled white hair enters the room, walks up to the bench, and, without fanfare, instructs everyone to be seated.

"Good morning, everyone. The motion before this court concerns a challenge by the defense to the calling of certain expert witnesses by the plaintiffs. We will determine today whether to preclude these witnesses from testifying or limit the scope of their testimonies." He glances at the plaintiff's counsel. "Mr. England, you may call your first witness."

After thanking the judge, Roger England calls to the stand the former FDA Medical Affairs Officer. For the next thirty minutes, England questions her, mainly concerning her knowledge of North Star's dealings with the FDA, specifically whether they ignored the FDA's requests for proper warning labels about the side effects of their drugs. When he is finished, George Payne stands and, smiling smugly, proceeds to cross-examine the witness. Despite his demeanor, however, Robert notes that he really doesn't challenge the woman's testimony. Nor does he question her qualifications, which are well documented by her years of employment by the FDA and her name on the correspondence between the FDA and North Star.

After she is excused, Richard Kramer, the case-specific expert witness, takes the stand. It takes England an hour and fifteen minutes just to outline his credentials. Robert is not surprised, for Kramer is a longtime friend as well as a trusted colleague who shares with him a desire to return integrity to healthcare. Although he does not have Robert's research and scientific background, he does have thirty-five years of clinical experience and at one time or another has presided over most of the oral and maxillo-facial surgery organizations and sub-organizations in the country. He has also been published in numerous surgical publications and is clearly suited to judge whether this patient's problems are due to the toxicity of Bone Protect.

Throughout Kramer's testimony, George Payne is conspicuously silent; in fact, he looks rather bored, even looking at the clock several times during the direct examination. When England is finally finished, the judge calls recess for lunch and everyone rises. Robert glances over at Payne to find the smug smile has reappeared.

When the court reconvenes at 1:30, it is immediately apparent that Payne will not go as easy on Dr. Kramer as he had the first witness. He trots out several articles, mostly published by paid consultants of North Star Drug Company, that suggest an alternative cause of the dead bone in this patient's case.

"Objection, Your Honor," England says, rising from his seat. "Mr. Payne is not supposed to be trying the case here."

"Overruled," Judge Lockhart drawls.

Payne smiles at England, then continues his onslaught against Kramer.

England objects several more times, only to be overruled by Judge Lockhart. However, the judge finally warns George Payne to limit his questions to those relevant to Dr. Kramer's credentials.

It is as England had predicted—Payne is trying to show the judge that Dr. Kramer's "tunnel vision" has prevented him from considering the alternative causes suggested in the articles. Listening to him, Robert realizes England was right about something else as well: Payne wants to drag out Kramer's testimony to the end of the day so that Dr. Merriweather will have to extend his stay in New York, change his air travel plans, and cancel some of his patients—anything to inconvenience and, hopefully, force him to drop out of the case.

For the next several minutes, the handful of people in the courtroom look on as George Payne tries to get Dr. Kramer to lend credence to North Star's Bone Protect articles, but Kramer refuses to budge.

"Do you mean to say, Dr. Kramer, that there is no possibility that the well-documented research in these articles is true?"

Kramer is silent for a moment, then he finally says, "Mr. Payne, I see it like this: is it possible that my beloved New York Mets might win one hundred sixty-two games this coming year? Possible, but as everyone knows, the chances are slim-to-none. I'd give these articles the same chance of being accurate."

There is a smattering of laughter in the court; even Judge Lockhart is fighting a smile.

Couldn't have said it better myself, Robert thinks as he suppresses a chuckle.

After that, George Payne continues to question Kramer, but it is just more of the same. He makes no headway, but he does succeed in wasting the rest of the afternoon. Finally, Judge Lockhart adjourns the hearing until the next morning and everyone shuffles from the courtroom.

After saying goodnight to England and the others, Robert

goes back outside to hail a cab. On the ride back to Heather's apartment, he sends her a text to let her know he's returning, then dials Issy's number. "Cancel my schedule for tomorrow and please apologize to my patients for me. Looks like I'll be spending another day in New York."

By 9 a.m. the following morning he is back in the courtroom, this time on the witness stand. There was a time when Dr. Robert Merriweather was nervous before testifying, but that was years ago. Today, he is just anxious to be done with this circus and get back to Miami.

At the bailiff's request, he states his name and occupation—Professor of Surgery and Chief, Division of Oral and Maxillofacial Surgery—for the record.

"Do you have any other titles?" England asks him.

"Yes, I am Director of Head and Neck Research, and I have an appointment at the University of Miami Bone Tissue Bank. I am also the President of the Tissue Engineering Society, which is a national organization."

England then holds up a piece of paper, hands it to Robert, and asks him to state for the record what it is.

"My curriculum vitae."

"Is this current?"

"Yes, as of two months ago."

"Are there any additions to it that would be useful to this case?"

"Yes, I believe so. Last month, I published a peer-reviewed article entitled 'A Decade of Cis-Phosphorous Osteonecrosis: What it has Taught us About Bone Physiology and Chemical Injury.'"

England emits a low whistle to indicate how impressed he is. At the defense table, Robert sees George Payne roll his eyes.

"Dr. Merriweather, how many peer-reviewed publications are listed on your C.V., and how many textbooks have you written?"

"Let me see here, they are numbered, one hundred thirty-two scientific articles and fourteen textbooks."

"And do any of the textbooks deal with cis-phosphorous drugs causing osteonecrosis?"

"Yes, there are two books that specifically address that subject and another two where it is one among many other jaw diseases I discuss."

"How many research projects have you conducted?"

Robert looks up to the ceiling. "Thirty-eight, mostly about cancer and other bone diseases."

"Dr. Merriweather, do you ever get phone calls or emails asking for advice concerning the cis-phosphorous drugs and osteonecrosis?"

"Yes, about five to ten each week."

"Are you on the editorial staff or reviewer list of any scientific medical journals?"

"Yes, eight journals."

"Dr. Merriweather, have you been on any task forces concerning the cis-phosphorous jaw problems?"

"Yes, the National Society of Oral and Maxillofacial Surgery task force and the National Society of Bone Research task force, but I resigned from that one."

"And why did you do that?"

"Of the twenty-five task force members, nineteen were paid consultants of cis-phosphorous drug manufacturers. Many were being paid by more than one company. Eleven were paid consultants to North Star and eight were paid by Apollo Pharmaceuticals."

"Objection, Your Honor!" George Payne springs from his chair. "This is irrelevant and prejudicial."

"Your objection is overruled, Mr. Payne," Judge Lockhart says, sounding more than a bit tired of Payne's antics. He too had hoped the hearing would be over the day before, and he'd be damned if it was going to go on a third day. "You'll get your chance to dispute the doctor's testimony on cross examination."

England shoots Payne a smile, then turns back to the witness stand.

"Finally, Dr. Merriweather, did North Star Drug Company ever reach out to you for your opinion?"

"Yes, they did in the very beginning."

"Dr. Merriweather, isn't it in fact true that North Star Drug Company asked you to become one of their paid consultants?"

"Oh yes, they offered me a physician-initiated research grant and an annual fee for my input."

"Did you accept their offer?"

"No, I didn't."

"Why not?"

"Because I warned them that Bone Protect, as well as its

forerunner, Bonafide, were causing jaw osteonecrosis and that the cases that all of my colleagues were seeing was only the tip of the iceberg. I warned them that it would become the very epidemic that we are seeing today. They took my position as a serious threat. Then they decided to try to discredit me."

George Payne rises again. "Your Honor, I must object to Dr. Merriweather making such accusations. It is an attempt to prejudice Your Honor against my clients. Not to mention the fact that no organization or national body has labeled this an epidemic."

Before the judge can rule, England quickly rebuts the argument. "Your Honor, Dr. Merriweather was merely answering my question as to whether North Star considers him an expert. The fact that they asked him to consult directly contradicts their present assertion that he should be precluded from testifying as such."

Nodding wearily, Judge Lockhart overrules the objection concerning North Star but instructs the court reporter to strike the reference to an epidemic from the record.

Despite this, it is another clear victory for England. "Thank you, Your Honor. No more questions." He turns back to the plaintiff's table, a small smile on his face as he meets Payne's eyes.

Robert nods his thanks at the bailiff, who has just brought him a glass of water. The easy part now over, he braces himself for George Payne's inevitable attack.

Payne locks eyes with Robert as he approaches the witness stand, not bothering to hide his disdain.

"Dr. Merriweather, you know me, don't you?"

"Yes," Robert replies coldly. "After nineteen depositions, I know who you are."

"Dr. Merriweather, you are not really a doctor, are you?"

"Well, Mr. Payne, you tell me. You just addressed me as Dr. Merriweather."

"Move to strike, Your Honor," Payne says, allowing the slightest bit of indignation to creep into his voice. "The witness is being argumentative."

"So stricken," Judge Lockhart says, looking more annoyed at Payne than Robert.

"Okay, Dr. Merriweather, you are not a medical doctor. Is that correct?"

"Correct, I do not have an M.D. I am, however, a Doctor of Dental Surgery."

"But you do not have the extensive medical training that a medical doctor has, do you?"

"As a matter of fact, I do. All oral and maxillofacial surgeons have extensive medical training. Plus, we are the only specialty of either medicine or dentistry that is trained and permitted to practice anesthesiology, other than anesthesiologists themselves."

Seeing that he is not rattling Robert, Payne moves on to another topic. "Dr. Merriweather, according to your C.V. you have conducted thirty-eight research projects. Were all of them on human subjects?"

"No, about half were animal studies, sometimes referred to as preclinical studies."

"Well, do you hold animal studies to be as important as human studies?"

"I certainly do. In fact, most all human studies are preceded by animal studies before they are allowed to be extended to human trials. That's why they call them preclinical trials. Animal studies are designed to show proof of concept. Human studies are designed to show proof of performance. That's the protocol your client failed to follow over and over again."

Now genuinely irate, George Payne snaps, "Move to strike, Your Honor."

This time, Judge Lockhart announces that the last sentence be stricken from the record and admonishes Dr. Merriweather for voicing an opinion not asked for.

"Dr. Merriweather, isn't it true that you have never written a research protocol or participated in a randomized human clinical trial for an industry-sponsored drug like Bone Protect or Bonafide?"

"No, that is not true, Mr. Payne."

Visibly taken aback by the answer, Payne is silent for a moment. Robert thinks he hears a snicker, but can't tell if it's from England or Dr. Kramer, who has returned to observe the proceedings.

"Uh, I mean real research that comes to an actual publication and product for the marketplace."

"The answer is the same, Mr. Payne." Robert allows himself a slight smile. "In fact, I wrote and participated in all three clinical trials of recombinant human bone regenerative protein—or rhBRP—which is now on the market as the commercial product of Applied Genetic Technologies known as Progen. Furthermore, I was the presenter to the FDA about rhBRP when it gained a unanimous approval."

"And can you tell us, Dr. Merriweather, why this is not listed on your C.V.?"

"Because a curriculum vitae is not about trials; it is about achievements. Anyone can write a protocol and enroll patients. The academic standard is that it has to be completed and results obtained."

Convinced he has found a chink in Robert's armor, Payne adopts his usual smug tone.

"Well then, you must not have obtained viable results, did you?"

"We most certainly did get viable results, Mr. Payne. This is why Progen was FDA approved. Once a research project comes to a conclusion, it is indeed placed on the participant's C.V. and these were on mine at one time. However, when a peer-reviewed scientific article about the study is published, the research effort itself is deleted from the C.V. and replaced by the reference for the scientific publication. In this way, a research effort is not credited twice. I believe you will find the citing to my publications about this very research on pages twenty-nine, thirty-six, and forty-four."

England snickers again, earning a nasty stare from Payne.

"Dr. Merriweather, clearly you have made quite a name for yourself in the world of academia." Payne says the word as if it tastes sour. "But can you show any real-world documented proof of your conclusions?"

"Absolutely," Robert says glibly. "The entire FDA proceeding is a matter of public record, including the research protocol and all the results. You can find it on the FDA's website."

A dull red flush rises to Payne's face. At this point, the

judge intervenes. "Gentlemen, I think this is a good time for a lunch break. Court adjourned until 1:30."

All stand as the judge leaves the courtroom for his chambers, then Robert steps down from the witness stand and walks over to a smiling Roger England. George Payne still looks furious as he and his group head to the witness preparation room just beyond the swinging doors of the courtroom. As Robert, England and Kramer pass by, they hear Payne shouting, probably at one of the associates for their shoddy research.

"That turned out to be quite fun," Robert says.

"Nice work, Robert," Kramer says, chuckling.

"Well, I had to come up with something to top your Mets comment."

"You guys are a couple of comedians." England laughed. "Now what do you want for lunch?"

Still laughing, the three men move out of the courtroom, with Roger and Dr. Kramer each suggesting a local place where they can get something quick to eat. They don't notice the short, fiftyish man with thinning red hair and a scruffy red goatee seated in the last row of the spectators benches. He waits until everyone has left the courtroom before quietly slipping away.

They return to the courtroom ninety minutes later to find the Halstead lawyers already there. Gone is Payne's smug expression; he now has the look of a man afraid of losing his bonus, if not his job.

Robert returns to the witness stand, reminding himself that this will soon be over. Sure enough, when the judge calls on George Payne, he just rises and says, "No more questions at this time, Your Honor."

Clearly relieved, Judge Lockhart then turns to Roger England and asks if he has any redirect for the doctor before he rules.

England rises from his chair. "Yes, Your Honor, just two: Dr. Merriweather, have you read the complete research studies of Bone Protect and Bonafide conducted by North Star Drug Companies Consultants?"

"Yes, I have."

"Will you be prepared to testify concerning the scientific conduct and validity of these studies in forthcoming trials?"

"Yes, I will."

As expected, the judge rejects the Daubert challenge and rules that all three witnesses are qualified to testify as experts at trial.

By 5:30, Robert is at LaGuardia Airport and holding a ticket for the next flight back to Miami. It's not until he takes his seat on the plane that he realizes how exhausted he is. He reclines his chair and closes his eyes, completely oblivious to the intent of the red-haired, goateed man sitting one row ahead of him.

CHAPTER 10
Heartburn

"The weather report said it was supposed to be 'unseasonably warm' up here," Detective Molinaro says as he and Gonzalez step out of the airport terminal and are greeted by a blast of icy wind. "I'm already freezing my ass off."

Gonzalez shrugs and shivers at the same time. "Maybe twenty degrees is unseasonably warm here. Besides, the weather reports are just a suggestion here." He points to the curb, where a stocky guy is leaning against an unmarked police car. "That must be our ride."

Gonzalez had collaborated with Detective Josh Barkley years before when they were both on the periphery of a joint Miami-New York task force that was tracking a serial killer. Their roles were limited to information sharing through phone calls and emails, and, although the two have kept in touch since then, they have never met in person.

Gonzalez and Molinaro walk over to the car, each rolling small pieces of carry-on luggage behind them. The stout man approaches them, smiling broadly, hand outstretched.

"Which one's Gonzalez?"

Gonzalez steps forward and shakes his hand. "Josh, nice to finally meet you in person."

"Same here, Rick," he says, turning to the shivering Molinaro. "Josh Barkley, homicide."

The two men shake. "Appreciate the ride," Molinaro says.

"No problem," Barkley smirks. "Glad to help our counterparts from South New York and North Havana."

"Typical New Yorker," Gonzalez quips, smiling, "always has a smartass remark." Seeing the confused look on Molinaro's face, he explains, "It's an old joke about Miami because of all the New York snowbirds that come down in the winter and all the Cuban immigrants like me who have immigrated up to Miami since 1959."

Barkley chuckles. "C'mon, you guys must be starving. Let's get you checked into your hotel, then we'll get something to eat before we get started."

"Hope the heat works in this thing," Molinaro mutters as they climb into his car.

An hour later they are standing in a dingy motel room in Midtown Manhattan. "Wonder what the department is getting billed for this dump," Molinaro says.

Gonzalez grins. "I've seen worse."

They throw their bags on the bed, then head back downstairs where Barkley is waiting for them, a manila folder in hand. They follow him around the corner to a diner that looks only slightly cleaner than the hotel. After ordering breakfast and coffee, Barkley gets right down to business.

"You were right to send me the security photo shots from the parking garage. There was nothing on the morning of the murder, but I did see something, or rather someone, else you might find interesting." Barkley slides the folder to the center of the table and opens it to reveal several black and white, rather grainy photographs. "This," he says, pointing to the top photo, "is your Dr. Merriweather, correct?"

Gonzalez and Molinaro nod, and Barkley slides the second photo out. "Here he is, talking to some suit."

"Yeah, so?" Molinaro says. "That's just the CEO from the hospital."

"That's not why I sent him the photos." Gonzalez holds the photo out so his partner can get a better look.

"What, the joker in the red baseball cap behind Merriweather?

Shaking his head, Gonzalez points to a blurry image in the corner of the photo. It is another man with thick, longish dark hair and a black leather jacket. He is sitting in a parked car a few rows from where Merriweather is standing, clearly observing him.

Molinaro shrugs. "Big deal. We can't see his face."

"Not in this photo you can't." Gonzalez pulls out the last photo, a magnified version of the man's face.

Molinaro looks at him, nonplussed, but Barkley sits up straighter in his chair.

"I agree with you, Rick."

Gonzalez nods, earning a frustrated glance from his partner.

"You guys wanna fill me in here?"

"It's Dimitri Petrakov—hitman for the Russians," Gonzalez says. "Works out of some crappy café in Brighton Beach, but in the past he had quite a few business dealings in Miami as well. I thought I recognized him but I wanted Barkley's confirmation."

"You saying the Russians are after Merriweather?"

Now it's Barkley's turn to shrug. "Who knows what the good doctor is into? Anyway, that's not even the best part. The Feds have a wiretap on Petrakov's cafe, which for the most part has been useless since he says nothing incriminating over the phone. But after you called me, I had a friend give me the transcripts for the past few months. I did find out that he calls his attorney frequently."

"Again, not helpful to us …" Molinaro snaps, annoyed that they had come all the way to New York on a wild goose chase. "We can't use anything he says to his lawyer."

"It's not what he said, it's who the lawyer is …" Barkley pauses for effect. "Barrymore Halstead."

"What?" Molinaro and Gonzalez say in unison, eliciting a chuckle from Barkley.

"You know, you two actually looked like twins just now."

"Cut the crap," Gonzalez says, but he's laughing too. "But what the hell would a white shoe lawyer like Halstead get out of representing a thug like Petrakov?"

Barkley takes a sip of his coffee. "You mean besides a boatload of cash?"

Molinaro looks at Gonzalez. "Does this guy ever stop with the wisecracks?"

Gonzalez slowly shakes his head. "Nope." He turns to Barkley. "Okay, so what do we do now?"

Barkley smiles. "How about we see how the other half lives?"

****

Wednesday morning finds Barrymore Halstead furious over the outcome of the Daubert hearing. A few minutes earlier, he chewed out George Payne, who is now licking his wounds in his own office down the hall. Halstead is still stewing about Payne's incompetence when the receptionist buzzes his phone. Halstead presses the speaker button and snaps, "Yes?"

"Mr. Halstead, there are three detectives here to see you."

What the…?

"Tell them I'm in a meeting. They can make an appointment for another time."

He is startled when a male voice barks back at him.

"Mr. Halstead, this is Detective Josh Barkley, and my colleagues and I are homicide detectives investigating a murder. We would just like a few minutes of your time."

Halstead sighs. "Christina, cancel my nine-thirty, and show the detectives in."

A moment later, Christina enters his office with three men in tow. Halstead takes in their ill-fitting suits and generic haircuts. Well, they certainly look the part. The shortest of the three men steps forward.

"I'm Detective Josh Barkley, NYPD, and these gentlemen are Detectives Gonzalez and Molinaro of Miami Homicide."

Halstead stands and pastes a respectful impression on his face. "Good morning, Detectives." He turns to Molinaro and Gonzalez. "How are you enjoying New York City? Quite a change from—"

Gonzalez clears his throat. "Mr. Halstead, we are not here on vacation. We are investigating a homicide."

"Yes, that's what Detective Barkley said earlier, but I cannot imagine why a homicide investigation would lead you to my office."

"Mr. Halstead, do you know a Dr. Robert Merriweather?"

Halstead gasps theatrically. "Has something happened to Dr. Merriweather?"

"Please answer the question, sir," Barkley says.

"Well, I have never met the doctor in person. However, he has been called as an expert witness in some of our high profile pharmaceutical cases."

"Has been called to testify against your client," Gonzalez clarifies.

"Yes. Again, I have to ask, has something happened to him?"

"No," Barkley said, "we are investigating the murder of Dr. Stewart Jacobson."

Halstead looks at them in genuine confusion. "Jacobson? I have no idea who that is, or what he has to do with Dr. Merriweather."

"We have reason to believe that Merriweather was the intended target."

"Well, I still don't see what that has to do with my firm...."

"With all due respect, Mr. Halstead, we know the stakes involved with these Big Pharma cases," Gonzalez says, "and we also know that Dr. Merriweather has been quite the thorn in your side."

Halstead chuckles. "Detective, are you suggesting that someone at my firm is targeting Merriweather to keep him from testifying? I have been practicing law for over three decades, and I can assure you that I don't win cases by offing my adversaries' witnesses."

"I'm sure you don't, sir—"

"However, to ease your minds, why don't you speak with George Payne? He is a senior partner here, and just yesterday he questioned Dr. Merriweather at a hearing."

"That would be great, sir," Barkley says. "Thank you."

Halstead rings George Payne's office, and a moment later he appears at the door.

"George," Halstead booms jovially, as if he hadn't just spent the morning tearing him to shreds, "come in and meet our guests." After introducing the detectives, he says, "These gentlemen would like some information about the firm's relationship to Dr. Merriweather, and I thought since you went toe to toe with him in the Daubert hearing yesterday, you might be the best person to help."

Payne nods, avoiding Halstead's eye. He knows his boss' emphasis on the phrase "toe to toe" is a reminder that Merriweather mopped the floor with him.

"Detectives, I have deposed Dr. Merriweather numerous times." He keeps his voice neutral. "He may think he gained some points during the hearing, but the actual trial has yet to take place. We're not worried."

Gonzalez holds up a hand. "Mr. Payne, we are not here to discuss your sparring match with Merriweather. We are only interested in finding out who may want to harm him."

Payne looks as confused as Halstead had a few moments earlier. Halstead quickly fills him in, then turns back to the detectives.

"So you see, gentlemen, Mr. Payne and I know nothing of use to you. Now, we are very sorry about Dr. Jacobson, but we really are very busy...."

"Of course," Barkley says, "We appreciate your time. Just so we can wrap this up, can both of you account for your whereabouts on Saturday, January 27?"

"Of course we can, Detective. We were in Denver attending to a matter wholly unrelated to this case." He goes over and picks up the phone. "Christina, please give the detectives our time sheets for January 26 and 27? Thank you." He replaces the phone and beams at the detectives. "She'll take care of it. Good day, gentlemen, and good luck with your investigation."

The detectives thank him and Payne, then make their way to the door, with Barkley bringing up the rear. Suddenly, he turns back to the attorneys. "Oh, Mr. Halstead, be sure to tell Dimitri Petrakov that Josh Barkley says hi."

Molinaro and Gonzalez turn to see Halstead's mouth working. Finally, he says, "I'm quite sure I don't know who you're talking about."

Barkley grins. "Oh, I must be mistaken. Good day, sir."

As soon as they leave, Barrymore Halstead drops the benevolent smile and turns to George Payne. "You fucking idiot. First, you botch the Daubert hearing and now you connect Petrakov to us."

"What?" George whines, "You've represented Dimitri for years."

128

"Yes, but I don't broadcast it, you moron."

Much as Halstead wants to blame Payne, he knows the detectives could have learned from any number of sources that he represents Petrakov's legal interests. After all, he had been doing so for more than two decades, when Petrakov was just a street thug and Halstead was hungry for clients. He'd gotten him acquitted of an aggravated assault charge, saving Petrakov from at least ten years in jail and earning Halstead the mobster's undying loyalty. Since then, he's advised Petrakov on his business dealings and handed off anything he didn't want to dirty his hands with to lawyers outside the firm. On the other hand, he was still angry with Payne over the Daubert hearing and, as was his way, would continue to abuse the man until the feeling passed.

"I told you not to use the office phones."

"But the cops couldn't have tapped our phones...."

Halstead looks at him in disgust. "No, but Dimitri's may be tapped. If not for your stupidity, the cops would never be sniffing around here."

Halstead reaches into the top draw of his desk and pulls out a burner phone. "You can get these anywhere, and they're untraceable." Halstead keys up a number from memory. "Mr. Petrakov, how are you today?"

"I am very well," Petrakov replies in heavily accented Eastern European English. "Am I going to see you today?"

"No, but I think you might be getting some other visitors. Just wanted to give you a heads up."

"Da, I understand. About that other matter?"

"That is on hold for now. I'll get back to you soon. Understand?"

"Yes, yes."

****

The three detectives pile in Barkley's car, each clutching a hot dog purchased from the food truck at the end of the block. Shivering, Molinaro slides into the back seat, looks dubiously at the dog, and counts the minutes until he is back on the plane to Miami.

"That," Barkley says, "is a traditional New York street lunch."

"Yeah," Gonzalez says, "don't think about it too much. Just eat it." He bites into his own dog, loaded with mustard, relish, and onion.

"Feel like we're stuck in an episode of Law & Order," Molinaro grumbles, then takes a bite. It is surprisingly delicious. "Mmmm ... not bad."

"Nothin' like a dirty water dog," Barkley agrees.

"Dirty wa—?"

"Just eat it," Gonzalez says again.

Barkley licks the last of the mustard off his fingers then eases the car into traffic. He glances at Gonzalez. "You up for a road trip?"

"Absolutely."

"Where are we headed?" Molinaro asks.

"Brooklyn."

Nearly forty-five minutes later, they pull up in front of the

Golden Ruble Café in Brighton Beach. It would have taken only twenty minutes, Barkley explained, had they not hit so much traffic just getting from Midtown to the Brooklyn Bridge. "We're lucky the BQE wasn't too bad," he adds, eliciting a grunt from Molinaro, who now, on top of being freezing, has heartburn from the hot dog.

When they walk into the dimly lit café, Detective Barkley immediately points to a back booth, where a man is sitting alone, pouring over a piece of paper. On the table next to him is a bottle of Stoli and a shot glass.

"There he is."

Scientists contend that modern humans share two percent of their genomes with their Neanderthal ancestors; however, one look at Dimitri Petrakov would make one think it is closer to fifty. Even sitting down, it is easy to see that he is short but stocky and powerfully built. Dark brown hair stops just short of his thick eyebrows and curls wildly around his collar. His thick hands and protruding forehead, as well as the hairy chest evident through a partially unbuttoned shirt, give further credence to a Neanderthal influence.

As they approach the table, two huge men dressed all in black move quickly towards them. Petrakov looks up, then waves the men away.

"Detective Barkley," he says, his mouth twisting into a cruel grin, "it has been a while...."

"You know this guy?" Molinaro asks.

"I've arrested a few of his associates over the years."

"Never arrested me, though," Petrakov says, the grin widening.

"There's always time for that," Barkley quips. "Mr. Petrakov, this is Detective Gonzalez and Detective Molinaro—they are from Miami."

Petrakov waves them to join him, and as they slide into the seat he lays down the piece of paper he'd been looking at. It looks to be a racing form. He gestures to the bottle, then calls to one of his men. "Bring the detectives some glasses."

"I don't think so, Dimitri," Barkley says, still smiling. "We'll take three coffees though."

One of the thugs disappears into the kitchen, leaving the other standing there, bulky arms crossed.

"Mr. Petrakov," Gonzalez says, "why do I get the feeling you've been expecting us?"

Petrakov shakes his head. "No, Dimitri just have nothing to hide. Often chat with police or FBI. Dimitri is simple businessman." The man returns with three cups of coffee and, with surprising grace, places them on the table. Petrakov waits for them to take a sip. "You like coffee? It's from original Russian Samovar."

"Yeah, it's delicious," Barkley says. "Now cut the crap. Did your lawyer call to tell you we were coming?"

"Lawyer? No, Dimitri doesn't like lawyers. You call them liars here, no?"

The detectives laugh; no arguing with him there.

"People here need lawyers because America is lawless society." Petrakov gives them another cruel grin, and the detectives realize that's the only one he has. "Many criminals and punks roam streets. Not like old Soviet Union, where order and curfews were enforced." He turns to

Gonzalez. "Not like Cuba, either. You are Cuban, no? There are no gangs selling drugs there, and people respect government."

Ignoring his commentary, Gonzalez says, "So Barrymore Halstead doesn't represent you?"

Dimitri gives them a casual wave of his hand. "He advises me on how to deal with America's burdensome tax laws."

"Mr. Petrakov, Detective Molinaro and I are investigating a homicide that took place in Miami. Would you mind telling us the last time you were there?"

"Dimitri never visit Miami, too decadent."

Just then, Molinaro pulls his phone out of his pocket, checks the caller ID, and answers it. "Hello? Hello? Dammit." He points to the phone on the wall behind Dimitri. "Mind if I use your phone? That was my doctor's office, and I have no signal in here."

"It is okay with Dimitri. You Americans look healthy, but inside too many troubles, and you take too many pills."

His patience rapidly coming to an end, Gonzalez halfheartedly asks Dimitri whether he knows Drs. Merriweather or Jacobson, all the while wondering what his partner is up to.

His cell phone still in his left hand, Molinaro moves to the rotary phone right behind Dimitri and begins to dial.

"Ms. Ruiz," he says, just loudly enough that the others can hear, "this is Detective Molinaro. You just called, said it was urgent?"

"Andy?" Isabella asks, "I thought we agreed to call each other by our first names. And I didn't call you, urgently or otherwise."

"Ms. Ruiz, did my test results come back bad?"

"Andy, what are you talking about? What test results?"

"Well, that's not too bad. I can take care of a little elevated cholesterol by changing my diet."

"Andy, what cholesterol? What are you talking about? Are you in some kind of trouble?"

"No, no I feel fine." As he speaks, Molinaro subtly angles his cell phone over Dimitri's left shoulder and snaps a quiet picture of the racing form. "Okay, then I'll see Dr. Brewster next week, Wednesday at three-thirty, thanks." Just as he is about to hang up, he hears Isabella muttering something about how all the cute guys are nuts. Smiling, he ends the call, then rejoins the others at the table. "Looks like it was nothing to worry about."

Five minutes later, the detectives finally leave the café and head out into the freezing air.

"At least the coffee was good," Barkley snaps, annoyed that they had gotten nothing from Dimitri. He presses a button to unlock the car door, and they all hurry to get inside. "Other than that it was a complete waste of time."

"Maybe not." Gonzalez twists toward the back seat and smiles at his partner. "That was good. I almost didn't see you take the picture."

"I learned that maneuver when I was in the FBI." He pulls out his phone again and brings up the picture, moving his fingers on the touchscreen to enlarge it. "These are not peri-mutual racing forms, and these are not numbers one would use in placing off-track bets. These are sixteen-digit numbers, followed by four numbers, then a hyphen and three more numbers. The first four numbers of some of these are familiar."

He reaches for his wallet and pulls out his credit cards. "Yes, these are credit card numbers—MasterCard, Visa, Discover, and even American Express. The four digit numbers are the month and year of expiration. Looks like old Dimitri is trying his hand at identity theft."

"Not surprising, but he is also up to no good with Halstead," adds Gonzalez. "I just know it."

They ride in silence back to the city, each man thinking about the best way to proceed with the case. As Barkley pulls into the parking garage of the hotel, he says, "This place has a pretty good restaurant—casual and, more importantly, with a fully stocked bar. It's still pretty early. Won't get crowded till later. What do you say we grab a quick dinner, have a few drinks, and go over what we know?"

"Okay," Gonzalez says irritably, "but let's keep it short. That special New York hotdog of yours has been repeating on me all afternoon."

"I thought it was just me," Molinaro says. "Besides, you're the one who told me to 'just eat it.'"

"What a coupla wusses," Barkley chuckles, drawing glares from both of them.

They make their way into the restaurant and seek out a table in the far corner. A waitress follows them to drop off some menus and take their drink orders—scotch and water for Barkley and a rum and coke for Molinaro. Gonzalez orders a sparkling water, ignoring his partner's raised eyebrow. Gonzalez has never passed up a drink before. Molinaro peruses the menu for all of two seconds before deciding on a burger and fries.

"What are you getting, Rick?" he says, glancing up at his partner. "Geez, man, you okay? You don't look so good."

Gonzalez nods. "I'll be okay. Just the day catching up with me." He rotates his left wrist then runs his hand up his left arm. "Even my arthritis is acting up."

After the waitress brings their drinks and takes the food order, Barkley raises his scotch and says, "Here's to catching Petrakov … for something."

"Here's to finding the bastard who bludgeoned Jacobson, whoever he is."

The two touch glasses, but Gonzalez stays still, his eyes fixed, his skin ashen gray.

Molinaro puts his glass down. "Rick?"

Gonzalez looks like he wants to speak, but instead he just winces in pain. Molinaro gasps in horror when he sees spittle at the corner of his partner's mouth.

"Rick!" he shouts.

Gonzalez slumps over, and Molinaro jumps up and grabs his shoulders just in time to stop him from hitting the floor. He lays him gently down, then places two fingers on his neck.

"Call 911," he calls to Barkley, who's already pulling out his phone. "He's got a pulse, but it's very weak."

Over the past few minutes, the restaurant has started to fill up. Now, an eerie silence falls over the place as all eyes turn to the man lying on the ground. The waitress runs to the hotel lobby, and a moment later, the concierge's voice is heard over the loudspeaker, asking any medical doctors to please go to the restaurant. Within minutes, an internist visiting from Atlanta walks in and rushes over to Molinaro. He is still monitoring his partner's thready pulse and trying to keep him from losing consciousness.

"I'm Dr. Clara Bergstrum. Has your friend complained of chest, back, or stomach pain today?"

"Yes, it started about an hour ago."

"Okay, any pain in his left arm?"

"Yes, but he said it was his arthritis acting up."

"Has someone called 911?"

"Yes," Barkley chimes in, "they should be here any minute. Is he having a heart attack?"

"Looks that way." Bergstrum turns to face the other patrons and shouts, "Anyone have an aspirin on them?"

A woman comes rushing over and starts fumbling through her purse. "I don't have aspirin, but I have these," she says, pulling out a bottle of Excedrin. "Are they okay?"

"Yes, they'll do." She looks up at Barkley. "I need you to go see I f the hotel has an AED."

"A what?"

"It's a portable defibrillator. I may need it to restore his heart rate."

She places the Excedrin to Gonzalez's lips. "Chew it first, it'll work faster that way." He nods, then bites down on the pills, grimacing. "I know it's bitter," Bergstrum says, then turns to Molinaro. "Grab his water."

Molinaro does as he's told, then gently lifts his partner's head so he can sip. Just then, the EMTs arrive.

"This man is having an acute myocardial infarction," Bergstrum tells them. "Get EKG leads on him and start an IV. He's just had some Excedrin, but I want you to give him nitro as well."

"Yes, doctor."

She looks down at Gonzalez. "They're going to give you nitroglycerin. Just keep it under your tongue, okay?"

Within minutes the EMTs have the IV in and EKG leads on. Dr. Bergstrum notes the depressed S-T segment of the EKG pattern, confirming her diagnosis of a fairly significant heart attack.

"Okay, let's get him out of here."

Moving at lightning speed, the EMTs hoist him onto the gurney and rush him to the ambulance waiting outside. They are followed by Bergstrum, Molinaro, and Barkley.

"I'll follow you," Barkley shouts, knowing Molinaro will want to ride with his partner.

"Okay." Molinaro looks at the EMT about to shut the ambulance doors. "Don't even think about it," he growls as he climbs in next to the gurney.

For the next seven minutes, he keeps up a steady course of encouragement to his partner as the ambulance navigates the crowded Manhattan streets. When they get to the ER, they whisk Gonzalez down the long tile covered sterile corridor.

"He's just hanging on," Bergstrum says, confirming what Molinaro already knows. "I'm sorry to tell you this, but there's a good chance your friend won't make it."

CHAPTER 11
Turmoil

The morning after he returns from New York, Robert awakens before dawn, his mind already teaming with everything he has to do. George Payne's tactics had robbed him of an entire day, a day packed with meetings and other obligations that would now have to be rescheduled. There was also one thing that could not be moved: an early surgery at Jackson South Hospital. After a quick run with Tubby to clear his thoughts and an icy shower to invigorate his body, he is singularly focused on the task before him. As he eases his car on to the road, the sun is just beginning its ascent, and bringing with it the promise of another idyllic Florida day.

By 7 a.m., he is walking the halls of Jackson South. Around him, he sees the usual pre-op flurry, with nurses and the anesthesia team scurrying around to complete the necessary forms and check last minute lab results. Robert nods at a few of them, then heads directly for the eye of the storm, the patient holding area. A seventy-ish woman lays on a gurney in bay number 8, her mouth a tight, anxious line, her eyes following the buzz of activity. Next to her sits an equally nervous looking man. Two weeks ago, Dr. Merriweather had diagnosed Beverly Elliott with Drug-Induced Jaw Osteonecrosis resulting from her prolonged use of Bone Max. When she sees him walking toward her, a look of relief crosses Beverly's face.

"Dr. Merriweather, I am so glad to see you! We have a couple more questions before we start."

Merriweather smiles. "Certainly, Mrs. Elliot, and this is your husband, I presume?"

"Yes, this is Jake. He couldn't make it for my appointment a couple of weeks ago."

The two men shake hands, then Dr. Merriweather stands directly in front of them. "I'll answer all your questions, but first I have one for you. Has anything changed since I saw you last?"

"A little," Beverly admits. "I've been very depressed. I snap at poor Jake like I never have before." She grabs her husband's hand and squeezes it. "The drainage from my face is less since you gave me that antibiotic, but the bone in my mouth, the bad taste, and the smell are even worse. Also, my teeth don't meet like before. That was one of my questions—why is that?"

Merriweather nods; he has heard this all before. "Mrs. Elliott, the antibiotic only treats the secondary infection that settled into the dead bone in your mouth. That dead bone is still there. Your jaw is broken, and from what you're describing, the bone segments must have separated, which is causing your teeth not to meet. As we discussed before, the break in your jaw is through a nerve—actually, it severed the nerve—that's why your lower lip and chin on the right side are numb."

"That was one of my other questions."

"Mrs. Elliott, today we are going to go in and remove the dead bone. To do this, we must amputate part of your lower jaw." He sees the look of fear in her eyes and holds up a hand. "It sounds worse than it is. It will relieve your pain and resolve the infections, the bad taste, and the smell as it heals the area. We will replace the missing bone with a titanium plate and realign your lower jaw so that your facial appearance will be normal and the teeth you have left will meet correctly. I am afraid that there are five teeth within the dead bone that will be lost. You will have to adapt to eating on the left side."

Beverly's shoulders slump a little from either sadness or relief. Merriweather figures it's a little of both. When she started taking Bone Max six years earlier, she had been a happily retired school teacher, traveling with her husband and enjoying her grandchildren. Like many women, she'd been told by her doctor that Bone Max was a wonder drug and that if she took it for the rest of her life, she'd be protected from osteoporosis and bone fracture in her spine and hips. Three years later, however, she began to feel agonizing pain in her jaw. Now the ordeal would finally end with a major surgery.

Jake looks even more upset than Beverly. "Dr. Merriweather, how did this happen to my wife?"

"Well, it's a long story. In the doctor's defense, he was only telling you what he had been told by the Apollo Drug Company. And, as your case shows, Bone Max does strengthen your bones and reduces the risk for a spine or hip fracture for the first three years. But after that it works in reverse and begins weakening your bones. It is essentially too much for too long. Apollo Drug Company ignored the cumulative effects of the drug, particularly in the jawbone. The FDA has recently put out warnings that everyone should be reexamined after taking Bone Max for three years and no one should take it for more than five. Unfortunately, that does not help your wife, but it will prevent others from going through this." He touches Beverly's arm. "There's nothing we can do about the past. Let's just concentrate on getting you well and back to your grandkids and traveling with Jake, okay?"

Just then, Robert sees Glanville and Sanders standing near the nurses' station and waves them over.

"Jake, Beverly, these fine doctors are part of my surgical team." He smiles at Beverly. "You're in very good hands." He turns back to Jake to break down the logistics. "The actual procedure will take about four hours, but there's an hour of prep before we begin and another hour in the recovery room afterward. In a way, you have the hardest job—waiting—but my volunteer Diana Edelson will come out and give you periodic updates on our progress, and I'll talk to you right after we finish. Now give her a kiss for good luck."

A few minutes later, Beverly Elliott is wheeled into Operating Room 2. The induction of anesthesia by Dr. Morales and his team goes smoothly, as does the intubation of a breathing tube through the nose, down the throat, and through the vocal cords to rest in the trachea below the larynx. The nasal intubation leaves the mouth unobstructed for oral surgery and keeps the tube away from the neck, where the incision will be made.

When she is safely asleep, the face below the eyes, jaw area, and neck down to the clavicle are prepared with an antiseptic solution, then sterile towels and drapes are placed to create a sterile field.

In the meantime, Dr. Merriweather and his team vigorously scrub their hands and arms with an alcohol solution, then slip into the gowns and gloves held out to them by the nurses. As they head out to the operating field, he smiles reassuringly at Dr. Melissa Sanders. As Chief Resident, she will be performing the surgery, assisted by Robert and Dr. Glanville.

"Okay, Dr. Sanders, outline your neck incision and place it in a natural skin fold. This lady may be seventy-one but she is just as concerned about a scar as you or I would be." He watches as she swiftly but strategically marks the area where she will make the cut. "Okay, go ahead and make your incision."

With a steady hand, Sanders begins running the scalpel along the skin. Beginning just below the right ear, the incision runs two inches below the jaw and ends to the left of the chin. The long incision is necessary to remove the large amount of dead bone and place the titanium plate.

"Good, now control your little bleeders with the cautery, but don't field cauterize. Just cauterize each bleeder separately to reduce thermal injury to adjacent tissue. Now get through the subcutaneous fat and identify the platysma muscle. Melissa, do you know what the corollary of the platysma muscle is called in mammals other than humans?"

"The Panniculus Carnosus...?"

"Good, Panniculus Carnosus, or skin muscle, is what dogs, cats, and lions, et cetera use to snarl and raise the hair on their backs when they are aroused. Thanks to evolution, the only part of this muscle left in humans is the platysma and our facial muscles, which allow us to express emotions by voluntarily moving our skin."

"Hey, Dr. Merriweather, are you operating or are you lecturing?" chides Dr. Morales as he peeks over the drape separating the operative field from the anesthesia machine.

"Well, this is a teaching program, after all," Merriweather replies. "I'm sorry if I woke you up back there or, heaven forbid, disturbed the reading of your stock portfolio."

He hears Morales' soft chuckle, then watches as Dr. Sanders continues cutting through the platysma muscle. Then, at Dr. Merriweather's direction, she ties off an artery and vein and proceeds to the edge of the lower jaw.

"Observe the scar tissue around the dead bone and the fracture," Merriweather says, "as well as the pus coming out of the bone. Let's do a culture. Is it more yielding to culture pus, or some of the infected tissue?"

"The infected tissue," Melissa replies, "because the pus is just dead white blood cells, and the majority of the bacteria is in the tissue that is infected."

"Very good. See all those splintered pieces of bone, culture one of them too. What are they called?"

"They're sequestra...."

"Very good again, Melissa. You're on a roll, but you still have to finish the year to graduate, you know."

Dr. Sanders strips the infected covering off the right side of the lower jaw. "Wow," she says, wrinkling her nose, "the bone looks and smells nasty."

"It certainly does," Dr. Glanville mutters. "Now, let's wire the teeth together to index her bite and adapt the titanium plate."

"Yes, Doctor Merriweather," Melissa says, then she and

Glanville adapt the titanium plate to the jaw. They have just placed four screws on each side of the planned bone removal site when the lights in the operating room start flashing on and off. Suddenly, a voice booms from the overhead speaker: "Code Gray, Code Gray. I repeat, Code Gray. Take protective action."

Everyone in the operating room looks around in confusion, each mentally going through the various codes. Code Blue is a cardiac arrest, Code Red is a fire, Code Pink is a missing baby, Code Black is a disaster code. What the heck is Code Gray?

Paula, the circulating room nurse, rushes to the computer bench to look it up.

"It's an intruder alert," she announces a moment later. "There must be an unauthorized person in the operating room area."

Just then, they hear a noise from a trash can being turned over just outside the room. Paula gasps as she sees a slender man with a red baseball cap peeking in through the side window by the scrub sink. He locks eyes with the nurse, then moves toward the door of the operating room.

"Help me!" she exclaims, grabbing Diana Edelson's arm and pulling her toward the heavy instrument cart. Together, they push it against the now half-open door, knocking the intruder backward.

"Hey, there he is!" they hear someone shout, then two security guards race past the operating room. "Get him before he goes through an emergency exit!"

"Paula, did you see who it was?" asks Dr. Glanville when the two women return.

Paula, her face white as a sheet, shakes her head. "Nobody I know. He had a red goatee and was wearing a baseball cap. I don't know what the hell he was up to, but I didn't like the look in his eyes."

Only Robert remains unruffled; to him, the man was simply an unwelcome diversion from his patient. "Okay," he says, "the excitement is over. Let's get back to business."

"Yes," Melissa says, but there is a tremor in her voice.

"Let's remove the plate," Merriweather continues, "resect the bone, and replace the plate using the same screws placed in the same screw holes."

About five inches of the right side of the lower jaw is removed using an air-driven saw; this bone is then replaced by the titanium plate, and the mouth and neck open wounds are sutured. The surgery ends with a dressing placed over the neck and the removal of the breathing tube.

"Good work, everyone," Merriweather says, trying to break the lingering tension. "Potentially dangerous intruder aside, the surgery went beautifully."

This is the best part, he thinks as he heads out to the waiting room to give Jake the good news. Then, after checking on Beverly in the recovery room, he returns to the clinic to touch base with Isabella.

"Hey, Issy. Any messages?"

Isabella looks up from her computer screen. "Several, but first you better see what's waiting for you in your office."

Dr. Merriweather raises an eyebrow at her, then walks into his office to find two uniformed security guards.

"Matt, José, what are you guys doing here? Is it about the

intruder?"

"It certainly is, Dr. Merriweather," José replies. "Before he tried to bust into your OR, he asked reception where your office was, said he had an appointment. When he was told you were in surgery, a few of the nurses saw him checking out the OR schedule. Do you have any idea who this guy was?"

"Heck no. I didn't even see him. We were in surgery at the time. He actually would have gotten in if Paula and Diana hadn't blocked the door."

"The bastard got out through one of the emergency exits and drove off."

"Tell them about the brick-throwing incident," they hear Isabella call from the outer office. "It may be the same guy."

José's eyes go wide. "You had a brick thrown at you?"

"Yes, with a threatening note on it, but not here. It was at my house."

"Look, Dr. Merriweather, we'll do our best to protect you on hospital grounds, but you really need to report both these incidents to the police. Who knows, they may even be connected to Dr. Jacobson's murder."

"That's what I've told him," Isabella calls out.

After the security guards have left, she gets up from her chair and walks into the office. "If you don't tell Andy about this stuff, I will. Someone is out to get you. You need police protection."

Robert raises an eyebrow at her again. "Andy? Do I detect a budding romance here?"

"Don't change the subject. You have been living in denial

for weeks. You might be a great doctor, but you are not indestructible. Think of everyone who cares about you— your kids, your dogs, Heather, me!" She smirks. "Not necessarily in that order, of course."

"Okay, okay, you made your point, and I will refrain from asking you about your love life. Now, about my messages...."

"Yes, the most important one is from Steve Carr. He wants you to come to the lab this afternoon if you can. It seems your rats are having some problems."

****

Merriweather checks on Beverley Elliott again, then he and Dr. Glanville head out to the animal lab, which is a thirty-minute drive from the hospital.

"I'm worried, James. Judging from Steve's message, it's possible that the rats that received Bone Max have exposed bone in their mouths and are reacting to the infection and pain, similar to the symptoms Mrs. Elliott was suffering."

"I hope not. I've always loved those rats. When we started the study, I was surprised how cuddly they were."

"Yes, their reputation as disease-carrying vermin has much more to do with circumstance than their true nature."

Merriweather explains that when civilization began to urbanize around 1200 AD, rats, which are among the most resilient creatures on the planet, adapted to the unsanitary and overcrowded conditions part and parcel to urban living. In fact, they prospered and proliferated their numbers due to the abundant food supply of leftover trash and hidden living places. There were few predators around, as even the cats couldn't get at them in the nooks and crannies of the cities. This environment also protected them from hawks and eagles, as well as the cold winters.

About the same time, Marco Polo found an overland route to China that facilitated the exportation of silk and other oriental goods to Europe. However, one of the unforeseen goods that traveled along this "Silk Road" was the oriental rat flea. Previously unknown to Europe, this flea carried the bacteria Yersinia Pestis, which caused the Bubonic Plague and would eventually kill more than fifty percent of Europe's population.

"Although the bacteria, which was spread through flea bites, actually caused the disease, the rats were blamed for the plague and targeted for extermination."

"Wow, I never realized all that. How do you know so much about this?"

"Historical medicine is not only fascinating, some of it is actually relevant today, if only to get our minds thinking about a problem from a different perspective. Just like we don't limit our expertise to the oral and maxillofacial area, we shouldn't limit our knowledge to one particular time period. There are many things to be learned from the past, especially past mistakes."

"Very true," Glanville says as they pull into the parking lot. "One thing's for sure. I'll be looking at our furry friends differently now."

They park on the fourth floor of the lot, then walk next door to the medical school. Once inside, they take the elevator down to the basement, where the lab is located. When the doors open, they find Steve Carr, senior veterinary technician, already waiting for them.

He steps forward to shake Merriweather's hand. "Thanks for getting here so quickly."

"Of course. Steve, you've met my clinical research fellow, Dr. Glanville."

"Yes, good to see you again, Dr. Glanville." Steve turns to another man standing nearby. "Let me introduce Julio, one of our vet tech interns."

The two doctors nod their greeting to Julio, then Steve leads them down a dimly lit hallway toward the rat lab. As they round a corner, Robert thinks he sees a shadow moving near the ceiling. Is that a bat? He is about to point it out to the others when Steve starts talking about the rats.

"Julio and I have been looking at them every day. Half act normal, and half are agitated as hell. I called you because some are frothing at the mouth and biting their front paws. Two have actually chewed off one of them. If they get infected and die before the completion of your study, it may screw up your statistical analysis."

"Heck yes, Steve. I am worried about that too, but I am more worried that they're developing exposed bone and that the pain is the driving force for their behavior. Can we examine a couple of the aggressive ones?"

"Sure, just give me a second."

He grabs four pairs of armored gloves and hands them to the other men before slipping them on himself. Then he reaches into a cage and expertly grabs one of the rats by the back of the neck. Merriweather's brow furrows in concern as the rat begins attacking the glove. Steve positions his hand over the skull and pins the animal to the top of the examining table. Merriweather and Glanville pick up routine dental mirrors to look into the mouth. It confirms Merriweather's fear.

"Indeed, there is exposed bone on the left side and frothy white saliva drooling out of the mouth. See, James, his fur is wet here."

Steve puts the rat back in the cage, then grabs a second, whose jaw has the same appearance. The third and fourth rats also display aggressive behavior, but have no exposed bone.

"Well, that is interesting ..." says Merriweather. "The cis-phosphorous drug may be causing bone pain even before becoming exposed. We saw that in a few of our patients as well." He nods his head toward the cages. "I would like to see a few more."

This time, Julio reaches in to grab the fifth aggressive rat. It is then that Merriweather realizes he is only wearing one glove.

"Julio, wait!"

But it's too late. As Julio brings the rat out of the cage it passes close to his ungloved left hand. The rat seizes the opportunity and clamps down on the webbing between the thumb and the index finger. Shrieking in pain, Julio desperately tries to shake the rat off. His efforts only infuriate the animal more; it shakes its head from side to side and finally succeeds in biting through the soft flesh. Julio shrieks again, and the rat drops to the floor.

While Steve Carr tries to corner it, Merriweather and

Glanville attend to Julio's wound. They run cold water over the open wound and hold a steady pressure on it to stop the bleeding. Julio's face is pasty white, and he looks like he might pass out.

"Gotcha!" Steve exclaims as he catches the rat and tosses him back in his cage.

Merriweather waves him over. "Steve, get some of your Betadine sterile prep solution. Let's try to decontaminate the bite area and get him over to the emergency room."

Steve rushes to a nearby table and grabs a bottle, then walks back over to the others. Julio instinctively tries to pull away as Steve pours the brown organic iodine liquid over the wound, then relaxes a bit when it does not sting as he expected. The doctors make a pressure dressing wrap for the hand and walk him over to the main Dade County Hospital Emergency Room.

As Steve Carr starts filling out the myriad of annoying forms necessary to register him, Robert walks toward the back of the ER, eyes flicking this way and that. Finally, he sees a well-built African-American man, gray at the temples, speaking to a nurse and swiftly approaches him.

Harold Yates had worked with Robert in the ER back when they were both residents. Over the years the two had remained friends and Harold, now Chief of Emergency Room Operations, had come to rely on Merriweather's "Team OMFS" for the oral and maxillofacial surgeries that comprised eighty percent of the facial trauma calls.

"Harold, I need your help."

Yates turns around, all smiles. "Robert, what a pleasant surprise. What's the matter, don't you have enough residents and junior faculty to cover the ER, or is some visiting dignitary in need of your services?"

Robert smiles grimly at the joke. Normally, the surgical chief did not cover trauma calls; however, in the case of a politician or other VIP, the Dean would request that the chief meet the patient's helicopter directly.

"Actually, Harold, one of the vet tech interns was bitten, rather savagely, by a research rat, one that may have a jaw infection. I am even concerned about rabies."

"Rabies, are you crazy? Not in research rats, Robert. They're quarantined and tested before you get them."

"I know it sounds crazy, but any animal can get rabies, even lab rats." He tells Harold about the bat he thought he saw earlier. "Harold, this rat was frothing at the mouth and psychotic, just like a rabid dog. I'm going back to the lab now to take specimens from that rat, but I'd appreciate it if you could get one of your guys to take care of Julio, get him started on antibiotics right away."

"Of course, Robert. Don't worry about things here, just get over to your lab and do what you got to do."

"Thanks," Merriweather calls, already rushing back to find Steve and Glanville, "I owe you."

He finds them standing by the reception desk.

"Look, I got the ER chief himself to take care of Julio. We have to go back to the lab now. Steve, have you seen any bats around the lab?"

"Yes," Steve says, "we have several of them. There is no way to keep them out. The building has several cracks and vents they use to enter in the morning and leave at night.

It's their cave away from home, if you will. What are you getting at?"

Merriweather relays his concern about rabies. "Some of those rats had frothing at the mouth, but no exposed bone. Although the greater likelihood is that they are experiencing bone pain due to a cis-phosphorous effect without exposed bone, the possibility of rabies is too grave to ignore. I'll need your help and that of Dr. Glanville here to perform a necroscopy and prepare the specimens."

The three of them head back to the lab, where Steve Carr prepares the dissection table, then euthanizes the rat that attacked Julio.

"How are we going to test for rabies?" Glanville asks. "I don't have the slightest notion of where to begin."

"You will after today," Merriweather replies. "Remember what I said in the car about broadening your knowledge base? Well, now's your chance."

"Great," Glanville mutters.

"Here's what we'll do: first we take saliva and blood samples, then we will need to crack the skull and the vertebrae to remove the brain and spinal cord without damaging either one. In the old days, animals were diagnosed with rabies by brain specimens, which showed Negri bodies under high power microscopes. Negri bodies are oval inclusion particles in nerve cells that were first identified by Adelchi Negri. However, they were not specific and are therefore no longer used to arrive at a confirmed diagnosis. Instead, we'll use direct fluorescent antibodies on the brain tissue and polymerase chain reaction testing of the saliva. If this rat had rabies, those tests will show it. Now, let's get on with it."

Once Steve Carr has collected the blood and saliva specimens and labeled each container, Merriweather guides Dr. Glanville in the delicate saw operation to split the skull and vertebrae to access the brain and spinal cord. Then, after severing the nerves arising from each, they remove both the brain and spinal cord, still attached to one another.

"Wow, look at that brain," Glanville says. "It's all shriveled up, and there are more holes than Swiss cheese. Is a rabies brain supposed to look like this?"

Merriweather shakes his head grimly. "Actually, no, not at all. However, while in school, I assisted in autopsies of spongiform encephalopathy—'mad cow disease'—and saw brains that looked just like this. Anyway, let's take some pictures of this before I take representative slices for microscopy. We'll also take these specimens over to the histopathology lab; they'll want the specimens fresh rather than fixed in formaldehyde."

After dropping the specimens off at the lab, they check in on Julio, who has been admitted to the infectious disease ward and is receiving intravenous antibiotics.

"Hey, buddy," Steve says, "you're gonna be fine."

Merriweather and Glanville nod encouragingly.

No one mentions the possibility of rabies or mad cow disease.

CHAPTER 12
More Than a Meeting

The harsh ring of the cell phone breaks the silence in Isabella Ruiz's living room, ripping her from sleep. She jumps up and looks around. It was just 11 p.m., and she had dozed off on the couch while watching television. She reaches for the phone lying on the coffee table.

"Hello?"

"Issy? It's Andy ... Molinaro. I'm sorry; it sounds like I woke you."

Isabella swings her leg over the side of the couch. "You did, but I don't mind. In fact, I am glad you called. What was that craziness the other day? Why did you act like you were calling to make a doctor's appointment?"

Molinaro chuckled. "Yeah, sorry about that. For now, let's just chalk it up to police business." His voice grows serious. "But that's not why I'm calling. I'm still in New York ... I have some bad news."

"Still in New York? Andy, what's the matter?"

"My partner had a heart attack, happened a few hours after I called you."

"Oh my God, Andy," Isabella gasps. "Is he okay?"

"I think so. It was touch and go for a while, but he's stable and in pretty good spirits, considering. His wife and his oldest son flew in today to be with him," Andy sighs. "Oh, God, Issy, they're saying he needs a triple bypass!"

"Andy," she says gently, "I know it's awful, but believe me, people have bypasses all the time. In fact, a lot of Dr. Merriweather's patients have had them. Your partner has blockages in the blood vessels feeding the heart. The doctors are going to take a vein from his leg and hook them up to those vessels above and below the blockages, allowing the blood flow to bypass them."

Isabella hears Andy's sharp intake of breath.

"It sounds worse than it is," she says. "Most everyone is able to resume normal activities afterward."

"Okay, but what is 'normal?' Would he be able to come back to the force?"

Isabella sighs again. "That I can't tell you. I'm sorry, Andy."

"Yeah, me too. And to make matters worse, my lieutenant is pressuring me to solve this Jacobson case, partner or no partner."

"Can't they get you someone else while Gonzalez recovers?"

"Nah, they're shorthanded right now." He pauses. "Issy, I know this is going to sound kinda weird, but would you be willing to help me a little bit, let me bounce some ideas about the case off you? I know Dr. Merriweather keeps you very busy, and you could say no if you want, but I'm—"

"Andy, Andy slow down," she says, laughing. "I'd be thrilled to help you."

"You would?"

"Yes! My ex was a detective, remember? He used to run

cases by me all the time."

"That would be great, but you know this has to be hush-hush. A husband sharing information with his wife is one thing, but if it got out that I brought in a civilian—"

She cuts him off again. "Andy, believe me, I understand. You bounce ideas off me, and mum's the word."

"Thanks, Issy. I'm on an early flight tomorrow. Can we get together around five? I need your help going over the inventory in Dr. Merriweather's office."

"Five sounds great."

"Good," Andy says, his tone lifting. "We'll order dinner. I'll call you when I land and give you directions."

"Okay, and Andy? I almost forgot to tell you. I have some disturbing news as well."

"What is it?"

"The day you called, someone broke into the operating room looking for Dr. Merriweather."

"What?"

"Yes, it happened in the middle of a surgery! The guy would have gotten to him, too, but his volunteer and a nurse blocked the door with an instrument table. Security chased him, but he got away. And, Andy, that was not the first time. Just two days before Dr. Jacobson's murder, someone tried to run over Robert's dog in front of his house, and they threw a brick at him with a threatening note attached to it."

"But—but," Andy sputters, "why hasn't he said anything before?"

Isabella snorts. "Robert is too macho to admit those things." She pauses for a moment. "Andy, I'm afraid for him. He just passes it off and buries his head in his work, but what if this is the same guy who murdered Dr. Jacobson? Andy, I think you should arrange police protection for him before something terrible happens."

Andy sighs. This case just keeps getting more and more complicated. "I'll check into that, Issy. Do you know if the good doctor still has the note?"

"I don't know."

"Well, see if you can find it before we meet tomorrow."

By seven-thirty Saturday night, the living room of Andy Molinaro's one-bedroom Coconut Grove apartment is strewn with laboratory reports, crime scene inventory reports, and the officers' notes. A two-thirds-eaten pizza and three empty plastic Starbucks cups lay on the floor next to the coffee table. Isabella is sitting on a plush brown sofa, pouring over the crime scene inventory notes while Andy sits a few feet away in a matching chair, a stack of case history notes on his lap. He pulls his feet off the ottoman and grunts.

Isabella looks over at him questioningly.

"I don't feel like we're making much progress here. Most of the prints lifted from the crime scene came from those who normally frequent the office—you, Dr. Brewster, Dr. Samanka, Dr. Glanville, Mrs. Edelson, Dr. Sanders, a couple of other residents, and two patients, both of whom were several states away when the murder occurred. No help there. Then there are the four sets that we can't identify. They're not in any database. The only blood that was found was Dr. Jacobson's and one stain of old pig blood." Andy grimaces. "What was your doctor doing with pig blood in his office anyway?"

Isabella laughs. "That's from pig jaws he had as part of an experiment. They've been in the corner for over two years, and he still hasn't gotten around to processing or analyzing them. He is always too busy or is starting a new project or is waiting to see a glimmer of interest in the eyes of one of his fellows or residents," she shrugs. "The jaws are preserved, but I guess some blood got onto the carpet when he first brought them in. I've been after him to take them to the animal lab, but he doesn't listen."

Andy doesn't look any less disgusted by her explanation. "Anyway, back to what we got here. No help with hair fiber analysis. No unusual dirt samples and no footprints in the blood droppings. Everyone's whereabouts check out, including the caregiver, Miriam. Rick and I got nothing from the slimy attorneys in New York … then of course, there's the Russian hitman, who was not exactly forthcoming with information." Andy snorts. "Although he did provide us with an interesting comparison between the U.S. and the former Soviet Union."

Isabella raises a questioning eyebrow at him, then returns to her files.

A minute later, she says, "Wait, Andy, I think I found something. There is only one bookend mentioned on the inventory list, but Dr. Merriweather definitely had both in the office. He got them as a gift when he lectured in Vancouver three years ago. I remember him complaining about how heavy they were and that he should have checked them in as luggage rather than carrying them on the plane. Didn't you say the medical examiner found metal fragments—iron fragments—in Dr. Jacobson's skull?" She waits for Andy's nod. "Well, the reason those bookends are so heavy is because they're made of cast iron."

"Issy, you're a genius," Andy says as he reaches for the autopsy report. "I'm going to double check, but I'm sure that was in there."

Smiling, Isabella walks over to him and leans over the report.

"Yup, there it is. The metal fragments were pure iron. You found the murder weapon!" He looks up at her and smiles. "You know what this means? This wasn't just any hitman, this was a very, very good hit man. He must have spotted the bookends and decided to use that instead of his own weapon to avoid us tracing it."

"Or …" Isabella says, looking at him dubiously, "it might have been that stalker who threatened Dr. Merriweather and broke into the operating room." She stood up and walked back over to the couch. "Or it could have been anyone else around here who was jealous of my boss or couldn't take his criticisms. And believe me, Dr. M can certainly dish it out when he feels it's deserved."

Andy nods. "Good point, but this is still an important find. I'll recheck the faculty and residents and look into the rest of the staff, see who was on the receiving end of Merriweather's ire. Also, the department wouldn't sign off on the full-time police protection at this point, but I'll tail the good doctor and see if I can catch this stalker guy. Issy, this is the first real break in this case. I could kiss you."

At this slip of the tongue, Andy feels his face burning.

"I wish you would," she says curtly, so much so that Andy almost misses the invitation.

"I'll also need to—" Andy cuts himself off and looks over at her with a lopsided smile. Then he slowly stands, walks over to her and tentatively leans in toward her.

Smiling at his shyness, Isabella pulls him toward her for a passionate kiss. After a moment, she pulls back and stares at him as if slightly but pleasantly surprised. He hooks a finger under her chin.

"It's been a long time."

Isabella nods. "For me too," she says, leaning in for another kiss. The Jacobson case completely forgotten, Andy hesitates less than a moment before taking her hand and leading her to the bedroom.

CHAPTER 13
Bad News All Around

Around the same time, Robert stands just inside the doors of Terminal One at Miami International Airport. He hears the announcement that the American Airlines flight has arrived from New York and begins scanning the passengers' faces. It doesn't take long to see the one he is waiting for—Heather always sits toward the front of the plane.

When she spots him, Heather Bellaire's mouth curls up into a weary smile. Rolling her small Vuitton carry-on behind her, she walks over, throws her arms around him, and leans against his body.

"You look tired, Heather. Was your flight okay?"

"The flight was fine, Bob, but I have had one hell of a week. I hope I won't be too grumpy for you."

Robert smiles and takes her hand as they walk out to the parking lot.

"Well, now you can just sit back and relax while I do the driving." He puts her bag in the trunk and opens the passenger door for her before going around to the driver's side. "To tell you the truth, I have had a trying week myself, but you go first."

Heather wiggles out of her overcoat. "I probably shouldn't tell you. It will just make me more upset."

"Heather, if you can't tell me, then who can you tell? Is it your ex-husband again?"

"Yes, it's William again. It's always William. He goes missing for two weeks. He doesn't answer my calls or calls from the boys. He misses the time he's supposed to be with them, which means they miss soccer practice. Then, when he gets back, he accuses me of being a lousy parent and demands that I give him my time with the boys to make up for his absence. Worst of all, he made such a scene in front of them that they started crying. I tell you, Bob, he gets more belligerent every day. He's always checking on my whereabouts … he probably knows that I'm in Miami with you now!"

Robert reaches for her hand.

"God, Heather, I'm so sorry."

She sighs. "I wish that was all that happened. On top of my William problem, I've been having ongoing issues with one of our writers."

"Really?" Robert asks, eager for a rare glimpse outside the world of medicine. "What book, and what kind of issues?"

Heather sighs again. "Oh, ego issues mostly, and you're going to love this: it's a book on reconstructing the dental papilla."

So much for escaping his work. "A whole book on rebuilding the little bit of gum tissue between teeth? Hardly sounds like a scintillating read."

She laughs. "I knew you would react this way. And while it might seem insignificant compared to the major surgeries you do, there is actually a market for this type of book."

Robert grins. "I'll have to take your word on that because I certainly won't be buying it."

"Wait, you haven't even heard the best part. The author wants to be referred to as the 'Rembrandt of the Gums' and wants the cover to depict him and Rembrandt together, with a Rembrandt painting and teeth in the background."

Robert looks over at Heather and, when he realizes she is serious, breaks out in uncontrollable laughter. "I can't believe it," he says, wiping a tear from his eye. "I just can't believe it. What an egomaniac!"

Heather snorts. "You wouldn't think it's funny if you had to deal with him."

Robert can't argue with her there. "Well, I can certainly see why you're exhausted. I'm afraid to ask if there's more."

"There is, but it is petty stuff, like late submissions from authors, problems with our graphic designer who just can't seem to get the cover right, and too many of my staff out sick or on personal leave when we're at our busiest."

"I'm truly sorry, Heathy. Now I feel guilty asking you to spend the weekend helping me."

"Don't be silly, Bob, I always enjoy being with you. I just need a good night's sleep. I hope you don't want to go out to dinner tonight; I am afraid I'm just not up to it."

"Aha," he says, holding up a finger, "I anticipated that." He reaches over, opens the glove box, and pulls out a menu for a Chinese restaurant. "You sounded so weary on the phone, I figured we'd get takeout. This place is really good, and it's right around the corner from my house."

She squeezes him arm. "That sounds wonderful."

"Sure … a little hot and sour soup for us to share. Then Mongolian beef for me, Kung Pao Chicken for you, followed by a fortune cookie that will undoubtedly relate a better week ahead than the one you just had."

Heather rolls her eyes heavenward. "I certainly hope so."

A half hour later, after picking up the food, Robert pulls into his driveway and follows it around the bend to the west side of his garage, very close to the spot where Tubby had been targeted nearly five weeks earlier. He brings the car to a stop and reaches up to press the remote door opener on the visor. After retrieving Heather's bag from the trunk, he finds her in his garage, looking around with an astonished expression.

"What's up?" he asks.

"Your garage," she says, "it's the quintessential man cave."

He laughs. "C'mon, Heather...."

"No, seriously—the weightlifting set over there, twelve scuba tanks, and, let's see, twenty-six fishing rods? There's not even room for your car!" She eyes him suspiciously. "Are you sure you're a surgeon?"

"Okay, have your fun. The weightlifting set is Ryan's—he uses it when he visits. See, there's three hundred fifty pounds on it. That's what he was bench pressing at the time." He holds up his biceps and clenches. "I would need a forklift to lift that."

"Right," Heather says, "didn't he win a weightlifting contest?"

"Yes, then he turned around and won a cooking contest the next day." Robert looks toward her, unable to relate how proud he is of his youngest son. He thinks to himself, *time to schedule a fishing trip for Ryan's birthday, or as soon as I can get away.*

He looks up to find Heather studying him and, forcing a smile, walks over to the rack of fishing rods. "And don't give me any shit about these." He holds one up. "See this one? It's the one you caught that thirty-two-pound lake trout with in Canada two years ago." He shakes the rod in mock anger. "You beat me out by one lousy little pound. I should break it over your head."

"C'mon, caveman, I'm starving." She holds out a hand to him, and they make their way toward the house. Before Robert even sticks the key in the door, they hear the barking of three hungry Labradors waiting on the other side.

"Hi guys!" Heather exclaims, bending down to pet them. "Hi, Tubby!"

Right behind him is Rocky, the even chunkier alpha dog, and Libby, with her shiny chocolate coat.

"Why don't you go and unpack?" Robert says after greeting the dogs. "I have to feed them first or we'll never eat in peace."

When they finally sit down to dinner, Heather says, "Now, you've heard about my nightmare week. What's going on with you?"

Robert scoops some Mongolian beef onto his plate. "Well, first some joker got through the operating room security doors when we were in the middle of a procedure. He was supposedly looking for me." He waves away Heather's look of concern. "There was eighty-five-year-old Diana Edelson and the circulating nurse pushing an instrument cart against the door to keep him out. Then some sort of 'Keystone Cops' scenario ensued, with our security guards chasing him around the hospital corridors. He finally got away through the emergency door that was supposed to set off an alarm but didn't." He chuckles. "The hospital was in quite an uproar that day, everyone speculating about who is 'after me.' I personally think it was a very persistent company representative wanting to show me a new instrument."

Instead of giving him the laugh he's expecting, Heather reaches over and punches him hard in the shoulder. He pulls back, a bit stunned.

"This is not funny, Bob! Someone is clearly out to get you and you'd better start taking it seriously. The cops think the guy killed Jacobson by mistake, right? That you were the target? Well, he might have been back to finish the job!"

She sits back in her chair, weary again.

Sobered by her outburst, he shrugs and stares down at his food. "Yeah, you're right." He looks up at her again, with just the hint of a grin. "He just can't seem to get the job right."

Heather gives him an annoyed look. "Since you won't be serious, let's change the subject. Anything else new?"

"Yeah, I'm worried about what's going on with our research rats."

"Oh, really?"

Robert nods, then in between bites of Mongolian Beef he tells her about the rat that had bitten Julio. Heather shivers when he tells her about the bats he'd seen.

"So you're concerned about rabies …" she says.

"Exactly. Bats are one of the biggest carriers of rabies today. I am concerned that Julio could develop rabies or will have to undergo those injections—twenty-one extremely painful injections. We euthanized the rat so we could remove the brain and spinal cord and test for rabies, but when I got to the brain, it was shriveled up and had more holes than Swiss cheese."

Heather takes a sip of water as if to wash the taste of the story from her mouth. "Boy, I am glad I just finished eating. Think I'll pass on that fortune cookie, no matter what the fortune says. But go on, did the brain look like rabies?"

"That's just it, Heather; it didn't. It looked like mad cow disease. I know it sounds crazy, but I've seen autopsies of mad cow disease cases. The brains are full of holes like a sponge. That's the medical term for it, spongiform encephalopathy. Now I have a nineteen-year-old kid in the hospital and I don't know if the rats have rabies, mad cow disease, or are just bothered by pain."

Heather reaches across the kitchen table for Bob's hand. "Sounds like we've both had a pretty awful time of it. Why don't you grab that bottle of Pinot Noir and two glasses and meet me on the sofa? We'll watch TV and forget our troubles for a while."

The two cuddle up on the sofa with their stocking feet propped up on the coffee table. Robert pours two glasses of the Pinot and clicks on the television to find the last ten minutes of the Twilight Saga.

He snorts. "Vampires. Just what I need to get my mind off bats and rabies."

Heather giggles, and the two endure it until the eleven o'clock news comes on.

"Welcome to eyewitness news at eleven," a Ken Doll

lookalike says. "I am Kent Davenport."

The camera then turns to a vivacious-looking Hispanic woman, who says, "And I am Iliana Fraga. We have a lot to cover on this busy news night, starting with North Korea's threat to resume missile testing and a deadly tornado ripping through North Texas near Wichita Falls, killing at least a dozen people."

The camera then turns back to a surprisingly chipper Kent Davenport. "Tragedy struck today in a Cleveland middle school when a seventy-one-year-old teacher killed four students and wounded several others before being restrained by security guards. It is unknown at this time what prompted this woman, who has been a teacher for forty-five years, to do this; however, the tragedy is causing many people to advocate mandatory retirement. And lastly, just when we thought the fears of mad cow disease were over for good, a new epidemic has broken out in Australia. Details after these messages...."

When they hear the last story, Robert and Heather turn and stare at each other in disbelief.

After several inane commercials selling everything from car insurance to cereals, Kent Davenport returns. "So far the mad cow disease epidemic has been limited to cats," he says, grin still in place. "The animal control department in Australia claims they have euthanized over one hundred and fifty thousand cats suspected of having the disease. Several brands of cat food have been tested, and authorities now suspect that one particular brand containing sheep brains added to the fish and chicken meals in order to reduce costs was to blame. It is feared that some humans may be at risk, particularly the homeless, who are known to eat cat food when they don't have the money for regular food. There is no immediate fear of mad cow disease affecting cats or people in the United States. The U.S. Department of Agriculture is currently monitoring pet shops, animal pounds and rescue organizations, and, of course, cat food manufacturers."

Robert grabs the remote off the coffee table and shuts the television off.

"The perfect note on which to end the perfect week," he says sarcastically. "C'mon, let's just go to sleep."

He holds a hand out and together they stumble to the bedroom.

Just before five the next morning, Robert slips quietly out of bed and heads to his study to review the articles and text he needs Heather's help with. As a publisher, she knows her way around the National Library of Congress and the Pub Med system well enough to access even the most obscure articles. This coming Thursday is the start of the North Star cis-phosphorous litigation series, and, as always, he wants to be prepared. Lord knows the barracudas at Halstead, Butterworth and Payne will be.

After about an hour of reading, his rumbling stomach gets the better of him and he moves to the kitchen. He's in the middle of preparing a surprise breakfast for Heather when he realizes he's out of coffee.

"Hey Libby, jump in the car with me. Let's go get coffee."

The little chocolate lab eagerly follows Merriweather out through the garage door and into the front seat of the car. When they get back twenty minutes later, he finds Heather enjoying a morning dip in the pool. He stands out of sight for a moment, just watching her. When they were together like this, it was so close to perfect he wondered why he had not fully committed. Then the real world would come rushing in: she lives a thousand miles away and has two young sons; she is also in the middle of some kind of battle with her ex-husband. But deep down, Robert can't deny that it is his ex—or his feelings for her—that is holding him back.

She's certainly beautiful, lying on her back, blissfully ignoring the two white labs looking on from the edge. Suddenly, her moment of serenity is interrupted by a rubber ball splashing down next to her. It's followed by the significantly larger splash of the two dogs jumping in after it.

"Oh!" Heather sputters, getting soaked by the spray. A second later, Libby leaps in as well. Heather hears laughing and looks over to see Robert watching her from the gate.

"You lout!" she says, but she's laughing too. Being a good sport, she plays with the dogs in the pool for a while before getting out to get dressed for the day. Upon her return, she finds her favorite breakfast of waffles and fruit waiting for her, as well as a hot latte from Starbucks.

"Bob, who did you say won that cooking contest anyway, you or Ryan?"

"So you like it?" he says, grinning proudly.

"Yes, and I like you as well. In just one night, the hassles of last week have vanished."

"Or have at least been put on hold," he replies, then leans down to kiss her head. "Either way, I'm glad you're here."

"Me too."

He sighs. "Okay, enough fun and games. Time to prepare for my testimony."

CHAPTER 14
Pretrial

Monday morning finds Heather Bellaire back at her desk, refreshed and renewed by her weekend in Miami. In an office across town, however, the mood is far less bright. The eight attorneys visibly cringe as they file into the large conference room of Halstead, Butterworth and Payne to find Barry Halstead at the window, staring out at the Manhattan skyline. He only did this on two sorts of occasions: after a victory, when he appeared to be looking out over all he purveyed, or when things were not going well and he was wondering when it was all going to collapse around his ears.

As they take their seats around the oval table of polished oak, the team tries to gauge the situation and can only assume it is the latter, especially when they see the boxes marked Lamb v. North Star Drug Company. Next to it, this morning's New York Times is spread open to the Health section. George Payne's stomach tightens when he sees the headline: "Plaintiffs Enlist Big Pharma Crusader in North Star Case." Just below it is a photo of Robert Merriweather leaving the court after the Daubert hearing. Shit.

"George," Halstead says without preamble, his eyes still fixed on the ant-like movement of the commuters below, "I've decided that I'm going to cross Merriweather myself. I got a few surprises for that pompous ass." Halstead lowers his voice to a mutter. "Thinks he's going to blow us out of the water with his facts and figures about Bone Protect? Well, I've got a little bombshell that's going to wipe that smug smile right off his face."

When they realize they were not called to the room to be screamed at, a collective, almost audible sigh of relief goes up from the attorneys, all save one. Hands gripping the edge of the table, George Payne tries to maintain a neutral expression, as he also knows his boss likes to study the expressions of his minions in the reflection of the glass.

"Don't worry, George," Halstead booms, confirming Payne's suspicion, "you're still lead on the case." Finally, he moves away from the window and comes to stand at the head of the table. "Now, at some point during my cross of Merriweather—I'll let you know when—I'm going to want these boxes brought in. Get some associates to plop them down in front of the witness box." Ignoring the question in George's nod, he continues. "Okay, regarding the strategy for your cross of Mrs. Lamb ... sympathy, sympathy, sympathy. George, I want you to ooze it from every pore. She's going to have the hearts of the jury—nothing we can do about that—and we don't want to look like we're beating up an old lady on the stand. You're going to let her know that while we are very sorry for her plight, Bone Protect is not the cause of it."

George nods again, this time more emphatically. It's the strategy he expected, and it is perfect in its simplicity. The Lamb case is their "bellwether trial"—or one deemed by the judge to be representative of the class of plaintiffs suing North Star. The winning or losing of such cases was then used to determine whether similar cases in the class should be settled and, if so, the reasonable dollar amounts to be awarded. If they could show that something other than Bone Protect caused Sandra Lamb's injury, it would go a long way towards reducing the overall settlement, or doing away with the cases altogether.

"Judge Lockhart has indicated that he will push for a settlement," Halstead adds, "and use any award as a template for the final settlement if we lose the class action suit." His eyes narrow as he looks around the table. "I don't have to tell anyone here what's at stake. This one we must win at all costs."

****

For the group of oral and maxillofacial surgery residents, fellows and faculty gathered in the small auditorium of Miami Dade Hospital, the climate is only slightly less stressful. It is the regular Monday morning "grand rounds," where residents from each of the four hospital services present the cases accomplished the previous week and those planned for the upcoming week. For the presenting resident, who must field a barrage of tough questions from Dr. Merriweather and his faculty, this questioning is an important rite of passage, as well as an opportunity to sharpen his or her skills in preparation for their specialty board examination. It is also akin to standing before a firing squad.

Merriweather watches a thin, sweating resident slink back to his chair after a grueling round of questions. Despite the fine job he had done in presenting the trauma cases from the week before, the young man looks a bit peaked. Dr. Merriweather addresses the group, suppressing a smile as he sees the subtle change in the body language of the others; each is afraid of being the next target of his interrogation. As he scans their faces, he is considering not so much whom to call on, but what topic he wants to cover.

"Dr. Montel, you presented on the man who had the car accident. He wasn't wearing a seatbelt, and as a result he suffered a frontal sinus fracture by hitting his head on the windshield, correct?"

Montel sits straighter in his chair. "Yes, sir."

"Now, Dr. Montel, what would you be concerned about if he also developed ecchymosis—or bruising—on the front of the neck?"

"Bleeding in the throat?"

"Is that an answer or a question, Dr. Montel?"

"It's an answer, sir," Montel says, hopefully.

"Unfortunately, you are wrong. I'll give you a hint. Let's say the man shakes his head yes or no to most of your medical history questions. When he does speak, his voice is strained and raspy."

"Possibly a laryngeal fracture, sir?"

"Yes, of course. But, Dr. Montel, once again, don't answer a question with another question. When you're taking the oral examination for the American Board of Oral and Maxillofacial Surgeons, you will want to show the examiners that you are confident in your answer. You will be more impressive if you are decisive." Of all the advice Merriweather has given his residents over the years, their demeanor during oral exams is what they have found to be the most helpful. "So, what are you concerned about in this patient?"

"Airway, sir. He could obstruct."

"Good, Dr. Montel. So what would be your course of action?"

"We could do an intubation or tracheostomy, sir."

"Dr. Montel, on a board examination, the examiners will want you to tell them exactly what you would do, not what you could do. Remember, be decisive."

"A tracheostomy under local anesthesia, sir."

"Nice job. Oh, and Dr. Montel, you don't need to call me sir all the time. Dr. Merriweather will do just fine."

There are a few quiet chuckles from the other residents, more from relief they're not the ones on the hot seat than a need to make fun of their colleague.

"Yes, sir," Montel says, his face reddening, "I mean, Dr. Merriweather."

After grilling a few other residents on such topics as ecchymosis, meningitis and the blood-brain barrier, Robert glances at his watch. "I think I've subjected you to enough torture for today."

He stands, followed by the relieved residents, who quickly head to the door so they can disperse to their respective units.

"Dr. Glanville, I'll meet you and Melissa at Dade South in an hour," Merriweather calls out. "Remember, we have that tongue cancer case scheduled for two o'clock this afternoon. Bring the CT scans and my consult dictation to the

OR with you, okay?"

"Sure, Dr. Merriweather, I'll see you there."

It is just after noon when Merriweather climbs into his car for the twelve-mile drive to the Jackson South Hospital clinic. He's always enjoyed grand rounds, especially when it is as productive as it has been today; he feels it sets the week off on a good start.

On the other hand, this is not the typical week. As he pulls into the parking lot and rushes to his office, Robert mentally runs through his schedule for the next several days: he'd be in the OR all day today, then tomorrow he would head back to New York for the North Star trial. He and Roger England planned to meet in the evening to go over his testimony, then Wednesday they'd be in court. Despite the inconvenience of traveling and being out of the office, he finds himself looking forward to squaring off against Halstead and his thugs, not to mention holding North Star and Apollo accountable for all they have done.

He finds Isabella pouring two cups of coffee and wonders for the thousandth time how she is able to sense his imminent arrival. She smiles as she hands him a cup, but he can see there is something on her mind.

"Good afternoon, Issy. How was your weekend?"

"Really good, but I got a couple of important things to tell you before you rush off to the OR."

Merriweather takes a sip of his coffee. "Okay, shoot."

"Doris Steadman's husband is in the waiting room, and he is very upset about something. He wants to see you. Can you squeeze him in before you go to the OR?"

"Doris and David Steadman? Sure, I'll see them in my office. Can you show them in?"

"Actually, it is only Mr. Steadman." Isabella shrugs.

"Okay, show him in. And Issy, you said you had a couple of things to tell me…?"

"Right. It's about Dr. Jacobson. Over the weekend, Andy Molinaro and I realized that one of the bookends you got at the Vancouver lecture is missing. Chief, it looks like that was the murder weapon."

Merriweather gasps, horrified.

"Yes," she says, "it's awful. The lab is checking the metal pieces found during the autopsy against the metal from the remaining bookend. We are pretty sure they will match."

Robert is quiet for a moment. "Well, at least we've learned that much." He gives her a hint of a smile. "So … you and Detective Molinaro are 'teaming up'?"

Isabella rolls her eyes at his innuendo. "I'll go get Mr. Steadman."

Robert can't resist a chuckle as she hurries from the office.

A few moments later, a teary-eyed David Steadman is at Merriweather's door. With a feeling of dread, Robert rises and walks over to him.

"Mr. Steadman? Are you okay?"

Bracing his hand on the door, Steadman shakes his head.

"It's Doris. She's dead!"

For the second time in ten minutes, Robert gasps in shock. "What? But she was doing so well when I saw her last month! What happened? Did her blood pressure go up again?"

Steadman shakes his head again, then begins to sob. "She committed suicide the day before yesterday."

"Oh no, Dave." Robert ushers the man into a chair, then sits down across from him. "I don't understand, she was coping with her situation so well. Did her exposed bone become infected again? Was she in pain?"

"That's just it, Doctor—everything was fine. She was fine. Then, the day before it happened, she started acting strangely. She wouldn't say much to me, then she started yelling, accusing me of plotting against her. I tried to calm her down, but she said she just wanted to be alone. The following day, she shot herself." Still crying, he put his head in his hands. "If only I had done something...."

"David, there is no way you have could have known she would take her life. She had no history of depression, right? Never threatened suicide?"

Steadman shakes his head.

Merriweather puts a hand on the man's arm. "Chronic pain can drive people to do desperate things, and she dealt with it for five years."

Isabella enters the room with a couple of tissues and a glass of water. Steadman accepts them with a grateful nod.

"I guess you're right, Dr. Merriweather. Look, I didn't come here to burden you folks with my problems. I just wanted to let you know and thank you for helping her. So many other doctors thought it wasn't a big deal or told us it wasn't the Bone Max that did this to her. They told her it would go away. I wish we found you sooner. Anyway, I'm headed off to the airport now to meet my son."

The two men stand, and Robert offers him a hand. "When

is the funeral? I'd like to attend, if I may."

Steadman offers him a weak but genuine smile. "Oh, Doris would have liked that. It's going to be on Saturday."

Merriweather nods. "Just leave the details with Issy and I'll be there."

As soon as he has left, Robert turns to her. "Make sure I'm on a Friday flight back to Miami, whether I'm done testifying or not. If those bastards from Halstead use their usual delaying tactics, I'll just fly back up there on Sunday." He shakes his head, still stunned by the news. "I want to pay my respects to Doris."

"I'm on it, boss." Isabella pauses. "All the more reason for you to testify against Apollo and North Star, right?"

Robert doesn't answer, and when Isabella turns around, she sees him already hurrying down the hall toward the OR.

****

It is shortly after six the next evening when Robert's cab finally pulls up in front of Gild Hall, the small hotel in lower Manhattan where Roger England booked him a room. Robert sighs wearily as he pulls out his wallet to pay the driver. A bumpy flight had been followed by nearly two hours of bumper-to-bumper highway traffic and the slow, painful navigation of Manhattan streets. Robert would have preferred to stay at Heather's again, but as England pointed out, the Financial District, which is just a short walk to the United States District Court where he'll be testifying, makes more sense.

As he walks into the lobby, Robert pulls out his phone and calls England.

"Roger? It's Robert Merriweather. I'm just checking in now. When and where do you want to meet?"

"Glad you're here, Doctor," Roger says, and Robert can't tell whether he sounds stressed or energized. Probably a bit of both. "Listen, I'm still going over the witness list, so why don't you take a few minutes to settle in, then come to the Thompson Suite. Say, about seven?"

Forty-five minutes later, after a long, refreshing shower, Dr. Merriweather knocks on the door of the suite. He hears movement inside, then a young, harried-looking man answers.

"Welcome to the 'War Room,' Dr. Merriweather," he says, smiling.

"War Room, huh?" Merriweather says, raising an eyebrow as he looks around the luxurious suite. "You certainly picked a swanky spot from which to wage war."

"Only the best for you!" Roger England calls out. He is sitting on a tufted leather couch, completely surrounded by stacks of paper. A few feet away, there is a small conference table with a copy machine, printer, and paper shredder on it. On the wall hangs a Marlex poster board with the trial's timetable and the travel schedules of their witnesses. Standing around the table is Roger's partner, John Bays, along with another young man and an attractive, thirty-something brunette.

"Karen," Robert says with a wave. He is not at all surprised to find Karen Wasniewski there. She has been key to preparing the case—organizing the witnesses, coordinating their travel, making sure the lawyers have the supplies they need, and taking care of just about everything else. Robert knows she is as indispensable to England as Isabella is to him.

"Hi, Dr. M," she says. She points to the two younger men. "This is James and Ted, they're on loan from our sister firm in Des Moines."

Robert shakes hands with them. "Nice to meet you both. And it's nice to see you all once again." He looks pointedly at the stockpile of snacks on the coffee table in front of Roger. There's trail mix, M&Ms, Snickers, cashews, several different kinds of potato chips, pretzels, and beef jerky.

"Holy cow, there's enough food here to feed a small army." He looks at Karen. "Is your definition of a balanced diet a bag of potato chips in each hand?"

"Very funny, Dr. M. Would you like something to drink?"

"Anything with caffeine would be great, but I would love a Dr. Pepper." He moves over to the couch. "Roger, John, do you want to get right into it?"

"Yeah," Roger says, gesturing to a chair across from him. "Have a seat." He hands him a three-ringed binder. "These are the questions I will ask you on direct examination, but first let me go over a few things."

Robert sits down just as Karen returns with a diet Dr. Pepper and sets it down in front of him.

"You're a lifesaver," he says, raising the can at her. "Diet Dr. Pepper, the nectar of Waco, Texas. Thank you."

He pops the can open and drains half of it in one gulp

before turning his attention to Roger.

"Doctor, we've heard that Barrymore Halstead himself will be cross-examining you. He is out for blood and is as sneaky as they get."

"Aren't they all, Roger?"

"Yeah, but he's very, very good at being sneaky. We've also heard that he plans to pull a surprise of some sort on you."

"Oh really? Where did you hear that?"

England smirks. "I have my spies."

"Well, after several dozen depositions and numerous trials, not to mention those annoying Daubert hearings, nothing surprises me anymore."

"Just the same, Doc, we want to make sure you're prepared. You did read North Star's research protocols and the published results from their submission to the FDA?"

"You bet I did. It's a sloppy study, and boy did they bamboozle the FDA. It's a sad day when you realize the FDA is so understaffed and underfunded that they have to rely on the honesty and integrity of the drug companies." Robert snorts. "It's like relying on the integrity of rattlesnakes to not bite you."

Roger nods. "You're right, Doc. And since we're on the subject of rattlesnakes, keep in mind that the trick to dealing with Halstead is to get the jury to like you. They may not remember all you testify to, but they will certainly remember whether they like you or not." He smiles. "You're a likeable guy, so just be yourself. Keep your composure, and don't let Halstead bait you into a running argument. He gains the advantage if you do. Also, stick as much as possible to lay language so the jury can understand the problem. Again, this has never been a problem for you—it's just a reminder. This jury has five women and three men, all of whom are working, middle class people. They have been paying close attention throughout the trial, taking a lot of notes, et cetera. Now, Halstead will surely try to convince them that you are profiting from your testimony. You are still directing all the legal fees to the university, aren't you?"

Robert nods. "Yes, or to a fund for my residents. I don't receive any of the money."

"Okay, good. Halstead will undoubtedly take the stance that Mrs. Lamb's injury was caused by an 'unfortunate infection' and that Bone Protect—and, by extension, North Star—is being scapegoated." Roger sees Robert's expression and holds up a hand. "I know it's a ridiculous claim, and the research bears that out, but you cannot underestimate Halstead. He might be a sleaze, but he is a talented sleaze. He plays juries very well."

"I'm sure he does," Robert concedes, "but I'm confident that Dr. Kramer will be able to deal with it during his testimony. I've seen him do it before—even coached him on it. However, I'm sure Halstead will trot out my 1993 article on osteomyelitis of the jaws, just like old George Payne—in—the-ass always does. Just remember to ask me how many times I mentioned exposed bone in that article. The answer is zero, because osteomyelitis of the jaw rarely evolves into exposed bone. That's what distinguishes it from cis-phosphorous drug-induced jaw osteonecrosis." Robert drains the last of his soda. "Like I said, Dr. Kramer will run with that one."

Roger nods as he scribbles notes on a yellow pad. "Great, Doc, just review that tonight. Along with the questions for direct, there are also answers you have given in the past. You don't need to be word for word, but you do need to be consistent. Any difference in your testimony as compared to the depositions you gave Halstead will be used to undermine your credibility." He raises his bleary eyes to Robert. "I know this isn't your first rodeo, just going over the drill."

Indeed, Robert thinks as he accepts another can of soda from Karen's outstretched hand, *I could probably run the rodeo by now.* First, Roger would spend some time going through Robert's credentials to impress the jury. Then he'd ask Judge Lockhart to certify him as an expert in bone science. Then he'd take Robert through the mechanism of Bone Protect's damaging effects on bone before having him systematically eliminate other possible causes of jaw osteonecrosis, particularly infection.

"We'll finish with your opinion about North Star's research into Bone Protect," Roger says. "Now, this is new material, so it's what I want you to focus on during your review." He stands and claps his hands. "Now, you must be exhausted. Take a look at the binder, get some sleep, and we'll go over my questions and anything else tomorrow at breakfast. Say seven-fifteen, down in the restaurant in the lobby?" He winks at Karen. "They have great bagels."

Robert looks at the others and chuckles. Karen is chomping on a pretzel, and the men are sharing a package of beef jerky. "You guys are really something. See you all tomorrow."

Their mouths full, they respond with waves and "Mmms." Still chuckling, Robert closes the door behind him.

Sure hope it's brain food.

A couple of hours later, Robert closes the binder and rubs his eyes. He could go over it once more, but it would be a wasted effort, similar to over-studying for an exam for which you already know the answers. The thing he needs most right now is rest. But after slipping into the comfortable bed, he finds sleep eludes him. There is something, not related to the trial that he is forgetting....

A moment later it comes to him, and he reaches toward the nightstand to grab his cell phone. He hears four hollow rings, then Ryan's voice, sounding all too mature, asking the caller to leave a message.

"Hi, Ryan," Robert says when prompted by the beep, "It's Dad. I know you're busy, but your birthday's coming up and I was hoping you might find the time for a fishing trip. Let me know."

He ends the call with a sigh, hating the formality in his voice and longing for the day when seeing his sons for their birthdays would be a given.

Just focus on the trial, he mutters, eyes drooping. That night he dreams of a boat capsizing and the two men on board being swept out into rough seas.

CHAPTER 15
Opening Statements

The next morning, after a hearty breakfast and a thorough review of their game plan, Robert, Roger England, John Bays, and Karen Wasniwski take the brisk ten-minute walk to the courthouse. Robert shivers as icy wind whips around the buildings as if through a wind tunnel. It brings to mind the winters of his childhood in the Midwest, the snow fights he and Carl used to have. They had never felt the cold then; now, he shoves his hands in the pocket of his coat and wonders how anyone could choose to live in this climate.

"Are we almost there?" he asks England, who laughs at him.

"Real different from Florida, huh? Yes, it's just up ahead."

After going through security and, to Robert's annoyance, having their cell phones checked, they enter the crowded elevator. Robert sees George Payne standing at the back and gives him a curt nod, which Payne does not return, then they ride to the tenth floor in awkward silence.

When they walk into Judge Lockhart's courtroom, the eight rows of visitors' benches are nearly full, which is not surprising given the media attention the case has garnered. Big pharma cases always did, not only because of the public interest at stake, but of the names of the high profile lawyers involved.

As England and Bays organize their evidence sheets and prepare for the opening statement, in walks Barrymore Halstead, dressed to kill and ready for battle. Robert takes in the Armani suit with the monogrammed red handkerchief in his breast pocket, the golden cuff links, and the Rolex watch.

Sleaze certainly pays well.

He is barely able to refrain from rolling his eyes as Halstead makes a show of shaking the hands of the opposing counsel. The attorney's eyes flicker over Merriweather, then he extends a hand.

"At last we meet, Doctor. Good luck to you today."

"And to you as well," Robert says curtly as he reluctantly shakes the lawyer's hand.

At 9 a.m. sharp, the bailiff cries out, "All rise," and the courtroom goes quiet except for the rustling sounds of everyone getting to their feet. A second later, Judge Lockhart enters the courtroom in a flowing black robe and gavel in hand.

"Please be seated," he says in a gravelly voice, then settles himself upon the bench. "Mr. Halstead, it's nice to see you in my court again. It has been a long time. This must be a special occasion."

"Indeed it is, Your Honor."

"Just my point." Judge Lockhart's eyes flick over the room. "Ladies and gentlemen, before we begin, I want to remind everyone that I will not tolerate any outbursts or any other behavior that disrespects this court." He turns his attention to the plaintiff's attorneys.

"Mr. Bays, I understand that you will be delivering the opening statement this morning."

"Yes, Your Honor."

"Bailiff, please bring in the jury."

Everyone rises again as the five women and three men of the jury file into the room and take their seats. Each turns his or her attention to John Bays, who has moved to the podium at the front of the room.

"Good morning, my name is John Bays, and I represent Mrs. Sandra Lamb, the lady you see behind me to your right. In many ways, Sandra is just like the rest of us—a law-abiding citizen who loves her family and wants to live a happy, healthy life. Unfortunately, she has been suffering from terrible, debilitating health issues, which is the reason we're all here today. As you can see, Sandra's jaw is twisted to the left, and she cannot help her drooling. What you can't see is that she is missing the left side of her lower jaw and cannot feel her lower lip. You also cannot see the rubber feeding tube, hidden under her blouse, that goes into her stomach. The tube is necessary because she cannot swallow properly and must be fed through that tube. We intend to show that Sandra's suffering has been caused by Bone Protect, the very drug that was supposed to help her and protect her bones. Furthermore, we intend to show that North Star Drug Company did not inform doctors of the potential side effects of Bone Protect as mandated by the FDA, a warning that could have prevented Sandra's suffering."

"During the course of this trial, you will hear from several witnesses, including Mrs. Lamb's oral surgeon, who will tell you of the numerous attempts he made to spare her this pain, to no avail. You will also hear from other experts who will show that North Star ignored their own critical research findings about the devastating effects of long-term use of Bone Protect. Most importantly, though, you will hear from Mrs. Lamb herself. She will tell you about the agonizing pain she has endured over the past three years. She will tell you about the several surgeries she underwent, including the procedure to remove the entire left half of her lower jaw and the nerve that courses through it, which resulted in her numbness and the uncontrollable drooling."

John Bays scans the faces of the jurors and notes that, as expected, they are staring at Sandra Lamb with a mixture of horror and sympathy. This was the easy part; the hard part would be to make sure they awarded the poor woman what she is due. "Thank you, ladies and gentlemen, Your Honor."

As Bays returns to his seat, Judge Lockhart turns his focus to Barrymore Halstead. "Mr. Halstead, your opening statement, please."

"Thank you, Your Honor," Barrymore Halstead replies in an uncharacteristically humble tone as he stands up and heads over to the podium. Then, with a gentle smile, he approaches the jury bench, placing his hands ceremoniously on the bannister in front of them. He makes eye contact with each of them before he begins.

"Well, folks, if you believe everything you just heard, then we can all go home. But ladies and gentlemen, you know better than that. You know that we must examine the actual evidence, not just listen to the hearsay testimony of paid witnesses."

"During this trial, you will hear from several so called 'expert' witnesses who will testify about the 'evils' of Bone Protect. However, you will also hear evidence that indicates that other factors could have caused Mrs. Lamb's suffering. For example, when you hear from Dr. Castellanos, Mrs. Lamb's oral surgeon, you must ask yourself what role he may have played in the cause or the progression of the bone necrosis. After all, he wouldn't be the first well-meaning doctor who, despite the best of intentions, caused more harm than good. You will also hear about all the wonderful results patients have gotten with Bone Protect." Halstead shoots a dubious look at Merriweather. "Finally, you will hear about how the plaintiff's so-called 'experts' are reaping enormous financial rewards to disgrace the name of a fine pharmaceutical company."

Robert allows himself a small smirk. Let the games begin.

As Halstead thanks the court and returns to his seat, no one notices a slight, red-haired man slip into the courtroom and take a seat in the last row of visitors' benches. As he removes his baseball cap, he scans the crowd, his eyes finally landing on Dr. Robert Merriweather.

The judge adjourns the morning session early.

CHAPTER 16
The Trial

"I hope you all learned something this morning," Barrymore Halstead says just before bringing the spoonful of chilled vichyssoise to his lips. He closes his eyes as if savoring the creamy taste, but George Payne knows better. The soup may be good, but that is not the reason they are here. The French bistro a few blocks from the courthouse is notoriously difficult to get into, and Halstead loves the feeling of just walking in and demanding a table, which has been the case ever since he got the owner off on a tax fraud charge a few years back.

When he doesn't hear a response, he opens his eyes and coldly scans the others at the table. "The lesson to be learned is that emotion and theater always trump facts with the jury. Always." He brings another spoonful of soup to his mouth. "Remember, jurors are stupid. I mean, they're only jurors because they couldn't come up with a good excuse to get out of serving jury duty, right?"

The others nod, grunt, and "Yes, Mr. Halstead" with the appropriate amount of servility.

"You have to learn to read the jury—read what makes them tick—and play to that."

"But how did you learn to do that?" asks a young paralegal.

George Payne notes her obsequious tone and almost laughs

in her face. It is well known around the firm that the young woman is just finishing up her third year of law school and takes every opportunity to kiss up to Halstead in the hopes he'll hire her as an associate. Yeah, right. A night student from Pace working at a white shoe firm? Never gonna happen. If Halstead is aware of her motivation, he gives no indication. She is as irrelevant to him as a gnat. However, as she is now giving him the opportunity to keep boasting, he bestows an almost fatherly smile on her.

"It's an art to be sure, and one I've cultivated over more years than I'd care to admit. I originally read about the concept in the biography of another famous defense attorney—Clarence Darrow. Perhaps you've heard of him?"

The girl shakes her head. "No, sir."

This time, Payne rolls his eyes. He has seen the very same book on the paralegal's desk.

"Well, Darrow was defending a murder suspect with a long rap sheet. I mean, the evidence against this guy was overwhelming. To make matters worse, the prosecutor gave a brilliant summation. It looked like a slam dunk, and everyone was waiting for Darrow's next move. But he gets up there and gives just about the dullest summation in history. He talked for more than four days, bored the entire courtroom to tears! Several members of the jury and even the judge were seen dozing off. The prosecution was furious!"

The paralegal looks at Halstead in wide-eyed amazement. "But why would he do that, sir?"

"I'm getting to that," Halstead says, smiling as if he came up with the idea himself. "Of course the press crucified

Darrow for these shenanigans, but he didn't care. On the fifth day, he finally concluded his summation with two pointed statements to the jury. While the jury deliberated, a member of the Baltimore press asked Darrow why, except for his last statements, he made such a long and awful summation in contrast to the prosecutor's short, crisp statement. Darrow simply answered, 'And what did he say?' The reporter couldn't remember, and neither did the jury. His client was acquitted."

Everyone save the paralegal is silent, as they have all heard this story many times before.

"Wow, sir," she gushes, eliciting a grunt from Payne. She shoots him a dirty look.

"I've got the jury on my side now," Halstead adds, "especially that older woman on the end." He leans in. "You might think because she's around the same age as the plaintiff that she'd have sympathy for her, but what that juror really wants is to believe that the same thing can't happen to her. She wants to believe that the plaintiff or her doctors are to blame." He sits back and daintily wipes the corners of his mouth with a cloth napkin. "Just wait until I nail Merriweather."

In another, much less stylish restaurant, the attorneys for the other side huddle over trays of thick sandwiches, potato chips, and cans of diet coke.

"That Halstead is unbelievable," Karen Wasniewski says as she spreads mayo on her ham and cheese hero. "I just hope the jury didn't fall for all his bullshit."

"Wouldn't be the first time, Karen," Roger England replies as he tackles a pastrami on rye. "We just have to focus on educating the jurors on how Bone Protect damages bone, how the company knew—or should have known—that it would, and how they sidestepped the FDA. We need a strong start." Roger jerks his head toward Merriweather. "That's why we're putting this guy on first." Merriweather looks like he is a million miles away. "Robert, you okay?"

"Yes," Robert says vaguely as he looks down at the phone he retrieved when they left the court. He'd received an email from Steve Carr, the lead vet tech at the lab, and it seemed they still didn't know what was affecting the rats. For the moment, however, his biggest concern is Julio, the young veterinary assistant who was bitten on the hand. With some effort, Merriweather turns his attention back to the matter at hand.

"Yes, Roger, sorry. I'm fine." He slips the phone back in his pocket. "I just hope to live up to everyone's expectations once I'm on the stand."

"You will," Karen says reassuringly. She looks at her watch. "C'mon, guys. Judge wants us back in court by one."

By five minutes past the hour, the courtroom is once again packed. Everyone falls silent as Judge Lockhart emerges from his chambers and settles with his flowing robes on the bench.

"Mr. England," he calls without preamble, "your first witness, please."

"The plaintiff calls Dr. Robert A. Merriweather to the stand."

Robert rises from his seat in the front row of the spectators' bench and walks through the low swinging gate to stand in front of the court reporter.

The court reporter administers the oath and asks Dr. Merriweather to spell his name for the record, then ushers him to the witness box to the left of Judge Lockhart.

Robert can feel Halstead's smug stare and focuses instead on Roger England, who has taken the podium, his binder of prepared questions in hand.

"Dr. Merriweather, you are a full professor of surgery at the University Of Miami Miller School Of Medicine, are you not?"

"Yes, I am."

"What is the significance of that academic rank?"

"It's the highest academic level attainable."

"How many textbooks have you published, and how many are focused on bone?"

"Fourteen textbooks—ten focused on bone."

"How many of these books are on the specific topic of cis-phosphorous drugs and their effects on bone?"

"Four, with another—"

Rising from his chair, Halstead cuts him off. "Your Honor, the defense stipulates to Dr. Merriweather's credentials as an expert on bone science and bone pathology."

Robert keeps his expression neutral as he glances from Halstead to Roger, wondering why England looks so annoyed.

"Very well then," Judge Lockhart says, sounding almost relieved that the testimony will be abbreviated. "Mr. England, move on."

"But, Your Honor, the jury has a right to know the breadth

and depth of Dr. Merriweather's knowledge and experience."

"Mr. England," the judge says, not bothering to hide his annoyance, "how much more of an expert can an expert be? Dr. Merriweather's expertise can come out in his testimony. If you made an objection, which you didn't, I am overruling it, so please move on."

Robert watches as Barrymore Halstead turns back to George Payne. When he faces front again, he is wearing a smug, I-told- you-so smile.

Thinking he will never get used to the antics of lawyers, Robert turns once again to Roger England's heated face.

"Are you being paid for the testimony you are about to give here today?"

"No, I am not."

"Then where does the compensation money go, considering that all other witnesses, for both sides, are being paid their standard fees?"

"The amount of payment for expert witness testimony is set by university policy. It is paid to the university to compensate them for my absence and the loss of revenue while I am here."

"Does it contribute to any bonus or privilege you receive?"

"No, bonuses and privileges are based only on academic accomplishments."

"Does any of the money go to any other source outside the university?

"No. The university does allow some funds to be earmarked for resident education, but only through a foundation."

"Okay, Dr. Merriweather. Now, let's talk about bone and how cis-phosphorous drugs damage bone. First, explain to the jury how normal bone works."

Robert turns slightly to face the jury and goes into the "Bones 101" lecture he has honed over years of testifying at such trials.

"There are two hundred and eight bones in the human skeleton. Although bone is hard and may appear to be a non-living structure, it is in fact very much alive and must maintain itself. It does so by renewing itself twice each year. To explain this process, I'll ask you to first look at the skin on the back of your hand." Robert pauses for a beat as each juror holds up a hand and examines the back. "That skin will not be there one month from now. You see, skin cells only live for about twenty-one days. They form at the bottom layer of your skin and mature upwards. As they mature upwards your skin cells at the top die and are sloughed off. The new skin cells from the bottom replace those dead cells, almost like a conveyor belt. In this way, your visible skin is maintained. If this didn't happen, your skin would become old, dry, cracked, and finally fall off to expose the muscles and tendons underneath.

"Now, bone cells undergo a similar process, except that they are also encased in a calcium-mineral matrix. That means bone renews itself at a slower rate than skin—around every six months- or less than one percent each day. Your wrist bone, for example, will not be the same bone that's there in six months.

"Key to the bone renewal process is an important cell called an osteoclast—osteo meaning bone, and clast meaning dissolving, or what we in bone science refer to as resorbing cells. These osteoclast cells look and act like a little Pac-Man, and a group of them work together to seek out and bite through old bone. Now, when they dissolve the old bone, they create an empty space; however, in the process, they also release stimulating chemicals—proteins—that were embedded in the old bone. These stimulating chemicals turn the stem cells you so often hear about these days into bone-forming cells that replace the old bone that was dissolved away. This process is happening in all your bones every day and is needed to keep your bones healthy. If this does not happen, your bones become old, brittle, and prone to fracture. They may even become dead and exposed, as we are now seeing in the mouths of those affected by drugs like Bone Protect."

"How do the cis-phosphorous drugs like Bone Protect affect this normal process?"

"Simply stated, these drugs are cellular poisons. They kill the osteoclast cells. This is especially true of Bone Protect, due to its high potency."

"How do you know that Bone Protect kills osteoclasts, Dr. Merriweather?"

"We watched it happen using a vital microscope. The osteoclasts literally burst in our bone biopsy specimens."

"Is there anything, other than potency and basic toxicity, that concerns you about cis-phosphorous drugs in general and Bone Protect in particular?"

"Yes, all cis-phosphorous drugs last in bone for more than eleven years. They essentially accumulate in bone to dangerous levels and take a long time to be removed, if ever."

"And why are the jawbones especially vulnerable to these drugs?"

"Because, of all the bones in the adult skeleton, the jaw-bones go through the renewal process more often and faster."

"And why is that, Dr. Merriweather?"

"Because of teeth and dentures. When you bite down ..." Robert clangs his own teeth together for effect, "... your teeth put pressure on the jawbones. The tooth-bearing bone—whether they are natural teeth, dental implants, or dentures—must adjust to that every day. It does so by microscopic osteoclast resorption of this bone and the rebuilding of new bone. That is why all drug-induced jaw osteonecrosis starts in the tooth-bearing bone. After that, it may, and often does, spread to other parts of the jaw."

"What about other bones?"

"That's somewhat tricky. All bones are affected, but less so than the jaws. However, many older women are now experiencing fractures in other—"

"Objection, Your Honor," Barrymore Halstead exclaims as he rises from his chair. "The case before the court concerns a jaw injury."

"Your Honor, the case before the court is the damaging effects of Bone Protect on bone, not just jawbones, and Dr. Merriweather's research bears this out," retorts Roger England.

"Overruled, Mr. Halstead," the judge says wearily, then turns to England. "Mr. England, you may continue."

"Thank you, Your Honor. Doctor Merriweather, please tell us about the harmful effects of cis-phosphorous drugs on other bones."

"Yes, there is a growing number of older women taking cis-phosphorous drugs to prevent fractures from osteoporosis. However, taking them for more than five years, as most are asked to do, they experience just the opposite. That is, they suffer from fractures of the upper leg bone known as the femur."

"Again, I must object, Your Honor," Barrymore Halstead says, adopting an indignant tone. "Dr. Merriweather is not an orthopedist."

"Objection overruled," Judge Lockhart snaps. "Mr. Halstead, as you may recall, you stipulated that the doctor is an expert on bone science. You didn't qualify to any particular bone." The judge turns to address the jury directly. "The jury may consider the doctor's testimony on this subject as an expert."

Bolstered by the judge's favorable rulings and his rebuke of Halstead, Roger England moves to drive the final nail in the coffin.

"Dr. Merriweather, Bone Protect is FDA approved, yet you've testified as to some very negative aspects. In your expert opinion, is it a good drug or not?"

"It is a good drug in that it limits the spread of cancer by hardening bone, but its therapeutic effects occur in the first four doses. Beyond four doses, the toxicity begins to build and eventually produces the jaw necrosis problem and often leg fractures as well."

"How do you know this?"

"My research team and I studied it."

"Did you relate your findings to North Star?"

"Yes."

"What did they do about it?"

"They ignored it."

"Did North Star's research, conducted over a period of more than ten years, discover any of what you have just told us?"

"No."

"Why not?"

"They simply didn't look in the mouth. You can't see something if you don't look."

"Dr. Merriweather, how do you know the North Star researchers didn't look in the mouth?"

"It's right there on their safety sheet. The sheet calls for the study physicians to examine feet, abdomen, kidneys, liver, et cetera, but no structure in the mouth. Which, by the way, they would have done had they been following the lesson of bone pathology."

"Bone pathology? What do you mean by that?"

"Well, their researchers invent a drug that kills a normal cell in the human body. They know that this drug remains in the bone for more than eleven years. If they had looked in the same pathology texts that every medical and dental student is required to read, they would have found out what happens to bones—particularly jawbones—when the osteoclast is not present. They also would've learned about a genetic disease that does not develop normal osteoclast cells."

"And what disease is that?"

"It is called osteopetrosis—osteo meaning bone and petrous, which is Latin for 'hard as a rock'. This disease produces the same exposed jawbone and leg fractures caused by cis-phosphorous drugs."

"That's a pretty complex biology, Dr. Merriweather. Is there a way you can explain it so the rest of us can understand?"

"Absolutely. Let's say I invent a drug that eliminates pain—all pain—and it does so by killing nerve endings. I would likely be nominated for the Nobel Prize. However, if I first read the same pathology books I just mentioned, I would find degenerative diseases of the nervous system such as multiple sclerosis, Lou Gehrig's disease, Parkinson's disease, and myasthenia gravis, all of which my drug may cause as a side effect. Well, I better look into this before I market it."

"So you're saying that had North Star looked into these pathology books, they would have been alerted to look for exposed bone in the mouth?"

"Yes. Their research design was both ignorant and faulty."

George Payne observes the copious note-taking of the jury and shifts uneasily in his chair. Next to him, Halstead looks like the picture of quiet smugness. Payne gets whiff of expensive cologne mixed with cigars as Halstead leans toward him. "Stop worrying, George," he whispers. "Things are going exactly as planned."

George looks at him quizzically. "They are?"

Halstead nods. "Yup. Pay attention."

Payne turns back to England in time to hear the next question.

"Dr. Merriweather, have you found any other faults in North Star's research?"

"Yes, many. First, they never did a dosing study. They later found that their dose was way too high, but they covered that up. Second, they never determined when the maximum effect occurred, as we did. Third, they never measured the drug's accumulation levels in bone, not in their animal studies or their human clinical trials."

England turns to the jury. "As Dr. Merriweather just testified, North Star's incompetent research did not immediately reveal the risks associated with the dosage. However, we have uncovered proof that the company later found out this dose was too high and covered it up." He then looks up at Judge Lockhart. "Your Honor, I'd like to submit Exhibit A into evidence." He hands the judge several papers stapled together.

Judge Lockhart looks at them, nods, and hands them back to England. "Go ahead."

England then hands the papers to the court officer, and a moment later it pops up on the individual monitors in front of each juror, as well as a larger screen behind the jury box. It was a series of emails with the North Star logo on top.

"Dr. Merriweather, if you will, please read these official North Star emails for the jury. This first email was written by George Stevens, North Star's Director of Marketing. It reads, 'Request immediate strategy meeting regarding the recent reduced dosing data. Am very concerned that such a reduced dose would be as beneficial as our marketing dose. Should this data come to light, it would cut our profits in half.'" England pauses to note the looks of disgust on the jurors' faces. A second later, another email flashes on the screen.

Continue Dr. Merriweather. "Marvin Fletcher, Assistant Medical Director, wrote: 'We need to shift the focus to patient's cancer and chemotherapy as the cause of their dead jawbone problem. It would be particularly beneficial to target smokers. Bone Protect must be removed from the equation, or North Star will not survive the scrutiny.'"

Roger England smiles as he brings up the next email. "It seems the officials at North Star were especially concerned with preventing Dr. Merriweather from testifying." This time, he hears a gasp of surprise come from one of the jurors.

"Please read this one, Dr. Merriweather. 'We have to stop Merriweather at all costs. His lectures and publications are starting to make our prescribing physicians more cautious. He has already cost us a 25% reduction in physician use and several hundred million in revenue.' This email was sent by Ronald Kirschenbaum, North Star's Chief Financial Officer."

"And finally, this is the correspondence between Marilyn Patterson, Director of Research, and North Star's CEO, Anders Christiansen. As you can see, they are discussing the best way to represent, or, in this case ..."—England shoots at look at Halstead—"... misrepresent Bone Protect to the public. It was decided that a marketing campaign focused on doctor endorsements was the best way to go."

England steps out from the podium and approaches the jury box. "We have seen that North Star knowingly misled the public about the drug." He turns to Robert. "However, my final question to you, Dr. Merriweather, concerns the FDA. What does North Star's faulty research, about which you testified before I presented these emails, say about the company's published safety profile, the very one they submitted to the FDA?"

Robert glances at the jury, then looks back at England. "It is a false safety profile, a complete lie."

"No further questions, Your Honor."

As England heads back to his seat, Barrymore Halstead leans over and whispers to George Payne, "Bingo."

CHAPTER 17
Halstead's Bombshell

This time, Judge Lockhart grants them only a brief break before the cross-examination. The jury shuffles off to their break room, but nearly everyone else in the room remains in their seats. There is an undercurrent of tension in their chatter as everyone is wondering how the defense will respond to the stunning information revealed during England's questioning of Merriweather.

Robert remains in the witness box but stands to stretch his legs. Looking out over the room, he sees Heather Bellaire, dressed in a smart navy business suit and white blouse, slip into the courtroom and come to stand behind the plaintiff's bench. Their eyes meet and they exchange smiles—hers managing to convey support, his letting her know that he appreciates her being there. Heather glances around for a place to sit, then, suddenly, her eyes widen and she turns and abruptly walks out of the courtroom. Concerned, Robert looks around for something or someone that might have startled her but notices nothing amiss. He is about to stand up and follow when the side door opens and the jury files back into the court. With a frustrated sigh, Robert sits back down.

"All rise," the court officer bellows, then the judge once again walks over to the bench.

"Be seated." There is the sound of shuffling as everyone

gets settled, then Judge Lockhart looks over at the defense table. "Mr. Halstead, you may begin."

Adopting a relaxed posture, Barrymore Halstead stands and buttons his suit jacket, then approaches the podium, making sure to maintain eye contact with the jury. He sounds almost friendly when he turns to Robert.

"Dr. Merriweather, at last we meet. I've heard so much about you, yet I don't believe we've ever had the pleasure."

Robert fights the urge to roll his eyes at the phony banter. "No, we haven't."

"Well, if it's alright with you, we are going to get acquainted over the next few hours."

"Do I have a choice?" Robert mutters almost under his breath. He hears a chuckle from one of the jurors and what sounds like a snicker from Judge Lockhart.

Halstead looks over in mock confusion. "I'm sorry, Dr. Merriweather. I didn't hear your response."

"Oh, sorry. I said, 'No, I don't mind.'"

Halstead looks at Robert with a friendly smile and piercing eyes. Then, without further ado, he looks down at the papers in front of him.

"Doctor, didn't I just hear you testify that you personally receive no money for your testimony in any of these cis-phosphorous cases?

"Yes, you did."

"And are you sure about that testimony, Doctor?"

"Yes, I am sure."

"Well then, how do you explain this?" Halstead signals the

young paralegal, then a copy of a check appears on the large screen, as well as the smaller ones in front of the jurors. "As we can clearly see, this check is from Roger England's law firm and is made payable to Dr. Robert Merriweather. Is that true, Doctor?"

"Yes, it is."

"Then how can you testify that you receive no money from these legal cases? You do know what perjury is, Doctor?"

"First, Mr. Halstead, I am well aware of what perjury is. Second, your staff member cut off part of the check. The check is made payable to the Robert Merriweather Foundation, not me personally."

The stricken-looking paralegal hurries to adjust the image, which confirms that the check is indeed made out to the foundation. Halstead shoots the young woman a murderous look, then turns back to Merriweather.

"That's all well and good, Dr. Merriweather, but you are the only authorized signatory for this foundation, are you not?"

"Yes, I am."

"Well then, how do the good people of this jury know whether or not you write checks to yourself?"

With a smile on his face, Dr. Merriweather removes several sheets of folded paper from his suit coat pocket.

"I thought you might ask me that, so I brought these complete bank statements. They will document that no checks were written to me or any of my faculty from the inception of this foundation to the present."

The court officer steps forward to take the bank statements

from Dr. Merriweather, then hands them to the judge. After perusing them for roughly two minutes, Judge Lockhart announces, "These bank statements are in order. There is no indication that the doctor received any funds from this account. Mr. Halstead, move on please."

"Yes, Your Honor," Halstead says smoothly.

"Dr. Merriweather, you make a lot of money on the lecture circuit, don't you?"

"I do make some, yes."

"Some of those lectures are about cis-phosphorous drugs and what you call drug-induced jaw osteonecrosis, are they not?"

"That and other topics."

"Well, let's look at your curriculum vitae here. It says you lectured on jaw osteonecrosis to the Texas Society of Oral and Maxillofacial Surgeons last year. How much money did you receive for that?"

"Interesting that you mention that one, Mr. Halstead, because I actually didn't receive any money from that lecture. I did it as a favor for a close friend of mine who happened to be the program chairman for the meeting."

"Well, then, what about this other osteonecrosis lecture in Snow Mass, Colorado last April?"

"Snow Mass, yes. Over the course of a day and a half, I gave a series of lectures on several surgical topics, including osteonecrosis, for which I received an honorarium of $2,500."

"Thank you, Doctor, but our records indicate that you stayed another day and a half. Why?"

"I worked with the executives of the Colorado Association to develop questions for a fair specialty examination for their new members."

"So you're telling us that you spent all your leisure time at a resort in Snow Mass, Colorado lecturing and developing test questions?"

"Yes, that is what I did."

Initially facing the jurors, Halstead swings around abruptly, his now opened suit coat spinning with him for effect. "Doctor Merriweather, do you ski?"

"No sir, but friends say I've been going downhill for years." Robert's answer, coupled with his deadpan tone, elicits laughs from the weary jurors, but it's Judge Lockhart's chuckle that sets Barrymore Halstead's teeth on edge.

George Payne quickly rises from his chair. "Your Honor, at this time, I would like to request a moment to speak with my co-counsel."

The judge's face turns from humor to annoyance. "Very well, Mr. Payne. You have two minutes."

The mask drops from Halstead's face as he walks back to Payne. "What the hell are you doing, George?" he growls under his breath.

In a rare act of assertiveness, Payne whispers, "I told you Merriweather is a tough customer. I've been down this road before. You're not going to get anywhere trying to impugn his ethics, and you're not going to trump him in bone science. You're losing the jury. You need to hit him with the big ticket item to discredit his testimony, now."

Halstead pauses. "For once, George, you are right. I need to get him on the defensive."

He stands up again. "We're ready to resume, Your Honor."

"Please do," the judge says curtly.

Halstead returns to the podium, the folksy smile now gone.

"Okay, Dr. Merriweather, let's get to the heart of the matter, shall we?"

"Yes."

"You testified earlier that North Star's research on Bone Protect was ignorant and faulty, didn't you?"

"Yes, I did."

"That's a strong accusation, don't you think?"

"Yes, it is. It also happens to be true."

"Do you expect this fine jury of intelligent men and women to believe that you and your small research team conduct more thorough research than the dozens of experienced researchers employed by North Star?"

"Mr. Halstead, it is not a matter of belief, but a matter of scientific, evidence-based fact. North Star's researchers never found what my team did, and what the medical and dental professions are now seeing, in tens of thousands of patients with dead bone in their jaws and fractures in their legs."

"So you say. Were you ever asked to help design the research protocol for Bone Protect?

"No."

"Have you ever participated in a North Star research study?"

"No."

"Do you know how many researchers were on North Star's Bone Protect research team?"

"No."

"Would you be surprised to learn that it was a team of thirty-six highly trained researchers?"

"No, not at all."

"Was your university one of the many centers that tested Bone Protect in this research?"

"No."

"Have you ever served as a consultant to North Star?"

"No, I was offered a consultantship but turned it down."

Halstead turns to the judge. "Move to strike the last part of the doctor's answer as unresponsive."

"The jury will disregard the doctor's statement with regard to turning down a consultantship," Judge Lockhart instructs.

"Well, Doctor, do you know how many patients were tested in the Bone Protect research trial that was approved by the FDA?"

"I know it was more than ten thousand."

"Well, Doctor, if I told you it was ten thousand, two hundred and thirty-two, would you have any reason to disagree with that?"

"No."

"Do you know how many adjudicators looked scrupulously at the safety profile data and completed the FDA-required safety sheets?"

"Not exactly."

"Well, Doctor, there were ten. So, you don't know the exact number of patients in their clinical trial, you didn't contribute to the research design, neither you nor your university conducted any of the patient treatments, you don't know how many adjudicators documented the safety data, and you never even looked at the completed safety sheets presented to the FDA. Is that true?"

"Yes."

"Well, would you like to see them? Because here they are, all ten thousand two hundred and thirty-two of them."

Barrymore Halstead motions toward the back of the courtroom. Five muscular young men, each carrying two boxes, stride up the center aisle and unceremoniously plop them in front of the witness box.

Unfazed by the drama, Dr. Merriweather moves off the stand, walks over to the boxes and opens one.

"Your Honor, I am not finished here. Please ask Dr. Merriweather to return to the witness box."

Never a fan of theatrics, Judge Lockhart shoots Halstead a look of disdain before saying, "Yes, Dr. Merriweather, please be seated in the witness box."

"My apologies to the court, Your Honor," Robert says, as he grabs three binders and carries them back to the stand. Each binder represents the complete safety data from one hundred patients. As he sits down once again, he calls out, "Yes."

Barrymore Halstead looks at him quizzically. "Yes, what, Doctor? I didn't ask you a question."

"Yes, you did, Mr. Halstead. Just before your associates placed these boxes in front of me, you asked if I would like to see them. My answer is yes, and I am looking at them now."

"That was a figure of speech, Dr. Merriweather. Now, if we may continue...."

Roger England jumps up. "Your Honor, figure of speech or not, Mr. Halstead asked a question and our witness answered it. He has a right to review the documents that have just been placed in front of him."

"Gentlemen, we need a side bar," Judge Lockhart replies, then glances at John Bays and George Payne. "You two as well."

As the four men approach the judge's bench, static begins crackling over the courtroom speakers to muffle their conversation.

"Your Honor," England says, "the whole point of Dr. Merriweather's testimony is to show that despite North Star's Research and FDA approval, a serious side effect has become evident, a side effect that apparently escaped both of them. These safety sheets were not available to us before. The doctor has a right to examine them now. After all, Mr. Halstead introduced them himself."

Halstead inches closer and lowers his normally booming voice to a whisper.

"Your Honor, the defense has a right to fully cross—"

"Hey, these safety profiles are a fraud!"

Every head in the courtroom turns to look at Robert, who is holding a binder up.

"Doctor, you're out of order!" snaps Judge Lockhart. He picks up his gavel and holds it in the air as if to ward off further outburst.

"I apologize, Your Honor, but these safety profile sheets have been just pencil whipped. They contain no information other than a patient number, date of birth, and a signature at the bottom. There is no record of the dose, the time it was given, or the required entries about liver, heart, and kidney function." He gives an incredulous snort. "They don't even contain the patient's sex, height, and weight!"

"Doctor, let me see those safety sheets."

Robert places the binders in the outstretched hand of the court officer, who then delivers them to Judge Lockhart. For the next five minutes, the courtroom is silent as he studies them, then he finally lifts his head to address the jury.

"Ladies and gentlemen, I am calling for a recess at this time. Please return to the jury room while the attorneys and I discuss how best to proceed in light of this new evidence. I am instructing you to refrain at this time from making any conclusions about the testimony you have just heard."

He waits for the jury to leave the courtroom, then angrily turns to the attorneys. "In my chambers, right now. Dr. Merriweather, please remain seated in the witness box until we return."

Followed by the four attorneys, Judge Lockhart stomps into his chambers, where he sits on one corner of his desk, arms folded across his chest.

"Halstead, what the hell is going on here? Are these the

actual safety sheets North Star presented to the FDA?"

"Yes, Your Honor. I obtained them directly from North Star."

"But I suspect you didn't read them, Mr. Halstead. The doctor is right; the sheets in these binders, all three hundred of them, are signed but not filled out." He narrows his eyes at Halstead. "I don't have to tell you, Barrymore, that I take a very dim view of anyone introducing false evidence in my courtroom. Now, either you have an incompetence problem on your hands, or there is something else going on. If I find out that you knew about any of this beforehand, I will see to it that a thorough investigation is made into the practices of your law firm. Do you understand?"

For the first time all day, Halstead's emotions appear to be genuine. "Yes, I understand, Your Honor, but these are only three-hundred of the more than ten thousand drug safety sheets! In a study of this magnitude, some things are bound to slip through the cracks."

"Well, these better be the only ones." The judge sighs and stands up from the desk. "But right now we must deal with the whole shebang. Shall we, gentlemen?"

As they re-enter the courtroom, the buzz from the spectators' area immediately stops. A moment later, the jury is brought back in, and Judge Lockhart turns to address them.

"The court thanks you for your patience, ladies and gentlemen. Court is adjourned until 9 a.m. Friday. I instruct you once again not to talk to anyone, including your fellow jurors, about this case and not to draw any conclusions until all the testimony is heard."

As the jury stands to leave, the judge then turns to Robert. "Dr. Merriweather, please stay seated for now."

Robert nods, then, along with the judge and attorneys, he waits for the courtroom to empty. In the mass exodus, no one particularly takes notice of the man with red hair and a matching goatee. When the last spectator has gone, the judge looks at the four attorneys standing in front of him.

"Gentleman, please dismiss your associates."

Hearing this, the members of both legal teams gather their things and hurry from the room.

"Dr. Merriweather," the judge begins after they have left, "you have exposed a serious flaw in the evidence introduced here today. Now, I've given everyone a day off. Do you think you can review the remaining safety sheets in these boxes tomorrow and be able to testify to your findings when we reconvene on Friday morning?"

Robert glances at boxes containing the approximately ten thousand remaining safety sheets. "Yes, Your Honor, I would be glad to."

"Somehow I thought you would. I will have the conference room across the hall ready for you tomorrow morning at nine."

He turns to the attorneys. "I'll allow one person to be there to represent each of your firms. Choose that person, and have them here by nine as well. That's all for today."

Thoroughly exhausted, Robert steps down from the witness box and moves over to England and Bays. Together, they watch Barrymore Halstead stalk from the room, George Payne slinking nervously behind him. *I wouldn't want to be him right now,* Robert thinks as he looks at

Payne's slumped shoulders.

On Friday morning, a large group of spectators return to the courtroom only to find the entrance blocked by two armed court officers. When the jurors enter a moment later, they are equally surprised to find the room empty but for the judge, the lawyers, Dr. Merriweather, and two more armed officers. Once they are seated, the judge asks Robert to take the witness stand once more and reminds him that he is still under oath.

"I understand, Your Honor," he says, but he is scanning the empty room in hopes of seeing Heather. After the debacle at court on Wednesday, he'd called to find out why she left the courtroom so abruptly. She told him she had forgotten about a meeting for work, but her voice sounded off. Besides, Heather never forgot about a meeting. Something wasn't right.

"This court is now in session," Judge Lockhart announces with a pound of the gavel. "Doctor, today I will be the one asking the questions."

Robert nods, relieved he won't be dealing with Halstead. "Yes, Your Honor."

"Have you now reviewed all of the safety profile sheets presented to the FDA by North Star Drug Company?"

"Yes, Your Honor, I have."

"Please tell the court what your findings are."

"Well, of the ten thousand, two hundred and thirty-two safety profile sheets brought in by Mr. Halstead's associates, ten thousand and thirty-two were not filled out, only signed by one of the ten adjudicators. The other two hundred were completely filled out."

Judge Lockhart taps his pointer finger to his chin. "Of the two hundred that were completed, did any of them identify a complication assigned to either the upper or lower jaw?"

"No, Your Honor."

"Dr. Merriweather, given your experience with FDA submissions from the sponsored studies in which you participated, what is the explanation for these findings?"

"Your Honor, an FDA panel only sees and judges what is submitted to them by the sponsoring company. In all likelihood these two hundred fully completed safety profile sheets were the only ones that were shown to the FDA panel, with the remainder left in these boxes to create the assumption that they were fully completed as well. The FDA panel was then shown a false summary of the safety profile sheets identifying no serious side effects in the jaws or in other areas of the body, for that matter."

The judge's eyes flick quickly at the defense table before returning to Robert. "As Mr. Halstead related on Wednesday, you testified that North Star's safety profile was a lie and a fraud. Do you think this evidence corroborates your testimony?"

"I most certainly do."

The judge is silent for a moment, then says, "Okay, Dr. Merriweather, that will be all. The court thanks you for your extra assistance on this case. You may step down now, but please wait outside with the security guards in the hall."

"But, Your Honor," Halstead exclaims, jumping up from his seat, "I have not completed my cross examination yet!"

"Yes, you have, Mr. Halstead." Judge Lockhart then looks at Roger England. "Do I hear a motion?"

Before England can respond, Halstead calls out, "I move for a mistrial."

"Motion denied, Mr. Halstead." He glances at England again. "Do I hear another motion before the court?"

Roger England stands up. "I move for a directed verdict, Your Honor."

"Motion granted."

Now addressing the jury, Judge Lockhart says, "In unusual circumstances such as this court has experienced over the past few days and in the face of overwhelming evidence, it is the prerogative—actually, the duty—of the trial judge to decide the verdict. That said, I am deciding in favor of the plaintiff. I will also determine the amount of the award payable to the plaintiff, thereby removing that burden from you as well. You are now dismissed with the court's sincere gratitude for your service."

The jurors look at each other with a combination of bewilderment and annoyance at having missed work and school and whatever else, only to have the decision taken out of their hands. After they file from the court for the last time, the judge addresses Barrymore Halstead with a glare.

"Mr. Halstead, I am disturbed by the charade you attempted to perpetrate on this court. I am awarding a sum of five million dollars to the plaintiff for pain and suffering, with an additional eight million dollars in punitive damages. Furthermore, I am ordering you personally to appear before the ethics committee of this court's jurisdiction and explain how you came about introducing false evidence to this court. Court is adjourned." He raps the gavel again, the sound echoing loudly through the near empty courtroom.

Tears welling in her eyes, Mrs. Lamb places a thin hand on Roger England's. He gives her an exuberant smile and gives the hand a gentle squeeze. As John Bays escorts her out of the courtroom, England goes out in the hallway to bring a confused Robert Merriweather back in.

"Roger, why on Earth am I being guarded by armed men?"

"In a minute, Robert," England replies, jerking his head toward a stunned Barrymore Halstead and George Payne, who are heading toward them.

"Halstead looks completely different without that arrogant expression," England whispers, earning a small smile from Robert.

When they reach the front of the courtroom, Robert is surprised to find Judge Lockhart seated at the defense table. He gives Robert a curious look.

"Dr. Merriweather, it seems that someone doesn't like you. The bailiff here found these sketches lying on one of the benches Wednesday."

Eyes widening, Robert looks down at the three sketches, each a caricature of him in a different death pose. In one, he is hanging from a tree with a noose around his neck; in another, a man in a Philadelphia Phillies jacket is shooting him with what looks like a double-barreled shotgun; and in the third, the same man is stabbing him with a large knife, blood squirting out of several holes.

Robert looks up to see both Judge Lockhart and Roger England staring at him. "Your Honor, there have been threats made against me recently. Actually, my friend and mentor, Dr. Jacobson, was murdered in my office, and the popular theory is that I was the target. I haven't wanted to believe it, but, well, this seems to lend credibility to it. A Detective Molinaro in Miami is working on the murder case and knows about all the threats. Can these sketches be sent to him for fingerprinting and possibly a DNA analysis?"

The judge nods. "Yes, they can, Doctor, but I strongly advise you to ask this Detective Molinaro to provide you with police protection when you return to Miami. In the meantime, the NYPD will be accompanying you for the remainder of your stay in New York." He puts up a hand to silence Robert's objection. "No use arguing, Doctor. I'm not going to let you get bumped off in my city."

CHAPTER 18
The Hit Order

Robert reaches across the candlelit table to take Heather's hand. The small Italian bistro on the Upper East Side is one of their favorite eateries, and as he smells the heavenly aromas of freshly baked bread and marinara sauce, he realizes how hungry he is. And how tired. He smiles at Heather, glad he begged off when Roger England asked him to join Mrs. Lamb and the legal team for a celebratory dinner. No doubt dining at the Four Seasons would have been quite the experience, but he is just as happy to spend a quiet dinner with Heather. They have far too few nights together to waste one talking about legal strategies.

Still, Robert can't resist giving her a full account of the trial, including the fraud North Star perpetrated on the FDA and Judge Lockhart's directed verdict. Heather nods in all the appropriate places, but he can tell her thoughts are elsewhere.

"Are you okay, Heather?"

She looks at him for a moment, then blurts out, "I'm sorry to change the subject, but I didn't leave the courtroom to return to my office as I first told you. I left because I saw William sitting in the last row, behind Halstead's group."

Robert's mind immediately goes to the creepy sketches left in the courtroom, but he lets her continue.

"Bob, I am worried. I've always known he was bitter about the divorce, but to show up at a trial where you are testifying? He is obsessed with getting even with me or getting me back, maybe both, and sees you as the main obstacle."

"Heather," he says, trying to keep his voice even, "is William into art? I mean, does he like to draw?"

Heather looks at him quizzically. "Why, yes. He majored in English and made a hobby of sketching characters from English and Irish literature." She shrugs. "It was one of his few talents. Why do you ask?"

He gives her hand a gentle squeeze. "I wasn't going to tell you this, but now that you saw William … the bailiff found three sketches on one of the benches—they each depicted someone murdering me."

Heather gasps, but Robert holds up a hand to show her he's not worried.

"They're now being analyzed for fingerprints and DNA. I think it's safe to assume William drew them. The question is whether he is also the one who threw a brick at me that morning, and perhaps even the person who broke into our operating room during the surgery. Is there any reason to suspect William has been to Florida recently?"

Heather shakes her head. "I have no idea. He did disappear for a while, when he missed that weekend with the boys … I guess it's possible he went to Florida."

"Well, I'm sure the cops will now want to question him about the threats against me, and certainly Dr. Jacobson's murder as well."

Heather's eyes well up with tears. "Promise me you'll be careful."

He shakes his head. "I will be careful, but I have to leave early tomorrow morning. I've already been gone longer than planned, having spent an entire day reviewing those damned safety profile sheets. Besides, I promised to attend the funeral of one of my patients. She committed suicide."

"Oh, Bob, I am so sorry!"

"Yes, it's very sad, and definitely related to her jaw osteonecrosis." He snorts in disgust. "The agony these people are going through because of sheer negligence! Well, at least we scored a victory today, right?" He attempts a smile, but it looks more like a grimace. "I also have a research project that is falling apart, a whole mess of patients that need me, and let's not forget Julio, the young lab technician recovering from the rat bite."

"Okay, okay, I heard enough." Heather picks up her menu. "Let's enjoy our dinner …" She lowers it to give him a suggestive look. "… Then we can go back to my place and 'talk' about more pleasurable things."

****

Less than ten blocks away, Barrymore Halstead sits slumped in his drawing room, his manicured hand wrapped around a glass of King George Johnny Walker Blue. The Armani coat and tie now lay discarded on the tufted leather couch against the wall, next to the evening edition of the Wall Street Journal, which was taken to him a few minutes ago by his diligent and, as it turned out, unfortunate, maid.

"Didn't I tell you I did not want to be interrupted?" he screams, but his eyes are not focused on her; they are focused on the front page headline: "North Star Stock Plummets After Losing Trial."

"B-but Mr. Halstead," the young woman stutters, "You always want the evening paper."

His head snaps toward her as if he forgot she was in the room. "Get out! Get your things and get out!"

She runs sobbing from the room, but Halstead doesn't notice. He is already picking up the paper.

North Star Pharmaceuticals is scrambling to calm investors after U.S. District Judge Lockhart found for Sandra Lamb, plaintiff in the Bone Protect trial. The loss of this so-called bellwether trial indicates that the hundreds of other plaintiffs suing the pharmaceutical conglomerate will also be victorious....

Halstead skims the article, searching for his own name. It doesn't take long before he finds it.

Key testimony was provided by Dr. Robert Merriweather, a top oral and maxillofacial surgeon based in Miami. Merriweather, who has testified in hundreds of Big Pharma cases, bested Barrymore Halstead, founding partner of the prestigious firm....

He flings the paper on the couch and pours another scotch. "Goddamned fools! Why didn't they open those boxes themselves and find out the sheets were fraudulent? And those bastards at North Star ... what were they thinking?"

At the bottom of every lost case, he has always said, is a stupid client. "And damn that Judge Lockhart too. He was supposed to be on our side." He takes another sip of scotch.

It is not the fraud he is angry about; in fact, under normal circumstances, he would find their methods quite impressive. *But not telling their own counsel! How the hell am I supposed to mount a defense when I don't have the facts?*

"I don't lose!" Halstead screams, then hurls the glass against the wall. It shatters, sending bits of Waterford crystal all over the walls and couch. No doubt the other staff had heard it, but no one would dare knock now.

"I don't lose," he mutters as he sinks back into the chair. Suddenly, he is no longer in his suite, but in the bedroom of the dilapidated Brighton Beach rowhouse where he had grown up. He hears his father's heavy footsteps coming down the hall and scoots into the dank closet. Trembling with fear, he leaves the door open just enough so he can see out. *Maybe he won't find me this time,* he thinks with the flawed logic of a seven-year-old. A second later, the bright light shining in from a crack in the door is gone, replaced by the swaying figure of Anatoly Izmaylov. In his hands is a half-drunk bottle of cheap vodka.

"Boris," he singsongs, "Where in the hell are you, boy?" He takes a swig from the bottle. "Heard your lunch money was stolen again today.…"

Suddenly, the closet door swings open and his father reaches in and grips Boris' arm like a vice. "What did I tell you about being a pushover? You think I came to this country so you could lose my money to some bully? It's about time you learned some lessons about life, boy. You either win or be beaten."

"Please, Da," Boris screams when his father pulls harder on the arm.

The words are no sooner out of his mouth when he realizes his mistake. Any show of weakness only angers his father more. A second later, he is yanked out of the closet with such force, it dislocates his arm from its socket.

"I'll make a man out of you yet," his father screams in his native Russian. "'I will win,' say it! Say it again!"

Boris repeats the phrase, over and over, but not before his father has given him a split lip and a black eye. It wouldn't be his last beating, but it would be the last time he cried out. The next day at school, he heads for the playground. All the kids are there, including the boy who had been shaking him down. Without hesitation, he walks up to the boy and punches him right in the jaw. But it isn't the punch that attracts the attention of Dimitri Petrakov, a thug a few years older than him, but the way Boris keeps kicking him even after the boy is down.

"You tough kid," Dimitri says, putting an arm around him.

Boris smiles; he had never been called tough before. That day he begins hanging with Dimitri's crew—engaging in petty thefts and running their school, but eventually it becomes apparent that Boris has more to offer than a fist.

"You too smart for this," Dimitri says one day, his arm gesturing toward the street.

That was the beginning of his transformation into Barrymore Halstead. College, law school, learning everything about culture and fine things, and finally, making sure people did not know of his true background. It has been a long road, but it only took one minute, one loss, to take him back to that closet in Brooklyn.

He opens his eyes, sighing with relief when he finds himself back in his drawing room. "I will win," he whispers, "I will win."

His gaze returns to the newspaper. Merriweather. Just the thought of that high and mighty do-gooder makes Halstead's blood boil.

"I'll fix that son of a bitch," Halstead says as he rises from his chair. Swaying, he stumbles over to his desk and pulls open one of the drawers to reveal several burner phones. Looking for one in particular, he pulls it out and presses a single button. The phone only rings twice, then a familiar voice comes over the speaker in heavily accented English. "Hello, Golden Ruble. This is Antoli, speak please."

"Antoli, Barrymore Halstead here. Put Dimitri on the phone."

"Okay, Mr. Barrymore, I transfer you to boss."

Halstead rolls his eyes at the hold music, a rock song with some guy screaming in Russian. He can imagine Dimitri sitting in his office, stacks of credit card numbers, pin numbers, and social security numbers splayed out in front of him. Finally, the horrendous song is cut off, replaced by Petrakov's gruff voice.

"This is Dimitri."

"Dimitri, it's Barrymore. Are you alone?"

"Dimitri always alone in the world." He laughs. "Cost of being big boss."

Ignoring the comment, Halstead gets right down to

business. "Do you remember that job a while back? The one down in Miami?"

"This is medical job, yes?" Dimitri snickers. "I was supposed to warn doctor about certain risks to his health. Then murder happens in hospital and I could not get close to him."

"Thanks for the recap, Dimitri," Halstead says dryly. "Well, that job has now become a medical cleanup. I want you to take care of it now. The sooner the better."

"I will send someone—"

"No, you will not send anyone. I want you to take care of this personally."

"May not be safe for Dimitri. Cops were here, you know."

"They were just nosing around. I need you on this."

Petrakov pauses a moment, then says, "Dimitri can do job, but it will cost you."

"How much?"

"Five hundred thousand, cash. Half now, half when the job is done."

"Okay, but remember, this is a cleanup job. The mess just disappears. Understand?"

"That is what Dimitri do best. You send down payment money by Monday, then I leave."

Halstead accepts the terms with a grunt, then throws the disposable cell phone in the bucket of ice water next to his chair. Feeling in control for the first time all day, Halstead smiles as he pours himself another three fingers of scotch. Perhaps he'd get a good night's sleep after all.

CHAPTER 19
The Road to Miami

The following Monday morning, after receiving Halstead's payment, Dimitri Petrakov and Nicolai jump into a brown 2008 Chevrolet Cobalt and head toward the Verrazano Bridge linking Brooklyn and Staten Island. They make good time on the Staten Island Expressway and over the Goethals Bridge, yet by 1 p.m. they have only reached central New Jersey.

Nicolai stares listlessly out the window, thinking that if he sees one more row of pine trees, one more planned community, he'll go crazy.

"Dimitri," he whines, "why we not take Jersey Turnpike? We go faster on Turnpike."

Dimitri shoots him an annoyed look. "Nicolai, you know better than to ask this. Turnpike has toll booths, and toll booths have cameras. Do you want cops to have record of us leaving New York? I do not think you want this." He reaches over to grip his shoulder. "We take back roads only. When we get gas, we cover our faces and license plates. We will not stop, so get some sleep. You drive tonight."

Despite the numerous stoplights, overly cautious soccer moms, and school zone speed limits, they manage to make it to North Carolina by five. As they swerve through the winding rural backroads, Dimitri suddenly notices flashing blue lights in his rearview mirror. There is a state trooper behind them, and he is rapidly closing the distance.

Dimitri nudges Nicolai, who is once again dozing, his head against the passenger side window.

"We have company, Nicolai."

The cop signals him to pull over, an order which Dimitri immediately complies with. The state trooper then parks his car directly behind the old Chevrolet and runs the New York license plates. Dimitri knows the plates will come up clean, but his jaw is still on edge as he discreetly positions the 9mm Glock pistol hidden beneath his right leg.

"You want me to take care of him, boss?"

"No, you idiot. He probably has one of those … those.…"

"Dashcams?"

"Yes, dashcams. You just stay put unless I say otherwise. You understand?"

"Yes, boss."

When Dimitri glances in the rearview mirror again, he sees the state trooper sauntering toward them. He lowers the driver's side window and places both hands on the steering wheel, where the cop can see them.

"Evenin', gentlemen," he says, managing to convey, despite his genteel Southern drawl, that they are not welcome in his jurisdiction.

"Good evening, Officer …" Dimitri says, oozing charm.

"It's State Trooper Hatfield," he replies curtly. "License and registration, please."

Dimitri gives him an obsequious smile, then pulls the fake ID from his wallet and hands it to the trooper.

"Mr. Paul Simon?" the trooper says skeptically as he glances from the license to Dimitri's face.

"Yes, this is me. I shorten my last name when I come to this beautiful country, I wanted to be more American."

The trooper gives him a dubious look. "More American, huh? I'll be back in a moment."

As he heads back to his car to check the name on the license, Dimitri slowly exhales. "Asshole." He glances at Nicolai, who is lighting a cigarette with shaking hands. "Calm down, Nicolai," he growls. "The paperwork will check out. Idiot cop will have nothing unless you give him something."

Sure enough, Hatfield returns, a slightly disappointed expression on his face. He hands Dimitri the license and registration.

"Do you know why I stopped you today?" Dimitri isn't given a chance to answer. "I stopped you because you were going over seventy-five in a fifty-five mile an hour zone. Now maybe that's acceptable in New York City ..." Hatfield sneers as he says the name, like it's a dirty word, "... but here I can assure you it's a very serious matter."

Dimitri scrunches his face in confusion. "Officer, I not hear so good. What you say?"

With a roll of his eyes, Hatfield leans in toward the open window to repeat his admonition. His look of annoyance turns to surprise as, in one quick, fluid move, Dimitri's left hand shoots up to grab him by the neck-tie while his right pulls out the gun from under his thigh. He fires two quick shots into the trooper's forehead.

Hatfield's limp body is then caught by Nicolai, who had

exited his passenger side door as soon as Dimitri grabbed for the necktie. He quickly drags the body into the nearby ditch as the blood-splattered Dimitri exits his side and opens the trunk to grab the lug wrench from the spare well. He then runs over to Hatfield's car, slips inside, and smashes the dashcam and on-board computer. Satisfied that all record of the incident is gone, he flicks off the flashing lights and returns to the Cobalt.

"Dimitri, we are going the wrong way!" Nicolai exclaims as his boss pulls a U-turn to head north.

"No, Nicolai, when the body and abandoned police car are found, they will notice it pointing to south. They think to go in that direction to find us. We fool them. We go north for now. We also will stop at lake we passed before. You clean blood from car, and I wash blood off me and change clothes." He sighs at the unfortunate turn of events. "We find other back roads to Miami Beach."

****

The same Monday morning finds Robert Merriweather back at the hospital, buried in backlogs from the week before. By six-thirty, he is already meeting with his residents to review the last week's grand rounds.

"Okay, who is going to impress me with what you learned about the blood-brain barrier since last week?"

"I looked up a couple of articles, sir," Dr. Montel announces, then quickly corrects himself. "I mean, Dr. Merri-weather...."

Robert smiles at the mistake but finds he is not in the mood to tease the young doctor unnecessarily. Instead, he says, "Great! Tell us all what you learned."

"Well, the blood-brain barrier is not a specific structure, like, for example, a wall. It's actually a modification of the cells that make up the blood vessels surrounding the brain. Compared to blood vessels in other organs, the cells in the blood vessels surrounding the brain fit more tightly together—in fact, they are sort of interlocked. Because they are so tightly compressed, they only allow small molecules like sugars, alcohol, and smaller-sized antibiotics to freely pass from the bloodstream into the brain. Large molecules like proteins, penicillin, and most antibiotics cannot squeeze through these tight spaces and are therefore excluded from the brain."

"Good work, Dr. Montel." He glances around the group. "See, everyone, what you can learn with a little scientific curiosity and a little extra effort? Now, can anyone tell us how the blood-brain barrier comes into play when a diabetic receives an overdose of insulin?" His gaze falls on one of the third-year residents. "How about you, Dr. Hundley?"

"Okay, I'll try."

"First, tell us how insulin works in general."

"Insulin works by facilitating...."

As Hundley goes through his explanation, Robert glances up to find Glanville pointedly staring at him. The young man clearly has something to report.

"Very good," he says when Dr. Hundley has finished. "It looks like you certainly did your homework. Now, you all know I was at one of the cis-phosphorous trials last week...."

He smiles at the burst of applause that goes up from the residents. "I guess you all heard about the verdict as well. Not only was it revealed that the North Star Drug Company falsified their approval submission to the FDA for Bone Protect, and not only did the judge order a directed verdict for the plaintiff and a huge payout ..." The applause grows louder. "... But the lead attorney, Barrymore Halstead, has been brought up on ethics charges, and North Star Drug Company is being investigated by the US Department of Justice." He pauses. "But this is no time to become complacent. The outcome of the trial, while good news, is also a reminder that most drugs are not researched thoroughly with regard to their side effects. While these drugs are often valuable, even necessary, the dose that is advertised and the length of time for which they are recommended to be taken may not be correct. When prescribing medication, you should limit it to the smallest dose possible and for the shortest time possible to achieve the results you and your patients seek."

After a quick glance at his watch, Dr. Merriweather stands up. "Again, good work, everyone. Now if you'll excuse me, I have some catching up to do after my absence." He then turns the remainder of the grand rounds conference to his faculty member, Dr. Brewster.

"Okay, James," Robert says to Dr. Glanville as the two walk down the hospital corridors, "fill me in."

"I have some good news, some bad news, and some really bad news."

"Tell me the good news first. It'll give me time to brace myself for the other stuff."

"Okay—the good news is that Julio has healed from his rat bite and all specimen testing for rabies was negative. He will be back to work next week."

At hearing the young vet tech will be okay, Robert is filled with relief. "That is good news."

"Yeah, and the rat brain was also negative for mad cow disease, so it looks like Julio will be fine. Now here comes the bad news: we still don't know what is driving the rats crazy. And now are you ready for the really bad news, Dr. Merriweather?"

He manages a weak smile. "I'll take it like a man. Shoot."

"The rats have gotten worse, at least half of them. Some have even been chewing off parts of their tails and paws. Others have been doing flips in their cages. I saw it myself. Steve Carr says we have to euthanize the rats and take our specimens this week or they will destroy them."

Merriweather nods. "I can't blame him. Let's do it after our surgery today. Like always, we'll have four specimens—mandible, maxilla, brain and spinal cord—coded for each rat. I figure if we start by four and get either Greenberg or Montel to bottle and label the specimens, we should be finished by nine."

That night, with Doctors Glanville and Montel by his side, Dr. Merriweather completes the grim task of euthanizing the remaining thirty-nine research rats and cataloging their specimens. It is after ten when the three satisfied but fatigued doctors head to Cazolli's, a pizza parlor close to the medical school, to review their findings over a pepperoni pizza with extra cheese.

****

It is three in the morning when Dimitri Petrakov and Nicolai pull into the parking lot behind the Purple Stallion Gentlemen's Club. It took them eighteen hours to get to Miami Beach, but after getting pulled over by the cop, Dimitri was even more paranoid about the roads they took and how fast they went.

They can hear the house music blaring before they even reach the gaudy gold double doors; they are no sooner inside when an equally gaudy heavyset man rushes to them. It is Sergey Chernov, the owner and manager of the club, as well as Dimitri's first cousin.

"Cousin Dimitri! Nicolai! You finally made it!" Sergey booms, enveloping first Dimitri, then Nicolai, in a fleshy embrace. He is practically yelling, yet they can barely hear him above the din of the music. The noise, coupled with the reflection of the strobe lights and mostly naked dancers, is enough sensory overload to make the two exhausted travelers dizzy.

"Good to be welcomed by family," responds Dimitri, as he submits to another hug.

"Come into my office," Sergey says with a sweeping gesture. "We can talk over my best vodka, straight from Mother Russia."

Dimitri nods, then he and Nicolai follow Sergey to a spacious office in the back of the club. After closing the door behind them, Sergey grabs three glasses and a bottle of Tovaritch and pours three generous drinks. He holds up his glass to toast their arrival, then they throw the drinks back.

"See," Sergey says as he pours another round, "not like that American crap."

"Hmmm ..." Dimitri nods, managing to convey both his appreciation for the vodka and his desire to get down to business.

Sergey settles his considerable girth in the chair behind the desk. "Okay, I would love to pretend you're here for fun, but we know differently, right? Men like us, we are always working."

Dimitri nods again. Sergey has always talked too much, and Dimitri has learned to just let him ramble for a while. In due time, Sergey gets around to telling them what he has learned of Dr. Merriweather's known associates and daily routine.

"Dimitri, your target is well-known and is rarely alone. It won't be easy to get him at the hospital, especially since you have to make this look like a disappearance." Sergey shrugs his enormous shoulders. "You could go to his home. He lives alone but has three dogs you would have to deal with. Neighbors could hear...."

"Do you have anything of value to tell me?" Dimitri asks as he grabs the vodka bottle.

Sergey shrugs again. "He does like to fish and go skin diving. You could—"

Dimitri cuts him off with a raised hand. "I've heard enough for tonight." He throws back the vodka. "However, you give me good idea. Ocean is big place, good for hiding body. Now ..." He stands up and stifles a yawn. "... Dimitri must get sleep. You have nice beds for us, no?"

CHAPTER 20
Prelude to the Hit

The next morning, Robert is up even earlier than usual, intent on catching up with the backlog of emails and electronic medical records that have accumulated during his absence. Just before six, he pulls out of his driveway and heads for the office, unaware of the white utility van with the words "Air Conditioning Services" on the side following two car-lengths behind him. Twenty minutes later, he is behind his desk, enjoying the quiet solitude before the rush of the day begins. After an hour and a half and piles of tedious paperwork, he is relieved when Isabella interrupts him.

"Good morning, Chief, I see you've jumped in with both feet. Congrats, by the way. I heard all about your big victory against North Star, not to mention that jackass Halstead."

"Thanks, they certainly had it coming." He stands up. "Anyway, why don't you put your things down and come back in here? We need to have a talk."

She nods. "Be there in a jiff."

She heads straight for the coffeemaker and turns it on before setting her sweater and purse on her chair. By the time her computer has booted up, the aroma of coffee is wafting through the office. She pours two cups and carries them to Robert's desk.

"So what's up?" she asks, sitting across the desk from him.

"I've been hearing that you took some personal time while I was gone.…"

"Yes, yes I did."

"Issy, I think it's great that you took time for yourself, God knows you deserve it. But you have to let the university—someone—know that you're taking a sick day, a personal day, a vacation day, whatever." Robert pauses uncomfortably. "I also hear you were at the police station with Detective Molinaro. Issy, what's going on? Are you still my secretary, or are you a detective?"

Isabella looks half angry, half amused. "C'mon now, Dr. M, you know better than to ask that. You know I love you like a father."

Robert smiles. "I'll accept that, although I'd be happier if you had said you love me like a brother. Speaking of such, are you and the good Detective Molinaro a couple now?"

She shrugs. "I don't know if I'd use the word 'couple' yet, but there is something there. I'll also admit I should've let administration know I was taking off yesterday, but Andy called me with some disturbing news about you."

Robert realizes he should probably be alarmed, but all he can feel is annoyance. "Oh brother, now what?"

"He told me that the bailiff went back and searched the bench where he'd found the sketches … apparently there was a drawing pencil with bite indentations on it. He turned it over to that detective Andy and Gonzalez met while they were in New York. The crime lab processed it over the weekend, and they now have a full DNA profile of the guy who drew them."

"Well, who is it?"

Clearly frightened, Isabella looks him in the eye. "There is no match in their database, but given Heather's statement about seeing her ex in there ..." She pauses. "Why didn't you tell me about him? He sounds like a real nut."

"It wasn't my place to say anything, Issy."

"I understand," she says in a way that indicates otherwise. "Anyway, they suspect it's William Bellaire, especially since, to top it off, no one knows where he is. He hasn't shown up at work for over six weeks now, his car is gone, and his apartment manager in Philadelphia hasn't seen him either. Andy has asked the Philly police to get a search warrant for his place."

She peers at him intently, trying to gauge his reaction.

"All this," he replies with exaggerated coyness, "for lil' ole me?"

Isabella smacks her hand on the desk. "Dammit, Dr. Merriweather, don't you know how serious this is? Joking about it isn't going to make it go away. You know what I was doing yesterday? Trying to help Andy help you. He even had me call Heather to see if she had anything of William's that they could use for a DNA match. As soon as we got off the phone, she ran home and got some old comb of his—some of his hair is still on it and, hopefully, some of the roots for DNA analysis. You see, like the rest of us, she's also worried about you."

Robert shifts uncomfortably in his chair. "Okay, okay, I'll try to take this more seriously. Just do me a favor and from now on, let the administration know if you're not going to be in." His voice softens. "I couldn't do this job without you."

By 8:30, Dr. Merriweather is on the floor with his surgical team. As with every clinic day, they are incredibly busy, seeing not only twenty-six previous surgery patients whose progress they are monitoring, but another eight who they are treating with antibiotics and other medications in an effort to control their disease without operating. Finally, there are seven new patients, three of which are seen due to exposed bone in the mouth from a cis-phosphorous drug. One case in particular is tragic. After reviewing her history and an examination, Dr. Sanders presents her to Robert.

"Mrs. Burnett, this is Dr. Merriweather, the doctor your oncologist referred you to. Dr. Merriweather, Mrs. Burnett is here today because of constant pain and intermittent bouts of swelling from exposed bone in the mouth."

Next to her, Robert sees a silver-haired man of about sixty, who probably would look much younger if not for the concern tightening his handsome features.

"Mrs. and Mr. Burnett, I hope we can help you. I know Dr. Sanders has done an initial interview with you, and right now she's going to fill me in on some of the details. As you listen, please fill us in on anything that she's missing. I see here that your oncologist is Dr. Jo Ling, correct?" The Burnetts nod. "Good choice, Dr. Ling is excellent." Robert turns to Dr. Sanders. "Okay, go ahead."

"Mrs. Burnett is a fifty-eight-year-old woman with a history of illness that includes breast cancer in the left breast. It was initially diagnosed in 2004, and at that time she underwent a radical mastectomy and radiation therapy to the left side of the chest. She proceeded with no evidence of disease until metastatic spread to her scapula and pelvic bones were noted by Dr. Jo Ling. She was then started on two chemotherapy drugs: tumor statin and apopto-side, as well as six milligrams of Bone Protect each month. Her metastatic spread to these bones has been stable and produced no symptoms. However, Mrs. Burnett began developing exposed bone in the mandible by the fall of 2009. It began on the right side of the lower jaw but has since spread to include most of the alveolar bone all the way around to the left side."

Robert nods. "Yes, Dr. Ling and I discussed that over the phone. Mrs. Burnett, I understand you now have exposed bone on the left side of your upper jaw too. Is that right?"

"Yes, and I don't know which one hurts me more." She looks at the ground. "Both smell really bad. Oscar won't even kiss me anymore."

"Does your face ever swell up?"

"Yes, and when it does the pain is even worse. My oral surgeon gave me antibiotics for it. They initially helped, but now nothing seems to work."

"Dr. Ling said she stopped giving you the Bone Protect last year. Did that help any?"

"No, not at all." Her eyes well up with tears. "Dr. Merri-weather, what can I do? Does this ever go away?"

Robert places a gentle hand on her arm, then turns to Dr. Sanders. "Anything of note in the rest of her medical history?"

"No, Dr. Merriweather. She is otherwise healthy, no other medical conditions, no allergies … even the breast cancer is in remission."

"Mr. and Mrs. Burnett, I'm going to review these x-rays

you brought with you, as well as that special x-ray we just took of your jaws. It's known as a cone beam CT scan, and it allows us to actually see inside your bone. I'll be back in just a few minutes."

Dr. Merriweather and Dr. Sanders, along with Dr. Glanville, who has just joined them after removing sutures from one of the recent surgery patients, head to the resident's work room, where they pull up the digital computerized x-rays.

"Guys, this is pretty significant," begins Dr. Merriweather. "Look at the bony destruction from left to right in nearly her entire lower jaw. And look at the destruction in the left upper jaw. The maxillary sinus is almost completely obliterated, and there is complete bone loss around all of her upper and lower teeth. Those teeth must be mobile. Are they, Dr. Sanders?"

"Yes, except for the upper central incisor and some teeth on the upper right side, they are at a three-plus out of four." Robert nods in agreement. Sanders is using the one-to-four scale utilized by all dentists to assess how loose teeth are. Teeth at a level four are basically about to fall out by themselves.

"Okay," he says, "looks like we can resolve this with surgery, but she will lose all of her lower teeth and about four on the upper left. I think we can avoid an amputation surgery for now, but we'll still need to remove a lot of bone. Let's return. I'll examine her, and unless I see something different, I will explain what drug-induced jaw osteonecrosis is and what the surgery entails. At least we'll probably be able to eliminate the pain, odor, and taste of dead bone in her mouth."

The three return to the examination room and immediately sense the tension in the air.

"Oscar, don't contradict me. I'm the one with the jaw problem, not you."

"Jennifer, I wasn't contradicting you. I was only reminding you that Dr. Ling wanted to stop the Bone Protect years ago." He turns to Robert. "The National Society of Bone Research recommended that Bone Protect should be used continually or else the cancer would spread more. Now, all these years later, we find out there are studies saying the cancer can't spread in bone after just four doses of Bone Protect. My wife had over fifty doses!"

Mrs. Burnett snorts. "Well, I don't think she ever tried to help me. She was only treating me every month to make more money, and you were in cahoots with her, I know it."

Mr. Burnett looks ready to burst into tears. "Jennifer, how can you say that?"

That's when Robert steps in. "Mr. and Mrs. Burnett, for now why don't we focus on the problems in your jaw? I will say, though, that I know Dr. Ling, and she is one of the most caring and compassionate oncologists in the field. She would never—"

"Stay out of this, doctor," Mrs. Burnett snaps. "Oscar, you've been trying to get rid of me since I got this cancer. You want me out of the picture."

Suddenly, she leaps out of the examining chair and flies at her husband, flailing with both fists. Despite her frail condition, it takes quite an effort for Dr. Glanville and Dr. Merriweather to pull her off him. Even as they hold her back, she struggles against them, issuing a vicious barrage of accusations and threats at her shocked husband.

Robert turns to the nurse standing in the corner of the room. "Kathy, please get me a syringe of Versed, five milligrams, now."

Over the next few minutes, Mrs. Burnett's tirade continues, despite Dr. Glanville's grip and her husband's efforts to calm her.

"Mr. Burnett, I am hesitant to sedate her but I think we have to, for her safety and yours. Do I have your consent?"

"Yes, certainly, I can't imagine what's come over her. She's just not like this."

Dr. Merriweather quickly wipes her upper arm with an iodine-based antiseptic, then gives her the injection. Even then it takes five minutes for her to calm down enough for Dr. Glanville to release his grip and set her back into the examining chair. From there, Kathy, who has already brought the portable monitors to the room, hooks up an oxygen saturation monitor, a blood pressure monitor, and cardiogram leads.

"Mr. Burnett, your wife is alright, but I suggest we admit her to the hospital. I want a psychiatrist familiar with the stress of long-term pain and cancer to visit her. She may benefit from his consultation and perhaps some medications."

"Yes, of course. I just can't believe this. She was coping so well. You know, doctor, we've been married for forty years now. Can I stay with her?"

"Yes, through our admission process and in her hospital room too."

After getting her into a wheelchair, Kathy and Dr. Glanville wheel Mrs. Burnett to Admissions. Dr. Merriweather and Dr. Sanders then go to see the remaining afternoon clinic patients. Soon after, a short but powerfully built man approaches the appointment desk and begins speaking with Paula, a chipper if slightly naïve brunette.

"I need appointment with Dr. Merriweather."

"Okay, sir, what is your name and what's the reason for seeing Dr. Merriweather?"

"My name is Dimitri Petrakov, and I have bad teeth."

"Mr. Petrakov, I can give you an appointment with one of our other faculty. Dr. Merriweather is our Program Chairman and limits his practice to patients with tumors and cancer or their related problems."

"No, I need only to see Dr. Merriweather. I think my tooth has cancer."

Pamela offers him a kind smile. "Now, Mr. Petrakov, teeth don't get cancer. I'll give you an appointment with Dr. Samanaka for tomorrow."

"No, I only want to see Dr. Merriweather. I will see him Saturday, if he not fishing." He smiles proudly. "I am also fisherman."

Pamela's smile grows wider. "So you know Dr. Merriweather? As a matter of fact, he's going fishing this Saturday as a birthday present to his son Ryan."

Petrakov rolls his eyes skyward as if considering his options. "Okay, I take appointment with Japanese doctor, but not tomorrow, next week."

"That's fine, Mr. Petrakov." She looks at her computer screen.

"How about next Wednesday at three?"

"This is good."

Pamela's fingers fly on the keys. "Okay, you're all set."

"Thank you, young lady. I hope Dr. Merriweather has nice fishing trip. Where does he go?"

"Oh, he always fishes out of Key West—has a lot of luck there. He brings us fresh fish fillets every time he goes out."

Petrakov raises an eyebrow. "Really? What marina he use?"

"Murray's Marina on Stock Island. They just put his boat in the water and off he goes." She scribbles the date and time of his appointment on a card and hands it to him. "Please call us if you need to change your appointment."

"Thank you, miss." He offers her a crooked smile. "Someday maybe I go catch fish with Dr. Merriweather."

On Tuesday and Wednesday, Dimitri and Nicolai keep a close watch on Merriweather's activities. They follow him around during the day and at night, they position themselves in their white van, their binoculars fixed mostly on the garage where Dr. Merriweather keeps his fishing gear. By eleven Wednesday night, both men are so bored they are fighting to stay awake. Nicolai places the binoculars to his eyes and scans the neighboring homes, hoping to get a peek at some woman undressing or, better yet, in the shower. All he sees is a house cat sitting in the window, looking as bored as him. Then, suddenly, he grabs Dimitri's arm.

"Boss, other person watch doctor." He points to a car parked down the street. "Over there, in that car."

Dimitri takes the binoculars from Nicholai and, sure

enough, he sees a man with a goatee and a Phillies baseball cap. His eyes are fixed on Merriweather's house.

"You are right, Nicolai." Dimitri sits back, thinking for a moment. Has Halstead hired some kind of backup person, or does this Merriweather just have a lot of enemies? Or, worse yet, is the good doctor under police protection? "You stay here."

"What are you going to do?"

"I'm going to find out if he is cop."

Dimitri Petrakov quietly exits the driver's side and slips into the darkness. After circling the block, he positions himself in front of the man's car, approaching it in clear view so as not to raise any suspicions. When the man in the goatee looks his way, Dimitri gives him a smile and a friendly wave. As the man rolls down the window, Dimitri sees the bright red of his neatly trimmed goatee.

"Excuse me, sir. You see golden retriever run by here?"

"No, man." The goateed man glances back at Merriweather's house. "I haven't." To him, the conversation is over; however, Dimitri has other ideas.

"Oh this is just terrible!" Dimitri moans. "I just take him out for walk and he runs away. I knew I should have put him on leash!"

"You should have," the man says curtly.

"Are you sure … ?" Dimitri asks as he steps toward the car, taking in the man's clothes and demeanor. He also does the best he can to see whether there are any signs of law enforcement—there aren't.

"Nope," the man says, clearly growing annoyed at the interruption.

Dimitri takes another look inside the car. Something is glinting on the floor in the back, but he cannot tell what it is. "Okay, thanks anyway," he finally says. "Have a good evening." With that, he strolls off into the night, allegedly to search for his dog again.

"Nicolai, man in car not cop," he says when he returns to the van. "I think he is also after Merriweather, but he is amateur."

"Boss, good, let him do job. We collect money from Halstead."

"You're really stupid sometimes, you know that, Nicolai? I said he is amateur, not professional like us. He leave body, make big mess. Newspapers make big deal about murdered doctor. Eventually, heat comes down on us or our associates."

Nicolai looks at him. "So what do we do with amateur?"

****

From his vantage point, William Bellaire can see Merriweather moving about the kitchen. The doctor smiles as he picks up his cell phone off the counter and begins talking to someone.

"Piece of shit," Bellaire mutters, his face growing hot. "Probably talking to Heather."

A few minutes later, Merriweather ends the call, then moves out of view. *He'll be out in a minute*, William thinks; around this time each night, the doctor has been coming out to feed some feral cats and a flock of peacocks that were known to roam South Florida neighborhoods. But ten minutes pass with no sign of him.

Suddenly, the lights in the house begin to turn off. "Sonofabitch."

William starts his car and pulls away, thinking he will head back to the room he rented in Coconut Grove, watch some TV, and pass out. Maybe tomorrow will be more productive.

As he pulls into his small driveway, he is momentarily blinded by high—beams in his rearview mirror. He turns around, and just as he gets a glimpse of a white van, the car's front doors whip open, and William is pulled kicking and screaming from the front seat. He opens his mouth in protest, but before he can utter a word, he feels something being forced deep into his mouth. No matter how he struggles, it is useless against the much bigger and stronger Nicolai, who is holding him from behind. William tries to focus on a blurry shape moving in front of him. It's the man who'd lost his golden retriever. Sonofabitch.

It's the last thought William Bellaire has before Nicolai expertly snaps his neck, severing his spinal cord just above the third vertebrae.

Still holding the body, Nicolai waits for Dimitri to grab Bellaire's keys from his pocket. When Dimitri opens the door to the rental home, the two men carry the body inside. The place consists entirely of two small, cramped rooms; it was probably once a servant's home.

The two men lay the body on the bed, then slip back outside. Neither speak as they get in the van and head back to Miami Beach. As planned, they had committed a murder tonight.

Unfortunately, it wasn't the one that will get them paid.

CHAPTER 21
Trouble on the Water

"Hey, Dad!" Ryan Merriweather calls out as he pulls into the driveway.

Robert, who is already loading the diving gear into the silver mini-van, turns to his youngest son in mock surprise. "Six on the dot—you must really be looking forward to this trip."

Ryan's handsome face splits into a grin. "I know, I'm not usually the most punctual guy in the world, but c'mon, Dad, you see this weather? It's perfect!"

Robert can't suppress a grin. Although a grown man in his late twenties, Ryan was always like a kid at Christmas when they went fishing. For Robert, it was like getting to experience some of what he had missed out on since the divorce.

"Good, so let's get this stuff loaded and hit the road." He gestures toward the open rear hatchback door. "We'll need four scuba tanks, our spear guns, and some rods and reels."

Ryan slides out of his car and clicks the doors locked. "Okay, Dad, but I also want the lion fish lance. Maybe I can reduce the number of those damned invaders from the Pacific."

Robert points vaguely at the garage. "It's right over there. We'll also need two baitfish rods, two yellowtail rods, and two husky rods for the bigger snapper. Oh, and bring the Big Kahuna rod in case we get ambitious and try for a goliath grouper. It's loaded with a two-hundred-fifty-pound test line."

The two work quickly, not wanting to waste a precious moment. Twenty minutes later, the silver minivan is headed south on US-1, the only road through the Florida Keys.

"Hope you're still working out," Robert jokes as he places a hand on his son's muscular bicep. "I'm going to need your strength to bring in the anchor."

"Yeah, the usual routine."

"How much are you benching these days?"

"I'm up to three-sixty," Ryan says, unable to hide the note of pride in his voice.

Robert laughs. "Ouch, that hurts me just thinking about it."

As always, he is impressed by his son's dedication. After winning the weightlifting contest six years earlier, Ryan had talked about going professional. Robert never asked him why that particular dream had faded, but clearly Ryan still worked out like he was training for the next big competition.

"Well, I gotta keep my strength up, Dad, so I can spear bigger fish and dive deeper than you."

"Spearing fish and breath-holding dives are not about strength, as you know." Robert gives his son a sideways glance. "You'll have your chance to prove yourself tomorrow."

Ryan chuckles, as he does every time Robert issues a

challenge, then an awkward silence settles over the car. It gives Robert the chance he's been hoping for.

"So, what's new with you?" He glances at Ryan. "Are you seeing anyone special?"

Ryan pauses, as if surprised by the question, then says, "Yeah, Dad, actually I am. Her name is Priscilla and I've been seeing her for a few months."

As Ryan continues telling him about the young woman, it is Robert's turn to be surprised. Most of his conversations with Robbie and Randy had been more work related, but he now allows himself to hope that he's making headway with his youngest son's personal life.

"What about you, Dad? How are things going with you and … is her name Heather?"

Robert turns to him in shock. He had never told his sons or Veronica anything about her. "How did you know about her?"

"Oh, c'mon, Dad. She just happens to be at every event involving you? Every time you get an award?" He looks down at his hands. "We weren't sure until the chair dedication. The way she looks at you.…"

We?

"So, your brothers know too … and your mom?"

"Yes, and you don't have to worry about her, Dad. She's happy for you."

"Oh." Robert hears the disappointment in his voice and immediately tries to compensate for it. "Well, that's very good to hear!" He is quiet for a moment. "Heather is a lovely woman. I am very lucky." As he says the words he realizes, perhaps for the first time, how true they are.

"You sure are," Ryan quips, "She's hot!"

Robert looks at him again, then the two burst out laughing.

A few minutes later, Robert pulls up to the Islamorada Fish Company, an eatery just a few feet from the pristine Gulf of Mexico. Over a feast of shrimp cocktails and cracked conch, the conversation shifts to the recent trial in New York. Seeing Ryan's genuine interest, Robert tells him about his run-ins with Payne and Halstead, leaving out nothing but the strange sketches and the other threats to his life.

"It must be amazing to know your work helps so many people," Ryan says, almost wistful. "I hope someday I can find something I'm that committed to."

"It is an incredible feeling," Robert replies, his fork toying with the last bites of his meal, "and I have no doubt that you will find your own calling." He lifts his eyes to meet his son's. "Just remember not to let … other things … in your life fall by the wayside. You don't always get another chance, understand?"

Ryan gives him an almost sympathetic smile. "I do understand, Dad, and I'm really glad you could get away for this trip."

"Me too," Robert says quietly, not quite trusting his voice.

By the time they get back in the car, the sun is just beginning to set. The two fall silent as they approach the tall bridge, beyond which are what is referred to as the middle and lower keys, just taking in the beauty. The view works like a balm on Robert, melting away the stress from his shoulders and neck. After the months of juggling trial prep, patients and death threats—not to mention grieving his friend's murder—he hadn't realized just how bad he needed a break. He'd only told a few key people at the hospital where he was going, with instructions not to bother him unless it's an emergency. *It's nice*, he thinks as he pulls up to his Marathon Key condo, *to be flying under the radar for a change.*

****

Already in Key West, Dimitri Petrakov and Nicolai sit across the table from each other in Sloppy Joe's bar from the old days of Ernest Hemingway, a bottle of vodka between them. Dimitri feels Nicolai's eyes studying him, as he always does when he's confused about something. Lately, Nicolai has been even more confused than usual.

"What?" Dimitri snaps as he whips his head up.

"Boss, why we in Key West?"

"We know they go fishing tomorrow. We take special boat. Doctor will go fishing early. We be ready to follow."

****

By 7:00 the next morning, Ryan and Robert arrive at Murray's Marina, rested from the kind of sleep one only gets when near the ocean. They head right for the fuel dock and, as the forklift operator promised Ryan when he called the day before, find their boat, the Fish R Nervous, in the water and ready to go. *Best money I ever spent*, Robert thinks as he looks at the lovely vessel, a twenty-seven-foot, twin-hulled sea cat powered by twin one-hundred-seventy five horsepower Evinrude outboards.

Despite the early hour, the sun is strong and Ryan runs a hand across his forehead as he loads the boat. Once that's done, he buys the necessary bait for hook-and-line wreck fishing: shrimp, frozen thread fin herring, frozen squid, and, most importantly, the seven-pound blocks of frozen fish parts and fish oil known as chum. In the meantime, Robert hooks up the GPS navigational box and depth finder, then tops off the fuel tanks in preparation for the forty-five-mile run into the Gulf of Mexico. Both work quickly and efficiently in their respective tasks, a routine perfected over their many trips together. Their preparations complete, they climb aboard, with Robert positioned at the boat's center console, the steering wheel, with its adjacent twin throttles, at his front right and the padded live well that would house the bait fish at his back. He slowly motors out of the canal connecting the marina to Boca Chica Bay, creating no wake in observance of manatee protection. As soon as the boat has cleared the restricted area, he moves full speed to the middle of the bay.

"Dad, let's anchor in an area of maximum turtle grass. That's where we will catch the most pin fish."

Robert nods, smiling again at his son's boyish exuberance.

"Good idea, Rye."

Pin fish are considered the ideal live bait for mangrove and mutton snapper fishing. It doesn't take the pair very long to catch forty pin fish between three and eight inches long; then they head out at full speed to the Tango Wreck.

As they pass the last marker of the Calda Channel and

head into the open waters of the Gulf of Mexico, Robert and Ryan are delighted to find the seas flat calm. Cruising at a steady thirty-five miles per hour, they make a beeline for the Tango, a rarely-fished wreck lying in eighty feet of water and home to a variety of big game fish.

As he follows the course set by the GPS, Robert briefly turns his head toward the stern to be sure Ryan is getting the rods and reels ready. He doesn't notice the boat following on the same course far in the distance.

An hour and a half into their trip, Robert lifts his head from the GPS screen.

"Ryan, less than a mile to go. Get out the cinder block and buoy marker." At his son's nod, he adds, "Remember, throw it over on my mark. We'll try to place it on the down current side of the wreck."

As Ryan moves toward the cinder block, Robert looks down at the depth finder screen. When he sees the red-or-ange color indicating the exact location of the wreck, he begins to slow the boat.

"Okay, here is it," he says excitedly, "a great mark! Drop it now."

Ryan throws the cinder block tied to ninety-foot of rope over the stern.

Dr. Merriweather swings the boat around, letting the cinder block hit the bottom and the white Styrofoam ball tied to the end of the rope settle in the current.

"Remember our plan, Dad."

"I remember, and judging by this current, looks like we're gonna do some fishing first."

As always, whether they dove or fished first depended on the current and the tide. Now, as they observe a modest current and with slack tide predicted in three hours, fishing makes much more sense.

Robert positions the boat up-current from their buoy marker, leaving the motor idling while Ryan drops the anchor and ties it off. Ryan then moves to the boat's stern and, sandwiching himself between the two outboards, loads a block of chum into a meshed bag, ties it to the very edge of the stern, and throws it into the water. It will thaw out and float over the wreck, luring the hungry fish toward the surface.

"Hey, Dad, looks like we got company."

Robert looks up to see a sleek thirty-footer with a single V-shaped hull and three two-hundred horsepower outboards heading toward them. A moment later, the boat pulls alongside their starboard side. Robert and his son exchange amused glances as they take in the two men on board, for it looks like the last place they belong is on a boat. Both are dressed all in black, with a fair amount of gold adorning their necks, wrists and fingers.

"Ahoy there, friend," says the shorter man with a thick mop of hair and an even thicker Russian accent. "We lost, GPS broken."

I'll say you're lost, Robert thinks. "Where you headed?"

"Need to find way to Key West." This, from the boat's driver as he ties up to one of the starboard cleats on the Fish R Nervous.

"I see you have a compass," Robert replies. "I can give you a compass bearing straight to Key West."

"Oh, you are too kind," the passenger says with a humble nod of his head.

"Of course." Robert turns to his GPS and begins programming it for the mouth of the Key West northwest channel.

"Dad—look out!"

He whips toward the stern to find Ryan in the grips of the other boat's passenger. The Russian had clearly assessed Ryan's strength and had come up behind him to immobilize his arms.

"What the—?"

Robert takes a step toward the passenger only to hear the unmistakable click of a gun.

"I wouldn't do that, Dr. Merriweather," the man says as he boards the Fish R Nervous, a 9mm Glock in his meaty hand.

We're being robbed, Robert thinks as he slowly raises his hands to indicate he will not put up a fight.

To his surprise, the man just laughs. "Doctor, you come here to catch the fish. We make it so you feed the fish."

In spite of the heat, Robert feels an icy chill run up his spine. So, it was finally happening. For months he had dismissed the threats, the warnings of the police, and the concerns of Heather and Isabella, only to meet his end in the middle of the Gulf of Mexico. He might have been able to accept this, had his naiveté not put his own son in danger.

Ryan struggles against his captor, but he might as well be bound by steel cords for all the good it does. It's the Russian's mocking laughter, though, that sends Ryan's foot smashing down on Nicolai's leather boot. Ryan feels the grip tighten, then smells Nicolai's stale breath as he growls, "You can die with pain or without. Piss off Nicolai and there will be pain."

The Russian then lifts his head up and chuckles.

"I like this one, Dimitri. He has—how you say—chutzpah."

"Shut up, Nicholai."

Nicholai averts his eyes, confirming to Robert that the man with the gun is in charge. Clearly he is some sort of hitman, but who had hired him? The only person he can think of was Heather's ex, but would he really go through this kind of trouble to get rid of a romantic rival?

His hands still in the air, he leans back to rest against the steering wheel and dashboard. How would he get out of this? The twin throttles pressed against his backside gives him an idea. Keeping his expression blank, he puts his feet against the live well and pushes upward, throwing the throttles into forward gear. The Fish R Nervous lurches forward, taking the Russians' boat with it.

Robert watches as Dimitri is thrown violently against the front wall of the motor well, then hears the satisfying crack of the thug's ribs breaking. As second later, though, he is shocked to see Dimitri reach for the gun that had fallen into the motor well in front of the starboard motor. But the effort cost him; gasping in pain, he pauses just long enough for Robert to throw the boat back in neutral and grab his spear gun. He steps forward and stabs Dimitri in the left shoulder, right between the deltoid and the pectoral muscles.

"What you do to me!" Dimitri screams in horror as he tries unsuccessfully to move his arm.

Ignoring him, Robert turns toward the stern, the last place Ryan had been before the thrust of the boats threw him and his captor over. Unseen below the surface, Nicholai fights his air hunger and tries to maintain his grip on Ryan, but it is of no avail. The advantage has now shifted to Ryan, an accomplished free diver capable of holding his breath for more than two minutes. Nicholai loosens his hold and, while Ryan calmly kicks to the surface, the non-swimmer thrashes helplessly. His heavy boots now filled with water weigh him down further. He desperately tries to unlace the unwieldy obstacles for his chance to breathe air again. He finally kicks off his boots but is too late. The lack of oxygen and the buildup of carbon dioxide in his brain stem cause him to hallucinate. Then, as the lights go out of his consciousness, one last reflex gasp allows the salt water of the Gulf of Mexico to enter his lungs, ending his panic. On the surface, Robert is gripped with fear when he sees the torrent of bubbles surfacing off the stern.

"Ryan!"

He continues to scan the water, looking for signs of his son, but all he can see are a few diminishing bubbles signifying the end of the struggle below. He feels the panic rising like bile in his throat. Have to do something.

He rips off his shoes and is about to dive in when Ryan's muscular torso breaks through the surface.

"Oh, Ryan, thank God!"

Ryan manages a smile. "C'mon, Dad," he gasps, "Did that guy look like he could hold his breath very long?" Just then, he notices the spear gun in his father's hand and hears moaning coming from the deck.

"I used it on this guy," Robert explains, pointing the gun directly at his would be killer.

Ryan swims back to the boat, then stops and points off the bow on the port side. "Dad, look, the Marine Patrol."

"Great timing," Robert mutters sarcastically, then looks down at Dimitri, who is gripping his useless left arm with his right.

"You broke my shoulder! You doctor, right? Why you no help me?"

Robert shoots him an incredulous look. "Help? You're damn lucky I don't stab you in the other arm. Besides, I didn't break your shoulder—I lacerated the cephalic vein so you wouldn't be able to cause any more trouble. Just keep your right hand on your left shoulder and press down to control the bleeding. You'll be alright."

The Marine Patrol boat, its blue lights flashing, pulls up just as Ryan reaches the top of the dive ladder. Robert rushes to him, but is interrupted by a familiar voice calling his name.

"Dr. Merriweather, are you all right?"

Robert turns and blinks, thinking he must be seeing things.

"Detective Molinaro? Issy? What the hell is going on?"

"Detective, arrest this man!" shouts Petrakov, clutching his shoulder. "He tried to kill me!"

Molinaro jumps into Dr. Merriweather's boat and pulls the Russian up by the arm, ignoring Petrakov's grunt of pain as he roughly cuffs his hands behind his back.

"Very funny, Dimitri. Dimitri Petrakov, you are under arrest for the murder of North Carolina State Trooper

Johnny Hatfield, the attempted murder of Dr. Robert A. Merriweather, and, for good measure, identity theft. You have the right to remain silent and I hope you do. You have a right to an attorney. If you can't afford an attorney, one will be provided for you. Do you understand?"

"Da, da, I understand," Dimitri whines, "but, please, someone help me." He jerks his head toward Robert. "Not him, a real doctor."

Robert gives him a pointed look, then ties a clean boat towel around Petrakov's shoulder to stop the bleeding.

"Where's his bodyguard?" Molinaro jerks his head toward Dimitri. "He never goes anywhere without him."

"Oh, you mean Nicholai?" Ryan quips. "Probably floating down current."

Molinaro raises an eyebrow at Robert. "Tough kid."

"Sure is," Robert says, trying to control his voice as he wraps both arms around Ryan. "And he gave me quite a scare today."

The four of them watch as the officers of the Marine Patrol load the still complaining Petrakov into their boat, then motor off to pick up Nicolai's body.

"Detective," Robert asks, "how did you know we were out here?"

"Well, Dr. Merriweather, we followed Petrakov, who was following you."

"But how did you know he was following me, and that he was planning to kill us?"

"Believe it or not, identity theft. When Rick and I were in New York, we paid a visit to Dimitri's café. While we were there, I took pictures of some stolen credit card numbers. Since it's a federal crime, the FBI had no trouble obtaining a warrant to wiretap his phones. Even though he and the guy who ordered the hit on you mostly used throwaways, there were a couple of calls made to the tapped landline at the Golden Ruble Café. They'll provide enough evidence to convict both of them."

"Who ordered him to kill me?"

"You don't know?" "Well, I have an idea but-"

"It was Barrymore Halstead-"

"Barrymore Halstead!" Robert and Ryan exclaim. Although Ryan hadn't known of the threats, he certainly knew the name of the notoriously slimy attorney his father had faced off with in court.

"Yes. He ordered it a week ago Friday, right after the trial ended. In fact, the federal marshals are probably arresting him this very moment." Molinaro studies Robert for a moment. "Who did you think it was?"

"I thought it was Heather's ex-husband. He is not exactly pleased that we're seeing each other." Suddenly, the full ramification of what had happened hits Robert. "So Petrakov killed Dr. Jacobson by mistake?"

Molinaro shakes his head. "'Fraid not. We've placed Petrakov in New York at the time of the murder, and there is no evidence that Halstead was contemplating the hit back then. I'm afraid Dr. Jacobson's murderer is still out there, and we still believe you were the intended victim. Your girlfriend's ex is at the top of our list for that crime."

Still reeling from all this information, Robert says, "One last question, detective. If you were following Petrakov's boat, why did you get here so late? They could have killed both of us by the time you arrived."

"I'm really sorry about that. On the way out here we came across a vessel in distress. A boat had capsized and the three aboard didn't even have life jackets. We had no other choice but to rescue them and transfer them to another Marine Patrol boat."

"Then how did you find us way out here?" Ryan asks.

Molinaro smiles at Isabella. "You can thank Deputy Ruiz for that."

"Deputy Ruiz?" Robert snorts. "Oh brother!"

She gives him a mock glare. "Listen, Chief, my fast thinking saved you today. A while back, I'd typed your favorite GPS fishing coordinates into your logbooks, and I knew that you were going to the Tango wreck today ... so, I accessed my computer from the on-board computer on this boat, got the coordinates, and here we are."

"Well, I—we—certainly I owe you one."

"Maybe a raise," Isabella mutters slyly.

"You might be right, but for now, maybe you'll settle for dinner." Robert rubs his stomach. "Believe it or not, I am starving."

A few minutes later, the Marine Patrol boat pulls back up alongside them. Nicolai's body lies covered on the deck, while Dimitri Petrakov sits handcuffed to a bench front and center.

Molinaro and Isabella step back aboard the patrol boat, while a few of the federal officers walk across the Fish R Nervous and onto Dimitri's rented vessel.

"Dr. Merriweather, you and Ryan follow us back to Key West. These officers will bring up the rear in Petrakov's boat."

Robert nods, thinking he's never been so anxious to get back to shore. "Okay, but don't outrun us with those big engines. My top speed is only thirty-five knots, you know."

After Ryan brings up the Fish R Nervous' anchor, he and Robert retrieve their buoy marker, and the three vessels set off on the return trip to Key West. There, a police ambulance would be waiting to take Dimitri Petrakov to the hospital emergency room, and Nicolai to the morgue.

They are about two-thirds through their journey when the patrol boat suddenly stops. Robert slows for a moment, then speeds up again when he and Ryan see Molinaro on the deck, frantically waving his hands.

"What's the matter, Detective?" Roberts asks as he pulls alongside them.

"It's Petrakov. He was fine, then all of a sudden he said he's having a hard time breathing. Happened right after we went over another boat's wake. At first we thought he was bullshitting, but now I'm not so sure. Take a look?"

Robert jumps onto the marine patrol boat and sees that Petrakov indeed appears to be in distress. He's gasping for air, with eyes bulging and a mottled discoloration to his skin. Kneeling down, he opens the buttons of the Russian's shirt and puts his ear, first to the right side of the chest above the nipple line, then on the identical spot on the left side.

"Holy shit!" he exclaims, looking up at Molinaro. "He's got a tension pneumothorax!"

"A tension what?"

"Never mind. Just get me a first aid kit—and hurry!"

One of the officers disappears from deck, returning a moment later with a ten-inch metal box, which he tosses to Robert.

"Hope you have a syringe with a needle in here," Robert mutters as he opens the case. Finding one, he removes the syringe and rips the needle off, then begins feeling around Petrakov's ribs. He hears a collective gasp from the crowd as he forcibly jabs the needle between the second and third ribs, then a hissing sound, identical to a tire gauge releasing pressurized air, coming from the Russian's chest. Robert holds the needle in place as he monitors his pulse.

In less than a minute, Petrakov's breathing is not as forced and his color is better.

"His pulse is stronger now," Roberts says, "He should be alright, but I'll have to hold this needle in place the rest of the way and we will need to go slower." The officers nod. "Also, radio ahead for an ambulance with an emergency room doc and for the hospital to plan for a formal chest tube placement. Now let's go."

It's another hour before the boats finally reach Duval Pier. As the now quiet Petrakov is transferred to the waiting ambulance, Robert introduces himself to the emergency room physician.

"This guy seems otherwise healthy, has a minor stab wound to the deltopectoral area and a relieved tension pneumo- thorax. I temporarily alleviated it with an eighteen-gauge needle. So far it has held up, but I don't know for how long."

"Okay," the physician replies, "we'll get a chest tube in him

ASAP." He looks at the armed officers surrounding Petrakov. "Seems he's a dangerous fellow. We'll have the Key West cops accompanying us, making sure he's kept under lock and key. Thanks, Dr. Merriweather."

Had there been more time, Robert would have been tempted to reveal that his patient was a hitman, hired to kill him. The look on the young doctor's face would have been priceless.

A moment later, Robert, Ryan, Isabella and Molinaro watch as the ambulance screeches off, followed by two police cars.

A silence settles over the group as each tries to process all that had just transpired.

Finally, Issy breaks the silence. "That offer for dinner still good? Why don't we meet at the Square Grouper in little Torch Key?"

"Sounds good," Robert says with a nod. "Let's meet at eight." He glances wistfully at the sea. "Petrakov sure ruined a fine day for fishing."

"At least you lived to fish another day," Isabella jokes.

"Okay, eight it is. Oh, and Robert, it will be a working dinner. We still have the matter of Dr. Jacobson's murder to solve," interjects Molinaro.

CHAPTER 22
Closing in on the Murderer

That evening, the exhausted foursome gathers around a table at The Square Grouper. The restaurant, Isabella tells Robert, had been named after the floating bales of marijuana dropped from small airplanes during the heyday of the Florida Drug trade. It's a detail he finds ironic, given their brush with the criminal underworld earlier that day. They toast the capture of Petrakov, and the knowledge that Halstead will soon be trading in his Armani suits and gold cuff links for an orange jumpsuit and iron shackles.

"What was that numo-thor thing that Petrakov had?" asks Molinaro.

"A pneumothorax; it is a true life-threatening emergency. Probably happened after the patrol boat went over the other boat's wake. It must have jostled him and one of the sharp ends of his fractured ribs punctured his left lung." Seeing the detective is genuinely interested, he continues. "The open air sacs then leaked air between the soft lung tissue and the hard, unyielding ribcage. With each breath, more air built up between the lung and bony ribcage, creating greater pressure. The ever-increasing air pressure squeezed his lung ..." Robert squeezes his hand, "... just as you would squeeze a sponge into a little ball, preventing one lung from getting oxygen into the blood. Even worse, the ever-increasing pressure on his left side was pushing his heart into the right side of the chest, constricting the blood flow."

"So his gasping," Molinaro says, truly fascinated, "was because of the lack of oxygen in his blood, yet the gasping was only making it worse!"

"Very good, Detective, you would make a great oral and maxillofacial surgery resident. The needle I put into his chest cavity merely decompressed the air pressure and allowed the left lung to re-inflate and reposition itself so that the heart and its blood vessels would also reposition and begin pumping oxygenated blood throughout his body again."

"So that's what the hissing sound was and why he got better so fast." Molinaro shakes his head. "I'll never forget that sound. It was really something."

"Dad, that bastard tried to kill us," Ryan snapped. "Why didn't you just let him die? He certainly deserves it, after killing that trooper in North Carolina, and that's only one person we know of. It would save us taxpayers the money of a trial and years of paying for his upkeep."

From the corner of his eye, Robert can see Molinaro nodding his head in agreement. "You make a good point, Rye, but as a doctor, I can't think that way."

Ryan opens his mouth to speak but Robert holds up a hand.

"Healthcare is the most unbiased profession in the world. Disease and injury recognize no particular social status, even a criminal one. In the US, it means caring for anyone who truly needs it, no matter who they are and what our politicians say. As far as this Dimitri Petrakov is concerned, I am happy to leave his judgment to the courts and God."

After a tense moment, Ryan nods unconvincingly.

Isabella delicately clears her throat. "This is a very interesting debate, Chief, but speaking now as a 'deputy' and not as your secretary, we still have the business of Jacobson's murder—and the probable threat to your life—to discuss."

Molinaro takes a sip of his beer. "She is right, Dr. Merriweather. I got a text message from the New York City Crime Lab, and the DNA recovered from the sketch pencil was a match for William Bellaire. What's more, the description given to us by Heather Bellaire fits the description from the nurses and security guards who were there during the operating room break-in. It stands to reason that he's the one who murdered Dr. Jacobson—and that he is still after you. We know he is in the Miami area somewhere, and all units are looking for him, but we need you to be very careful until we get him into custody."

"Well, I hope you find him soon," Robert replies. "It will be nice to remove the target from my back ..." He gives a pointed look at Isabella, "and for you to remove your deputy's badge."

She looks at him with genuine annoyance. "No more jokes, Robert, not after today."

****

The following week begins as any other, with Monday morning grand rounds followed by an afternoon surgery, and an all-day clinic on Tuesday. By Wednesday morning, Robert has almost convinced himself that normal life has resumed.

He is just finishing up a procedure when the phone in operating room 2 rings loudly. The circulating nurse answers it, then a moment later, Isabella's voice comes over the intercom. "Dr. Merriweather, I hate to disturb you in the OR, but I have Diana on the line and she says it is very important. Can I put her through?"

"Yes, I was about to scrub out anyway. Hello, Diana, can you hear me?"

"I can hear you fine, but please take me off the speaker phone. I don't want anybody else to hear this."

Robert thinks this is a bit odd, but presses the button on the phone.

"Okay, the speaker phone is off. What's up?"

"I think I found the murder weapon."

"You did? Are you kidding me?"

"No, I have it here."

"Where is here?"

"Right here, where I am calling you from, my house."

"Diana, you're not making any sense. Where did you find it?"

"That's it, I really don't remember. I must have found it in the clinic yesterday when we were all rushing about and I was cleaning out the storage closet." She laughs weakly. "I am eighty-five years old, you know."

"Diana, is it by any chance a bookend?"

"Not so loud, Robert! The others in the operating room will hear you."

Robert holds the phone from his ear in surprise, wondering

at her odd behavior.

"Okay, okay, I'll call the detective running the investigation. He will want to have tests run on it. Whatever you do, Diana, don't touch it anymore. It's critical evidence."

His head spinning from the new revelation, Robert rushes out of the operating room to speak to Mr. and Mrs. Charles, whose son he had just operated on. At least he has good news for them—the tumor had been benign and the surgical margins clear. After telling the relieved parents they can see him in a few minutes, he rushes to his clinic. He finds Isabella at her desk, an extra large latte in her hand.

"Issy, did Diana tell you that she thinks she found the murder weapon?"

"Yes—the bookend—isn't that great news? Now if the DNA just matches Bellaire's, we'll finally be able to wrap up this case!"

Robert raises his eyebrow at her. "Issy, you're sounding more like a detective than a secretary—but that's a conversation for another day. Right now, I want to know how the hell Diana found it after everyone—trained professionals—went over this place with a fine-toothed comb. It's not like it's a small item—in fact, it's damn heavy."

"Don't underestimate Diana. She has been here longer than any of us and knows all the nooks and crannies, not only in this clinic, but in the entire building.

"I guess so. Did you get a hold of Molinaro?"

"Yes, but he's down in Key West, checking on Petrakov and hoping to record his statement. When he gets back tomorrow he'll pick me up and we'll go straight to Diana's. She has invited us—and you—for dinner. Can you come?"

"You bet. Just give me a call when he picks you up."

Back in his office, Dr. Merriweather begins sifting through the usual flood of emails. Some pertain to university business, while others concern upcoming courses and cis-phosphorous trial dates; most, however, are from fellow oral and maxillofacial surgeons asking his opinion about their own cases. He has just begun reviewing the detailed history of one such patient when Dr. Glanville peeks his head through the doorway. The normally serious young man looks almost giddy.

"The microscopic histology and chemical tests on the rat brains and jaws are back."

"Great. Where are they?"

"They're in the residents' room. I just now picked them up from pathology."

"Get the photographs we took of the specimens and take my microscope to the conference room—we'll look at all the data there. Just give me fifteen minutes and I'll join you."

Dr. Merriweather finishes reading his colleague's description of the patient, then reviews the images on the disc that had been included with the file. He quickly writes his opinion about the diagnosis and suggests two treatment options, then gives it to Isabella to type and send.

He is just about to go meet Glanville when her cell phone rings. A smile spreads over her face when she sees the caller ID.

Molinaro, he tells himself, still striding toward the door.

"What?" she gasps, then motions for Robert to wait.

"It's Andy. He just got some news about William Bellaire. Here, talk to him."

Robert takes the phone from her outstretched hand. "Detective?"

"Dr. Merriweather, I just got off the phone with the Coconut Grove police. They found William Bellaire with his neck broken. He's been murdered."

"What! Are you sure it's him? Why would anyone want to kill him?"

"I don't know, but they're sure it's him and they're sure it wasn't a robbery—still had his IDs and his money. Looks like a professional job, though, whoever it was broke into his place and waited there for him. I still think he's Dr. Jacobson's killer, but clearly there is something more complicated going on here. Anyway, I gotta run, but we'll talk more when I get back from Key West tomorrow. Tell Issy I'll call her later."

Robert nods his head blankly, then realizes that Molinaro can't see him. "Yes, of course. Thanks for calling, Detective."

He then hands the phone back to Isabella. "He said he'll call you later."

"Crazy stuff, right?" she says, looking as surprised as he is.

He nods again. "You can say that again."

He is still turning over this latest revelation in his mind as he walks down the hall. Poor Heather. She had wanted to be free of her ex-husband, but not this way. The worst part would be breaking the news to her kids. He pulls his phone out and sends her a quick text, telling her to call when she can. Then, after a few quick breaths to clear his mind, he walks through the conference room door.

After taking some time to review the info, Robert says, "Okay, James, let's get this organized. We'll put the microscopic slides together with each preserved brain specimen. I see you put down the waterproof tarp on the floor and the table top—good thinking. Did you get some scissors and scalpel blades?"

"I sure did, Dr. Merriweather. Not only that, I got the research logbook with the code numbers correlating the microscopic specimens to the preserved brain and spinal cord specimens. When we break the code, the book will be able to correlate whether each specimen is from a cis-phosphorous-treated rat or a placebo-treated rat."

"Great, James. You know, this is the grunt work of research, but contrary to what some would have you believe, it's also the critical part. It's what all the greats did—Pasteur, Koch, Pavlov, to name a few. Like them, we will analyze and make detailed notes of our observations before we break the code and find out which rat got what." He claps his hands. "Okay, let's do it."

Ten hours later, Robert looks at the clock and lets out a weary sigh.

"James, its 2 a.m., and I'm beat. I suspect you are too."

In reply, Glanville nods and stretches his arms above his head.

"I think we should call it a night," Robert continues. "We don't want to make mistakes due to fatigue, not to mention the fact that we have to be in surgery in six hours." He looks down at the specimens. "I think we're on to something here, but as much as I would like to keep going, I think we should get a good night's sleep and come back to break the code tomorrow."

Robert half expects James to argue the point, but he yawns instead. "Makes sense, Dr. Merriweather."

A few hours later, the two men are back at the hospital, this time scrubbing up for a long and involved surgery on sixty-two-year-old John Baker. Six years earlier, he was diagnosed with cancer at the base of his tongue. He was successfully treated with radiation therapy; unfortunately, the same radiation slowly killed part of his left lower jaw. It was now fractured with bone sticking into his mouth and through the skin of his neck. It also caused the skin of his neck and soft tissues in the mouth to become hard and unable to be stretched, like a scar. After the initial consult, Robert indicated that the procedure would end his pain, straighten out his jaw and help him to eat again.

It has been a long road to get to this point, however. First, Baker had to undergo thirty hyperbaric oxygen treatments to improve the healing abilities of the tissues damaged by the radiation, followed by laboratory blood tests, EKG heart tracing and chest x-rays, not to mention the seemingly endless red tape to get insurance approval.

"You're in the home stretch now," Robert tells him just before he's to go under anesthesia. "I know it's been hard on you."

Mr. Baker smiles gratefully. "You know, that hyperbaric oxygen stuff was actually pleasant. All I had to do was breathe oxygen in that submarine thing." Robert smiles; it's not the first time he's heard a patient refer to the hyperbaric oxygen chamber this way. "Met some nice people there—most of them had radiation problems too. 'Course some had foot and leg ulcers from diabetes. Anyway, I sure hope it worked for me."

"I am sure it did, Mr. Walker, but remember, it doesn't bring dead bone back to life. Hyperbaric oxygen only allows us to remove the dead bone and get your tissues to heal. Today, we will do that and replace your damaged skin with a patch of skin from your thigh. It will be hooked up to blood vessels in your neck to keep it alive and heal into you. The bone we remove will be replaced later; for today, we're going to replace it with a strong titanium plate that will act as an artificial jaw."

"Doc, it sounds complicated. Just fix me up. I got songs to sing, wine to drink, and women to chase."

Robert laughs. "I like your attitude, Mr. Walker, just don't tell Mrs. Walker about the last part." He places a hand on the man's shoulder. "I'll see you when you wake up."

Thirty minutes later, the surgery begins, with Drs. Merriweather and Glanville operating at the jaw level and Dr. Torborg, the microvascular surgeon, teamed up with Dr. Melissa Sanders at the leg. As Robert and Glanville work to remove the six inches of dead jawbone and some of the badly damaged skin, Drs. Torborg and Sanders are painstakingly dissecting out the correct blood vessels that will nourish the skin once it is transferred up to the neck area.

The surgery proceeds smoothly for several hours. Once the dead jawbone segment has been removed and the feeding blood vessels in the neck have been isolated for Dr. Torborg, the two teams switch places. Now, Torborg and Sanders, working under the operating microscope, suture the artery from the patch of thick skin from the leg to an artery in the neck that Merriweather and Glanville had prepared. This would supply blood-flow into the skin patch, also referred to as the skin paddle. Torborg and Sanders would also have to suture the draining vein from the skin paddle to a vein in the neck. The oxygen-rich blood from the arteries would keep nutrients flowing into the skin paddle, while the hooked-up veins would drain the oxygen and nutrient-depleted blood, just like normal skin. In the meantime, Drs. Merriweather and Glanville suture the thigh area, where the skin paddle was taken. Midway through the suturing, the phone in OR 8 rings, as it often does throughout a long surgery. The circulating nurse hurries to answer it.

"Dr. Merriweather, Isabella is on the phone and needs to talk to you."

Robert nods, then asks that she be put on speakerphone.

"Issy, what is it? I am almost through with my part. I'll see you back at the clinic in about twenty minutes."

"Okay, but I just couldn't wait to give you the good news. The case has been solved!"

"Wow, that is good news. I'll get the details from you after I finish here."

Robert brings his full concentration back to the work in front of him, but after the successful completion of the surgery he finds himself anxious to get back to the office. He forces Issy's phone call to the back of his mind long enough to give Mrs. Walker a progress report, then he's hurrying once again down the hall.

"Okay, I'm here," he says, plopping down in the chair next to Isabella's desk. "Tell me everything."

"Heather's husband was the murderer," she announces, spinning her own chair to face him, "and he was obviously after you. Andy ran his prints against those the CSI team lifted from this office, and they found a match. They couldn't match him before because he'd never been fingerprinted. Guess he never served in the military or had a government job and, as hard as it is to believe, he'd never been arrested." Isabella smiles slyly. "And now you're going to be proud of me."

"I am, what for? It sounds like Molinaro did all the work."

She narrows her eyes at him. "Simple. I took off my 'executive secretary hat' and put on my 'Detective Ruiz' hat. Turns out, Bellaire has actually been a patient here. He saw Dr. Zita in general dentistry back in January, a few days before your Chair Dedication Ceremony. According to our records, Dr. Zita did a single filling for him. Because Dr. Zita is here so rarely and does most of her teaching at our downtown clinic, nobody remembered him. Anyway, I called her and guess what?"

Robert crosses his arms in front of him. "I can't begin to imagine."

"She remembered him because he was weird, and because he asked about you several times. So many times that she brought him to your office and showed him all your awards. She also remembered that he insisted on wearing his baseball jacket and cap while she was working in his mouth. A red Philadelphia Phillies jacket and cap, just like the one they found on his body the other day. Probably the same clothes he wore when he broke into the OR a while back. Remember, the security guards and nurses all said the intruder was wearing a red baseball cap and red jacket."

"Issy, you are a real detective. Bellaire was a sad case to be sure." Isabella goes to argue, but he holds up a hand. "Now, I know he was a criminal, but Heather said he wasn't always bad. He just let jealously and obsession take him over. Of course, the real tragedy is Dr. Jacobson, he just was in the wrong place at the wrong time." Robert sighs as the full import of the events of the past few months hit him. "Wow, between Petrakov and William Bellaire, I dodged the bullet twice. I'm relieved that it's over, but I can't help feeling guilty. Dr. Jacobson died because of me."

Isabella pats him on the arm. "I know it's awful, but you can't go beating yourself up about it. Bellaire was insane." She pauses a beat. "There's more news too."

"Wow! It sounds like the Detective Ruiz hat is starting to fit better than the executive secretary hat."

"Do you want to hear the news or not?"

"Of course I do."

"It appears that Petrakov and his bodyguard were the ones that killed William Bellaire. Andy said the Coconut Grove Police matched their shoes and boots to the prints found in the mud outside the place Bellaire was renting there. That Nicolai guy that Ryan drowned was probably the one that broke his neck. You know he was a former KGB agent before Petrakov brought him to the US?"

"Hmm," Robert says thoughtfully. Something is gnawing at him. "But Issy, why would Petrakov even know who Bellaire is, let alone want him dead?"

"You're right! After all, they were both trying to put you in a body bag."

Robert raises an eyebrow at her. "Jeez, you're really starting to talk like a cop. But seriously, it doesn't make sense."

Isabella shrugs. "Maybe Petrakov didn't want Bellaire getting a piece of his action. I mean, Halstead must have been paying him a pretty penny to kill you."

"That does make sense," Robert agrees. "I guess they must have crossed paths somehow." He stands up. "Now that this nightmare is over, I need you to put your executive secretary hat back on and get to work. When Glanville gets back from the recovery room, we're going to get to work on our research project and forget about all of this. First, though, I am going to call Dr. Jacobson's family and let them know we found his killer."

"Got it, boss." Isabella puts her hands to her head and pushes upward, as if removing an imaginary hat. "But don't forget, seven o'clock tonight we're going to Diana and Norman's for dinner. Andy is still hoping to find Bellaire's fingerprints or DNA on the bookend she found. That would really put the icing on the cake, wouldn't it?"

Robert shakes his head. "As much as I hate to do it, I'm going to have to take a raincheck on that little celebration. Glanville and I are finding some interesting things in the rat study and we need to finish what we started. Please give my regrets to Diana and my usual salute to Norman. He loves it when I mention his WWII service. Oh, and be sure to bring him a cigar." Robert pauses. "And Issy, thanks for helping to put this craziness to bed. I feel like things are finally going to return to normal."

CHAPTER 23
Tying Up Loose Ends

Robert glances at the clock on the conference room wall. Seven o'clock. He should be at the Edelsons' right now, sitting down to one of Diana's delicious dinners. He can't bring himself to be too disappointed, though, given the excellent progress he and Dr. Glanville have made. They have worked through more than eighty percent of the specimens, and their notebook is filled with detailed observations regarding the appearance of brain tissue and how it correlates to the microscopic slides.

"James, hold up a minute. Are you getting the picture I'm getting?"

"I think so. There seems to be an even split between normal rat brains and those that have been destroyed or at least severely affected. Also, only one part of the abnormal brains seems to have been affected."

Robert looks up at him. "Exactly. Even though it deviates from the original protocol, we need to break the code now. If all the abnormal brains are in the cis-phosphorous group, we have found something significant and worrisome."

"Alright, Dr. Merriweather. I'll open the codebook and read the numbers and the treatment each rat received. You can match them to the specimens."

Fifteen minutes later, the specimens and treatments of each rat have been matched.

Robert smacks a hand on the table. "James, that's it! It is a perfect fit. All of the abnormal brains come from rats we gave the cis-phosphorous drug to. All the rats that received the placebo are normal. Do you know what this means?"

Glanville rubs his eye. "Not exactly, Dr. Merriweather, but I don't like that worried expression."

"I am worried."

"It means cis-phosphorous drugs cross the blood-brain barrier. Of course! I should have expected it. Cis-phosphorous drugs are small molecules. This isn't rabies or mad cow disease. The cis-phosphorous drugs are killing certain brain cells, just like they kill bone osteoclasts."

Glanville shakes his head. "Dr. Merriweather, how could you have known? There is nothing in the product handouts from either North Star or Apollo about neurologic or brain effects. They didn't even know that their drugs crossed into the brain!"

"Well, we shouldn't be surprised. They either never thought to look at the neurologic system in their animal studies, just like they didn't look into the mouth in the human trials, or they covered it up. Both are consistent with what I have learned about them from all these trials."

"What do you make of these consistent locations of brain damage in the cis-phosphorous group?"

"Not quite sure yet. I'm not as good with rat brains as I am with humans. Let's look at these areas under magnification."

The two surgeons put on their operating glasses with 4x magnifying lenses. Also known as loops, these lenses are the same ones they had used earlier that day to isolate small blood vessels for the microvascular flap during Mr. Baker's surgery.

"James, do you recognize the general shape of the damaged area?"

"Yeah, it sort of looks like a tonsil."

"Exactly, it's the amygdala, which is Latin for tonsil, and the other damaged area next to it is the hippocampus. Together they make up the limbic lobes, and they were first described by the French anatomist Broca in the late 1800s. The limbic lobes control our emotions and behavior—in fact, they are known as the 'seat of human emotion.' With these areas damaged, it makes sense that the rats went berserk."

"But how can we prove that the cis-phosphorous drugs actually caused the damage? You know the drug companies and their paid consultants will deny it and criticize us, as they always do."

"I don't care about the criticism, James, but we can directly answer that. What did you notice about the brain cells that were not yet dead but were in the process of dying?"

"The cells were swollen and their nucleus was fragmented, spilling chromosome particles into the cytoplasm." James pauses a moment. "Yes! They look just like the dying osteoclasts in the bones affected by cis-phosphorous drugs."

"You got it, James. We can prove it with the chemical testing results by comparing the amounts of cis-phosphorous drug in the damaged tissue to normal brain tissue using gas-liquid chromatography." Robert sharply inhales. "Wait a minute. If cis-phosphorous drugs affect the limbic lobes in rats, they probably do the same in humans. Didn't Mrs.

Steadman commit suicide, and didn't Mrs. Burnett have a psychiatric breakdown and attack her husband right in front of us?"

"Yes ..." James says slowly, not at all liking where this is going.

"And," Robert continues, "I also remember news reports a while back of older school teachers suddenly going psychotic and killing their students. It was always blamed on their age and stress in the workplace. Even I blamed the actions of our patients on their pain, just as I did the bizarre behavior of the rats. I wonder if these older women were being treated for osteoporosis with Bone Max. Even Diana was acting strangely for a while, and she had only been taking Bone Max for three years. Diana, yes Diana!" Robert suddenly stands up, startling his protégé. "James, cover this stuff up now, I have to call Issy and we need to get over to the Edelsons' right away."

****

"I knew we were going to be late," Isabella says, "but not this late."

"It couldn't be helped, Issy, you know that," Andy replies as he pulls up to the security gate of Diana and Norman Edelson's development.

"It's terrible, though, not even calling."

"You left your cell phone at home. It happens."

After being approved to go in, they continue to the house, where they find Diana waiting for them at the open front door.

"It's seven-forty five," she announces without so much as a hello. "Dinner has been ready for some time."

"We're sorry, Diana, Andy had to file a report at the precinct, and I forgot my cell phone."

Without a word, Diana steps to the side to allow them entry into the house.

"My apologies too, Mrs. Edelson," Molinaro says. "Issy told me you always set a beautiful table, and now I see she was right."

Diana wrinkles her face as if she smells something sour.

"Well you can enjoy it over an over-cooked dinner, Detective."

Startled by the normally gracious woman's cold response, Isabella tries to change the subject. "Where is Norman? Dr. Merriweather asked me to give him this cigar." She reaches into her purse and pulls out the stogie. "It's a Dominican, one of your husband's favorites."

"Oh, he's still upstairs, probably looking up World War II tales on the computer with no regard to the hour. I just hate it when people are late. He should be coming down the elevator in his wheelchair any moment now."

****

"Dr. Merriweather," James Glanville asks, his hand gripping the door handle, "why are you driving so fast?"

"It's a long story, James, but I think Issy is in terrible danger and she's not answering her cell phone."

"Danger? At the Edelsons'?"

"Yes. The police think that Heather's ex-husband killed Dr. Jacobson because he was stalking me and his prints were found in my office, but I now have a different theory."

****

"Well, while we're waiting for Norman, perhaps you could show us the bookend you found. Andy would like to have it sent to the lab for prints and DNA. If they find a DNA link to Dr. Jacobson, it will prove it's the murder weapon. We're also hoping to get some of William Bellaire's DNA off it as well. That would close the case."

"Of course, Detective," Diana says, a little more cordially. She crosses the room to an étagère, where, on the top shelf, sits one of the heavy bookends from Robert's office. Cradling it in both hands, she has a strange, almost proud expression as she walks back over to Andy.

"You didn't believe that I really found the murder weapon, did you, Detective?"

Andy smiles. "Of course I believed it, and here it is. What I don't understand is where you found it. We thoroughly searched Dr. Merriweather's office and the surrounding area."

Diana's mouth is a straight, grim line. "So many questions. It's almost like you don't believe I'm telling the truth. Very upsetting." Her long bony fingers reach out to the bookend. "Now, give it back to me. It's mine."

Molinaro stares at his hostess for a moment. Isabella had

never mentioned how strange she was. Not wanting to provoke her further, he hands her the bookend. As Diana heads to put it back on the étagère, Andy hears Isabella call out.

"Andy, Andy, there's blood coming from underneath this door!"

He turns to see her standing by the door to the elevator and rushes over.

"I pressed the button," she says frantically, "but it's not opening."

"I might be able to get it open," he says, placing his hands on the left side of the door and pulling with all his strength toward the right. Slowly, the door slides open.

The first thing they see is the blood. It is splattered all over the walls like crimson paint.

"What the—oh my God!" Isabella shrieks.

"What the-" Andy rushes into the elevator, where the lifeless body of Norman Edelson is slumped over in his wheelchair. The back of his head has been smashed in.

Andy reaches over to check Norman's pulse when he sees the blood on his own hands.

He shoots Isabella an incredulous look, then examines his palms again. "Where the hell did this come from? I haven't touched anything ... oh my God, the bookend!"

"Look out!" Isabella screams.

Andy turns around to see Diana rushing toward him with a wild expression and the bookend in her right hand.

Before he has time to react, Isabella steps forward and

pushes Diana roughly to the ground. Most women her age would have been hurt, perhaps even knocked unconscious, by such a fall, but Diana seems barely fazed by it.

"What gives you the right to snoop around my house," she screams, legs and arms flailing as she gets up. "You have no right. NO RIGHT!"

As Andy moves swiftly to restrain her, Isabella looks down in shock.

"Diana, what did you do?"

"I had to do it. Norman was asking too many questions too. He was late and he shouldn't have been at his computer desk when we are expecting company. He is just like Dr. Jacobson, staring at some dumb computer screen. Don't you know about all the brainwashing those computer games do? In my day—" Diana cuts herself off with a gasp. "Oh, Robert, thank God you're here!"

Isabella and Andy turn to see Robert walk in the front door, followed by a stunned James Glanville.

"Diana, that's enough. Just calm down." Robert slowly takes in the bloody scene in front of him. "I drove as fast as I could, but I guess we're a little late."

Robert gestures to Andy to release her, then he slowly approaches Diana and envelopes her in an affectionate but firm embrace.

"You'll be okay," he says soothingly as Diana melts into his arms. "Detective, we need to get her to the psych unit, but I'm asking out of respect for her and Norman that you let me, Issy and James do it. She doesn't need the indignity of handcuffs and a police car."

Andy shakes his head. "Dr. Merriweather, that is highly unorthodox, this woman is a murder-"

"I know what she did," Robert says, "but believe it or not, she is a victim too. So, please."

Andy waits a minute, then reluctantly nods.

"Thank you. Now can you please help James get her to my car? I'll be there in a second." Molinaro and Dr. Glanville each gently take one of her arms and escort her out the door.

Only Isabella stays behind. "You knew?" she asks, clearly shocked, "But how?"

"Our rat study, believe it or not. Dr. Glanville and I realized that cis-phosphorous drugs were inducing a psychotic rage in them, as well as in some of our patients. The drugs ruined the part of the brain that controls emotions, and gave them several times their normal strength. That's how Diana was able to attack Dr. Jacobson."

He walks over to the elevator and kneels down in front of Norman. "I'm so sorry, old friend," he says, then gives the fallen soldier one last salute before following Isabella to the door.

CHAPTER 24
The Aftermath

"Heather, it's so good of you to come down here and make the funeral arrangements for your ex-husband." Isabella places a sympathetic hand on Heather's. "I guess he had no one else, no family other than you and the boys?"

It's Saturday night and the two couples are seated at a quiet corner table at Vialetto's, having a meal to celebrate the end of the recent traumatic events, as well as to honor their victims.

"I am afraid not. His father is still alive, but he abandoned William and his mother when William was just a kid. I actually called his dad, though, it seemed the right thing to do. He didn't have much of a reaction. Sad, really. William's whole story is sad. He wasn't always so angry and obsessive." She sighs. "Anyway, I am going to ship his body back to Philadelphia for a brief service, if not for William, then for our sons. He'll be buried in his Philadelphia Phillies jacket and cap he loved so much."

"Did the boys come down here with you?"

"Yes, we are all staying at Bob's house. The boys are out fishing with Ryan down in the Keys."

"Ahh, the resiliency of youth," Molinaro says, shaking his head, unable to believe Ryan returned to the Keys so soon after nearly dying there.

After all that had happened, Ryan had insisted on staying with Robert a few more days, an offer his father had been more than happy to accept. He had even formally introduced him to Heather and her sons, and was thrilled when they immediately hit it off.

"And look what they caught." Holding up his cell phone for all to see, he shows several texted images of the two fifteen-year-olds holding a forty-pound Cobia and standing by an impressive catch of yellowtail and mangrove snappers. A grinning Ryan stands in the background.

Heather, Andy and Isabella ooh and ah appreciatively, then Isabella says, "So, Boss, what are you and Heather going to do now?"

"What do you mean?"

"You know. You two."

"Don't push us, Issy. You know all the research projects I have going, plus the patients, the surgeries, and of course, the residents and fellows. Heather also has a lot going on. Her publishing company is growing and she's at the heart of it." He turns to Heather and smiles as he reaches over to take Heather's hand. "But who knows, the future has a way of taking care of itself."

"I'm sorry, Chief, you know I can't resist." Isabella pauses. "And actually, I was just leading up to us."

"Us who, Issy?"

Isabella and Detective Molinaro look at each other and hesitate.

"That's okay, Andy. It's up to me to tell him anyway."

"Uh, oh! I smell an impending problem. You're not

pregnant, are you? I can't have you off for three months on maternity leave."

"No, no, you doofus, it's not anything like that ... but I will be permanently hanging up my secretary's hat." She looks from Robert to Andy, her eyes glowing. "I've decided to go for my private investigator's license."

For once, Dr. Robert Merriweather is at a loss for words.

Finally, he says, "What, are you two planning on being partners or something?"

"Yes, I mean, no," Molinaro sputters. "What I mean is, some cops retire and go on to be private eyes, so maybe ..." He takes a deep breath. "Now, if you meant partners in a personal sense...."

"It's okay, Andy," Isabella laughs, "They get your drift."

"I don't know, Issy," Roberts says chidingly, "This is the worst possible time for you to do this to me." His face splits into a grin. "All kidding aside, I can see you're passionate about this, and of course, I wish you the best." He looks at Andy. "I also wish the both of you luck, in whatever form your partnership takes."

He raises his glass. "To Detectives Molinaro and Ruiz."

"Let's not jump the gun, Boss," she says, but she's laughing as she raises her glass.

"My loss is your gain, Andy," Robert adds. "You're getting one hell of a great lady."

"No worries, Boss. I'm not leaving you in a lurch. I have already arranged for my replacement."

"Oh brother, I can just imagine. You've probably arranged for some matronly old spinster who's going to bitch at me at every turn."

"No, I know how you hate the human resources department, so I went over their head and hired Mishy for you."

"Your sister, Michele? She's only twenty!"

"Yes, but she types fast, knows computers and PowerPoint better than me. Most importantly, though, she knows all your quirks."

"I don't have any quirks, do I? She's also a hot young chick. The male residents will find every excuse to be in your, I mean, her office every minute. She will never have time to work with me like you do."

"That one you'll have to deal with yourself. As you always say, 'Put on your big boy pants and exercise your Y chromosome.' She starts two weeks from Monday."

Robert shoots Andy a look. "See what you're getting into?"

A round of laughter is interrupted by the waiter, who arrives to serve their food and refill their wine glasses.

As they dig in, Andy says, "Not to put a damper on the mood, but I guess I should update you on a couple of things about our friends Petrakov and Halstead."

Robert swirls some linguini onto his fork. "Shoot."

"Well, Petrakov has recovered well enough to be transferred up here to Miami. He'll likely spend two weeks in the hospital ward in the Everglades Federal Prison. From there we plan to extradite him to Raleigh, North Carolina, where he will stand trial for the murder of the state trooper. I am sure he will be convicted, as the evidence is overwhelming."

"Eye witnesses?" Robert asks.

"No ... well, in a sense. He thought he was smart by

smashing the dashcam on the trooper's car, but he didn't realize that they're now all digital. The memory card was retrieved and it shows the entire murder in graphic detail."

"That's excellent news, Detective."

"Yes. Obviously, the tape was very difficult to watch. It shows him pulling the state trooper's head into the car and shooting him in the head twice. The trooper never had a chance. It seems like a slam-dunk, so I suspect the prosecuting attorneys will go for either life without the possibility of parole or the death penalty. North Carolina doesn't allow much sympathy for remorseless cop killers."

"What about Barrymore Halstead?"

"As you know, Halstead is a real piece of work. He's actually claiming it was his partner, George Payne, that hired Petrakov. And of course, he's hired the best defense attorney his money can buy. Still, they're going to have a tough time selling the Payne nonsense, with the wiretap recordings. His attorneys are trying to get the wiretap evidence thrown out as a violation of his civil rights."

"Do you think their motions will be granted?"

Andy shrugs. "Who knows with our crazy legal system? Motions are hard to predict. Halstead's lawyers will argue that the wiretap was obtained for Petrakov's phone, not Halstead's. On the other hand, the two are clearly conspiring to commit murder … Whether it will hold up is anyone's guess, but at least for now, he is being held without bail at Riker's. I hear he is complaining about the food and his small cell every day. In any event, I'm sure he isn't endearing himself to guards or prisoners." He raises his glass. "I never congratulated you on the North Star victory."

"Sounds good, doesn't it?" Robert replies cynically. "They'll be fined hundreds of millions, and Christiansen will probably be fired by the Board of Trustees. Many of their paid consultants will be discredited, too. But those doctors will just go on to some other company that will fund them to do their research, the answers of which are predetermined by the drug company, and then go on and lecture about the benefits of this 'new-and-improved drug.' It's a real problem in medicine and dentistry today. With cutbacks in medical reimbursements, the medical profession and cash-starved universities are more tempted than ever to accept the rich rewards offered by billion-dollar pharmaceutical giants. Have you heard anything about Apollo Pharmaceuticals? After all, it was their drug Bone Max that caused Diana's psychosis and murder of Dr. Jacobson, not to mention the suicide of one of my patients and several others we have learned that are now suffering from mental deterioration."

"I believe you, Doctor, but so far there's no evidence that Apollo falsified their research like North Star did. In fact, it will be hard to prove that Diana Edelson's psychosis, or even those in your other patients, was actually due to these drugs and not due to aging or Alzheimer's disease, alcoholism, or something else without a biopsy. Your research is the only one that uncovered it. By the way, how is Diana?"

"Surprisingly well, actually. The real difficulty of this drug-induced psychosis is that these women behave normally most of the time, then abruptly go into a psychotic rage. They need to be kept on strict observation and without access to anything that could serve as a weapon. In essence, to protect others and themselves, they have to be confined liked prisoners. Diana is lucid now, but she doesn't even remember the two murders and she doesn't understand why Norman doesn't come to visit her at the mental health institute. What a sad ending for a war hero and a very classy lady who was so important to so many."

Robert finishes the last of his wine. "We have to publish our research results ASAP. The gas chromatography tests that Glanville and I ran showed that the parts of the brain that had deterioration confirmed high levels of Bone Protect, whereas the other parts of the brain showed none. Neither did any other tissues in the rats' bodies, other than the bones. I am positive—although I do not yet know the reason—that these cis-phosphorous drugs target not only the bone, but the two centers of the brain that control emotional behavior and stability. We need to find out why. There's too many postmenopausal women like Diana out there who are taking these meds and—"

Suddenly, Robert stops in mid-sentence. The others follow his gaze to the flat screen television hanging over the bar. Diana Edelson's warm, smiling face stares back at them, next to the words, "Miami Woman Arrested in Big Pharma Slaying." Although they can't hear the newscaster's voice, all four focus their eyes on the close captioning at the bottom of the screen: "… after the arrest of Diana Edelson, a wave of violent crimes committed by older women across the US has come to light. A Minnesota nursing home found that 17 patients were killed in their sleep last night at the hands of a female patient wielding a kitchen knife. Two elderly women kill a bank teller and hold hostages in a Virginia Bank. Negotiators say the women confess that they don't know why they're doing it. A National Organization for Women's rally on the Berkley Campus in California is disrupted when senior members attack security guards. A reunion of former Playboy bunnies at the Playboy Mansion in Geneva, Wisconsin turns violent, leaving several injured and Playboy Enterprise icon Hugh Hefner—in his words—'shaken to the core.' The investigation is ongoing as to whether these women were also reacting to the prolonged use of Bone Max. In other news...."

The four friends look at each other in disbelief.

"Well, Heather," Robert says, taking her hand once again, "the good news is, it looks like I'm going to be spending a lot more time in New York."

About the Author

Doctor Robert Marx is one of the world's most predominant stem cell researchers and bone marrow transplant specialists, and he has now written a bone-chilling fiction novel that is so compelling, it blurs the line of imagination and reality.

Professor of Surgery and Chief of the Division of Oral and Maxillofacial Surgery at the University of Miami Miller School of Medicine, Dr. Marx is well known as an educator, researcher, and innovative surgeon.

He has pioneered new concepts and treatments for pathologies of the oral and facial area as well as new techniques in reconstructive surgery.